When **Virginia Heath** was a little girl it took her ages to fall asleep—so she made up stories in her head to help pass the time while she was staring at the ceiling. As she got older the stories became more complicated—sometimes taking weeks to get to their happy ending. One day she decided to embrace her insomnia and start writing them down. Virginia lives in Essex, UK, with her wonderful husband and two teenagers. It still takes her for ever to fall asleep…

Also by Virginia Heath

Redeeming the Reclusive Earl
The Scoundrel's Bartered Bride
Christmas Cinderellas
'Invitation to the Duke's Ball'

The King's Elite miniseries

The Mysterious Lord Millcroft
The Uncompromising Lord Flint
The Disgraceful Lord Gray
The Determined Lord Hadleigh

Secrets of a Victorian Household collection

Lilian and the Irresistible Duke

The Talk of the Beau Monde miniseries

The Viscount's Unconventional Lady
Look out for the next book,
coming soon!

Discover more at millsandboon.co.uk.

THE VISCOUNT'S UNCONVENTIONAL LADY

Virginia Heath

MILLS & BOON

First published in Great Britain 2021
by Mills & Boon, an imprint of HarperCollins*Publishers* Ltd,
1 London Bridge Street, London, SE1 9GF

www.harpercollins.co.uk

HarperCollins*Publishers*
1st Floor, Watermarque Building,
Ringsend Road, Dublin 4, Ireland

Large Print edition 2021

The Viscount's Unconventional Lady © 2021 Susan Merritt

ISBN: 978-0-263-28939-8

05/21

MIX
Paper from
responsible sources
FSC™ C007454

This book is produced from independently certified
FSC™ paper to ensure responsible forest management.
For more information visit www.harpercollins.co.uk/green.

Printed and bound in Great Britain
by CPI Group (UK) Ltd, Croydon, CR0 4YY

To my adopted sisters The Harpies.
You all rock!

Chapter One

Rumours abound, gentle reader, concerning a certain young poet of great regard and the eldest daughter of one of England's premier portraitists after the pair were seen together again yesterday at the British Museum. Could this mean there is finally a betrothal in the offing for the unconventional Miss B. from Bloomsbury...?

Whispers from Behind the Fan
February 1814

'**A**re you absolutely certain you cannot do this alone?' Her mother's eyes were shooting unsubtle daggers at her father across the tight confines of the carriage in one last-ditch attempt to get him to change his mind. 'Surely I do not need to remind you, Augustus, that the eldest boy is a...' She dropped her voice to a pointed whisper and drew each letter in the air with her finger. 'D-I-V-O-R-C-E-E.'

Faith rolled her eyes, groaning aloud, exasperated in equal measure at both her mother's unnecessary overprotectiveness and her continued insistence at spelling unsavoury words out in the presence of any one of her three daughters as if they were all too stupid to piece the letters together. Typically, it was ignored.

'And he's a nasty piece of work to boot, by all accounts.' Her mother shuddered theatrically. 'Completely and utterly R-U-T-H-L-E-S-S.'

'I have been reading fluently for twenty years, Mama.' Faith watched her father stifle a laugh at her matter-of-fact tone. 'Although even if I was so daft as to be unable to decipher your *complicated* secret code, I can assure you that the world and his wife are already well aware of Viscount Eastwood's scandal.'

It was impossible not to be.

For the entirety of last spring and summer it was all anyone talked about. After all, it wasn't every day polite society got to watch a peer of the realm force a rushed petition through Parliament to offload his wife before she gave birth to their child.

Yet against all the odds, and no doubt thanks

to his family's superior connections, their moun-
tains of very old money and Lord Eastwood's
important position in the government, he managed to get shot of the poor woman in under
six months, on trumped-up charges of infidel-
ity, simply because he bitterly regretted marrying beneath him. Quite an achievement when
such things usually took years—if they were
ever achieved at all.

He had even managed to get the deed done
and dusted within a few days of the unfortunate woman going into labour. It had really been
quite something to behold. Unheard of, truth be
told. Unbelievably shocking, undeniably unpalatable, as it rendered the innocent child entirely
illegitimate, and thoroughly engrossing to follow in the newspapers. So much so, Faith had
been riveted, consumed with a visceral anger
she had found extremely difficult to mask because she empathised with the wronged wife entirely. Because she too had once been deemed
unsuitable by another viscount who was a presumptive earl-to-be, although thankfully her private shame and utter humiliation had not been
in the public glare, or even the personal for that
matter.

Her lily-livered, duplicitous and callous beau

had always insisted on secrecy, and like the naive, stupid young fool she had once been, she had blithely complied. And what really galled now was that she had even enjoyed all the intrigue at the time. The stolen moments, the illicit kisses, even those under her parents' own roof, had added a delicious frisson to her ill-fated romance which he had no doubt known was as seductive as his lies to an adventurous young woman who was as green around the gills as she had been. The only positive from the whole sorry debacle was that her dear family were still oblivious of her dreadful mistake.

Thank goodness!

Else she'd be in exactly the same leaky rowboat as the former Viscountess of Eastwood. Ruined as well as abandoned by the unworthy man she had thrown caution to the wind for—and doomed for all eternity to be maligned for ever as a result.

The stark similarities between her and this faceless, voiceless woman were uncanny. The only difference being that Faith hadn't managed to get her morally moribund presumptive Earl to marry her, which was probably just as well, all things considered, even though it hadn't felt particularly fortunate at the time. Which made

Lord Eastwood's ruthless behaviour all the more abhorrent. When one made one's bed, one should have the basic decency to lie in it. Especially when one had taken holy vows to keep the thing for all eternity.

However, as much as she disapproved of the callous Viscount's ungentlemanly behaviour, she couldn't deny she was curious to finally meet him in the flesh. Thanks to her parents' bohemian lifestyle she had met many scandalous individuals in their eclectic little corner of Bloomsbury, more still among the illustrious ranks of the aristocracy, but the cold and calculated Lord Eastwood was going to be her very first truly infamous one. Would his innate heartlessness be blatantly obvious from the outset or was it something he could mask? Her keen artist's eye wanted to know.

'I just don't like the thought of it, Augustus! My poor nerves are already shot to smithereens with the worry and you haven't even started working for the beast yet!' Her mother was clearly agitated as she gripped her father's sleeve. 'I think it would be much more prudent if you paint him alone, two men together, rather than expose our daughter to his badness. Faith can accompany me to my fitting today instead and perhaps later, in a few weeks once you have enough preliminary sketches of *him*...' She curled her lip in distaste. 'She can work on the background for you safely from home. Well out of *The Beast's* beastly clutches.'

'Roberta—you are letting your imagination run away with you again.' Her father knew full well a day spent idly twiddling her thumbs in the bowels of the Covent Garden theatre, while her soprano mother was fitted for her flamboyant stage costumes, was Faith's idea of a living hell. As much as she loved her mother, they were cut from a very different cloth. 'This is a huge commission, my darling.' He squeezed his wife's hand in reassurance. 'And once again, to clarify for the umpteenth time, I am not actually working for The Beast *per se*—but his esteemed father who is an altogether more agreeable kettle of fish. Only a tiny fraction of our time over the coming months will be spent exclusively with the Viscount.'

He held up his finger and thumb an inch apart for emphasis. 'The minutest fraction, which will be undoubtedly considerably less if his blatant lack of enthusiasm for the project is any gauge. When I met with the family last week, Lord Eastwood made no secret of the fact he was there on sufferance and made certain I knew he considered self-indulgent family portraits a complete waste of his valuable time and energy.'

'I dare say much like his poor unfortunate wife was.'

Faith's quip earned her a warning look from her father, one which obviously translated to *you are not helping*, before he covered it with a convincingly pained expression for the benefit of his own worried wife and changed tack.

'Such a large composition will take several more months if Faith doesn't assist me and despite the recent unfortunate scandal, it is still a prestigious and lucrative commission. I would be a fool not to give it my all. Especially as it's been in the planning for over a year and society is already abuzz about the sheer scale of the project. The Earl of Writtle is a favourite of the King and a great friend of the Prime Minister *and* the Foreign Secretary. They are the very pinnacle of society, and instead of choosing Sir Thomas Lawrence like all the best *ton* inevitably does, they wanted me. This commission is a tremendous coup, Roberta! I am unequivocally committed. Left stranded without Faith's help, I would need to work longer hours to get it completed in time to meet my other commitments. Significantly longer hours. I'd barely be home, Roberta...'

He let that reality hang for a moment, knowing his absence would bother her mother more than any association with a passing scandal ever could, when to all intents and purposes the Brookes family were a positive scandal in their own right anyway even without Faith's secret but massive *faux pas*. The mason's son turned artist, and the draper's daughter turned opera singer, were only tolerated by society because they also happened to be the very best artist and the very best opera singer in all of Christendom. Her father's rising star was shooting past all his rivals, including the painter-in-ordinary to His Majesty, Sir Thomas Lawrence. And now that he had been newly elected by the Royal Academy of Arts as their latest Academician, that star was destined to rise even farther.

'Aside from the eldest Lord Eastwood...'

'Please do not call him anything other than *The Beast* henceforth in my presence, Augustus!' Her mother refused to be placated. 'I have the measure of him and will never be swayed from it!'

'All right—aside from the beastly *Beast*, the rest of the Earl of Writtle's brood are delightful. You know they are. You have met them on many occasions. In fact, it was you who first introduced me to the family and saw the potential else I never would have accepted such a huge commission in the first place. You know I prefer the freedom of variety instead of months toiling over the same subjects. They were good people, you said. *Influential* people. And the Countess's greatest wish was to have her nearest and dearest immortalised in oils, you said…by me.'

Hardly a tremendous surprise when her father's work had become quite sought after in the last few years, especially his informal group tableaus, and the waiting list for a painting had been long. However, there was no denying since the Writtle commission and his recent elevation with the Academy, that list was now enormous. His schedule was packed and, keen to monopolise on his good fortune, her father had promised the Countess of Writtle her painting would be completed before the end of the Season and the grand ball the family always held at the end of May. Hence, he would have to renege on that lofty promise without an effective assistant who could effortlessly mimic his style and share some of the burden. Faith was his most promising student and the only one he trusted enough to delegate to.

'But that was a year ago, dear. A great deal has changed since then. Tell them you are suddenly unavailable, and this argument becomes moot.'

'Roberta…' Her father shook his head in disappointment. 'Aside from the fact that would be very poor form and potentially catastrophic for my good reputation, I pride myself in being a man of my word and I will not entertain the idea of letting anyone down—no matter who they might be associated with or what that associate might have done. And while I understand that all your concerns are because Faith is our daughter, it would be grossly unfair of us to tar all the Earl's family with the same brush now, wouldn't it?' Her father always saw the good in everyone—although from time to time that innate belief was grossly misplaced. 'What sort of people would *we* be if we deserted decent folk simply because of some selfish individual's actions which fall completely out of their control? Not to mention the Earl and Countess of Writtle are true patrons of the arts and we both know those are few and far between. They do not deserve such shoddy treatment and I will not be party to it.'

'You are right.' Roberta Brookes was nothing if not fiercely loyal to her legions of devoted fans, irrespective of whether they were paupers or peers. And despite all her current misgivings about Lord Beastly and his scandalous divorce, she really did have a generous nature and a heart of gold. 'Absolutely right… The Earl and Countess of Writtle are good people…'

'Of course they are!' He winked at his daughter as they both watched the older woman waver. 'Besides, my darling, Faith will be with *me*. What possible harm could come to her under the watchful eye of her own father?'

'But he is such a handsome and titled D-E-V-I-L and she is such a pretty thing. What if her head is turned? I worry for the sanctity of her V-I-R-T-U-E.'

While Faith blinked in shock at the ludicrous suggestion, not having the heart to shatter her prudish mother's illusions by telling her that she had stupidly given away her precious virtue to a lying blackguard years ago, her father's spontaneous bark of laughter was genuine. 'Have you gone completely mad, woman? You know our eldest better than anyone. It would take more than a handsome devil to turn her clever, discerning head. Edward Tate is possibly the handsomest man in London, and perhaps the entirety of England, and even he has failed to turn her head.'

'More's the pity!' Her mother was convinced the poet was the perfect match for Faith and did her utmost to encourage the match. But while Faith liked Edward—because they had been friends for many years before he decided he wanted more than friendship—she harboured no romantic feelings for him, even while trying.

'Or not,' said her father with a sly wink towards Faith, 'which rather proves my point. If anyone is going to give the nefarious Lord Eastwood short shrift, it is she. When has our Faith ever been able to keep her thoughts or opinions to herself?'

A character flaw her charming mother despaired of. 'We all know I am too outspoken, Mama, and I've never suffered fools gladly.' Not any more at any rate. Something she was immensely proud of, but she made a concerted effort to appear contrite. 'Although I really am trying to temper those unfortunate traits.'

An outright lie. While she was entirely capable of being polite and biting her tongue as far as her father's business was concerned, if a pithy comment was required, she was still more than happy to be the one to give it. Especially to someone with a lofty title. She abhorred the arrogant sense of superiority men from the aristocracy always had and loathed more that they always assumed any woman not of noble birth was always considered fair game. After the Earl-to-be had shattered all her childish illusions, and in the five years since he had skipped to pastures new without so much as a backwards glance, she had already accumulated enough indecent proposals from similar men of *illustrious* rank to fill a book and all without any encouragement on her part. Therefore, it was hardly a surprise she was entirely jaded with the breed.

'I can assure you, it will be a cold day in hell before I allow a scoundrel to seduce me. No matter how handsome he is.'

'It will take more than a fine face to tempt our eldest, Roberta, you know that. Unworthy scoundrels aside, how many decent suitors outside of that foppish poet have tried and failed to woo her over the years? She's ridiculously choosy.'

Another thing Faith was proud of. Once bitten, twice shy and all that. Not to mention she would rather cut off her painting hand than allow history to ever repeat itself.

'Well, there is that…' Her mother glanced at her and sighed, although probably more out of frustration at her eldest daughter's acid tongue than relief she possessed one. 'I have seen no recent evidence to suggest that cynical attitude towards all gentlemen will ever change.' Though not for the want of her trying. Roberta Brookes believed in love and marriage. By Faith's age she had been married for three years and had already given birth to two of her three daughters. She struggled to understand her eldest daughter's reluctance to entertain anyone, while Faith could hardly explain to her all the exceedingly good reasons why that was.

Her mother sighed again, clearly in two minds still but on the cusp of backing down. 'But I suppose, in this instance, I am prepared to acknowledge her unhealthy cynicism, lack of tact and determined forthrightness might come in handy around The Beast.'

'Undoubtedly it will.' Her father wrapped his arm around his wife and kissed the top of her head. 'You see, you really are worrying unduly, my darling, and you really shouldn't when you have quite enough on your plate already with rehearsals.'

Faith nodded, even though they had had the same circular argument about her involvement in the Writtle commission for over a month now, going toe to toe with her lovable but stubborn mother was never the way to win her around.

'*Così fan Tutte* has been your dream for so long, Mama... Please don't spoil it by worrying about me.' In the Brookes household, great stock was put on dreams and ambition because if both her parents hadn't dared reach for the stars, they would still be masons and drapers eking out a hard living exactly as their own parents and grandparents had done before them. 'You need to focus all your energies on giving London the *virtuosa* performance everyone is holding their breath for. In return, you have my solemn pledge I shall avoid *The Beast* at all costs and if I cannot avoid him, I shall remain unequivocally so pithy, cynical, tactless and forthright he is left in no doubt how much I heartily disapprove of him. If my head is turned in any direction it will be upwards—so I can better glare at him from down my nose.' For good measure she decided to demonstrate this, earning her another amused nod from her father.

'Intimidatingly haughty, darling. Well done! The beastly Beast won't know what's hit him when he sees that. Doesn't she look fearsome, Roberta?'

After a long, withering sigh, her mother finally nodded. 'Very well. I shall reluctantly capitulate. But only as long as I have your word, Augustus, that Faith is supervised by you at *all* times while you work on this commission.' Her narrowed eyes turned to her daughter. 'And that you, dear girl, desist being your usual headstrong self and let him! I want both of you to make that promise here and now or I shan't rest.'

Her father winced as their eyes locked. They both knew keeping to that pledge was going to nigh on impossible. In the two years Faith had been her father's occasional assistant, they had found their own way of working harmoniously and it was rarely together. No work got achieved otherwise. She liked to talk incessantly or sing to herself while she painted, and he preferred total silence which she abhorred. Therefore, when she assisted with his larger commissions, she created the whimsical and sentimental backgrounds which made a coveted Brookes tableau unique while he, as a complete and often irrational portrait perfectionist, concentrated on honing the pose and the expressions of the people in multiple sketches which he used to paint in the foreground later on in blissful peace. Usually entirely oblivious of the poor sitter who must be bored stiff with all the relentless posing while he captured them just so.

While their combined efforts always complemented one another perfectly and there was no denying they made the perfect artistic team, rarely, if ever, did they paint in the same room. If they were forced to do so, it would only be a matter of time before one of them murdered the other.

'You have my word I shall keep her close by.' He winced again over his wife's head as he said it, looking decidedly ill at ease to be stretching the truth. He already had a rigorous schedule of sittings booked with each member of the Writtle clan—and those were just his preliminary sketches. There would be more. There were always more. Obsessive preparation was part of her father's process, whereas Faith liked to paint as the muse took her.

Conscious she was staring straight at her, Faith offered her mother her best approximation of a reassuring smile. 'And I promise that I shall never be more than a few yards away from Papa while The Beast is in the residence.' As long as twenty or thirty yards separated by a solid brick wall still constituted a few.

As soon as their carriage pulled up outside the Earl of Writtle's impressive Grosvenor Square town house, a waiting footman opened the door and Faith practically tumbled out of it in her haste to escape in case the begrudging permission she had just been gifted was swiftly rescinded. If her father's haste to join her was any indication, he too feared the distinct possibility of either an immediate retraction or a thorough interrogation which would ultimately expose the truth. Together they pasted twin smiles on their faces as they waved off the carriage and simultaneously breathed a sigh of relief as it disappeared out of sight.

'I hate lying to her.'

'Technically, you didn't lie, Papa. I *will* always be close by.'

'And technically, any justification which starts with the word *technically* is fundamentally problematic and would be unlikely to stand up in court. A lie by omission is still a lie as far as a marriage is concerned. One day, I pray you will keep your tart mouth closed long enough to fool an upstanding and unsuspecting man into marrying you before he learns you are a complete harridan who is best avoided—and then you will understand the turmoil.'

'I rather like being a harridan.' It was the constant weapon in her arsenal which could be relied upon to thwart the unwanted advances of any man who thought a girl not from the illustrious ranks of the aristocracy fair game. 'Unless, of course, dear Mama is right and the handsome D-E-V-I-L in there miraculously turns my head and makes me forget to be one.'

'I think that is as likely as me managing to supervise you at all times. Not even the Almighty Himself is capable of such a momentous miracle if you are suitably riled.' He slanted her a warning glance. 'That said, please don't go in there spoiling for a fight, Faith. Lord Beastly aside, this family really are good people and I would be mortified if you offended them. Remember, we are here in a professional capacity and as such, I expect you to comport yourself in a professional manner at all times irrespective of your private feelings. Even when riled.'

She frowned, a little offended. When it came to her work, she was always professional. That veneer had only ever slipped once and in her defence only because the randy old sitter had made inappropriate physical advances while she had been preoccupied with mixing some paint. 'If you don't mind me saying, Papa, that is an entirely unnecessary and unwarranted reminder. Of course, I will be the epitome of good manners and professionalism. Exactly as I *always* am. Even around The Beast himself.'

After a beat of silence, her father's expression softened. 'It was an unnecessary reminder and I apologise. Forgive me, Faith. I am afraid after being married for a quarter of a century, your mother's voice is in my head and...' He huffed out a put-upon grunt. 'Well...there's been so many dreadful stories about Lord Eastwood in the papers, who could blame you for having strong opinions regarding him? Especially as I have a fair few of them myself and he has done little when I have encountered him to allay those fears. I suspect, for the next three months, we shall both have to bite our tongues whenever we come into contact with him.'

As the footmen relieved them of their burdens, keen to dismiss the small tiff before they stepped into the fray, she took her father's arm and dropped her voice to a whisper as they followed the men up the pristine marble steps.

'Talking of Lord Beastly, do you think he will be gracing us with his presence today?' After everything she had heard about him, she couldn't help but be intrigued. 'I confess, I cannot wait to see if this particular devil actually does have horns.'

'None that I saw, but perhaps he files them down?'

'I suppose we'll have to check inside his boots for cloven hooves to be thoroughly sure.'

Their wholly inappropriate mumbled discussion came to abrupt end when a smart butler met them in the hallway and briskly took their coats before escorting them to the drawing room. There they were promptly welcomed by the smiling Earl of Writtle, his grinning Countess, their two beaming adult daughters each beside their two genial husbands and two equally charming, cheerful grandchildren who giggled up at them from an explosion of toys on the Persian carpet.

All in all, a perfectly lovely display of honest-to-goodness friendliness.

The only other person in the room, a tall man, stood detached from the rest of the family beside the fireplace, with jet-black hair and the greenest eyes Faith had ever seen, wearing a scowl which would curdle even the freshest milk. The scowl aside, there was no doubting her mother's initial assessment was correct.

The beastly Lord Eastwood was a handsome devil—if devils were your type.

Fortunately, they were no longer hers. Either equipped fully with or without horns. Unfortunately, some devil inside her apparently scrambled her wits and took control of her tongue the moment his big hand politely shook hers, making her completely forget her resolve to be polite and professional at all times. As soon as the strange heat from his fingers seared through her gloves and set her nerve endings bouncing uncontrollably, she managed to unintentionally say exactly what she was thinking.

'Lord Eastwood—I've read so much about you. I do hope, for your sake at least, some of it is untrue.'

Chapter Two

Because he kept finding his gaze wandering to her, Piers ruthlessly focused his eyes on his teacup as the conversation wafted around him. He had known agreeing to this was a bad idea months ago, when the very last thing he wanted was a whimsical painting of himself standing all alone in a giant portrait when the rest of his family all came in pairs.

Yet his mother had persisted and being a dutiful son he had agreed, assuming the ordeal couldn't possibly make him feel any worse about his current situation than he did—but, oh, how wrong he had been! Thanks to the vexing Miss Faith Brookes, he wanted to go and hide in his study, and preferably stay there until his mother's long-awaited masterpiece was complete.

Every time she glanced his way, which she did with alarming frequency, her delightfully arranged features altered. For everyone else she smiled, but while the smile was still loosely nailed in place for him, there was a look about her eyes which reminded him of the expression people got when they caught a whiff of something noxious, but were at pains to pretend they hadn't in case the noxiousness emanated from their host.

'And what is your idea of a perfect day, Lord Writtle?' To get a better idea for the background setting of the ridiculously enormous picture his mother had commissioned at eye-watering expense, the cause of his current bad mood was *delving into their souls* to ensure the *tone of the composition* accurately reflected the family.

A preposterous load of old nonsense as far as he was concerned, but typically melodramatic and arty, as creatives types were prone to be. After thoroughly quizzing his mother on everything from her favourite colour, to her preferred ways to spend her time, to her persistent obsession with family picnics during the summer months irrespective of the weather, the tousled-haired Miss Brookes was now chatting cosily with his father. And looking thoroughly at home and entirely comfortable in her own skin while she did.

He envied her that.

Once upon a time he had felt entirely comfortable in his, but those days were long gone. Truth be told, he'd happily trade in his old skin now for a new one which completely camouflaged him. Something bland and unassuming which failed to turn heads and elicit fevered whispers behind hands or fans—but always behind his back. He no longer wanted to stand out like the vivacious Miss Brookes. In a perfect world, he would blend in seamlessly with the wallpaper.

Although looking at her now, he was certain he had never stood out quite as much as she. Yes, he was tall and dark and had been considered exceedingly eligible in his day, but she had a uniqueness about her which drew the eye and left everyone else feeling a little more uninspiring and insipid in comparison.

It was probably all down to the hair, he decided.

The unusual shade hovered midway between gold and copper and clearly the curls which were piled loosely on her head were formed naturally. They were too haphazard, too riotous and too invitingly tactile to have come from any man-made curling iron. Ironed curls behaved. Hers looked sinfully wayward.

'Obviously I also enjoy music, Miss Brookes.' His father was smiling at her, utterly charmed as she scribbled copious notes into a book. 'Especially when it comes from your talented mother.'

'You are too kind, my lord. I shall be sure to pass your compliment along to her later.' His mother had mentioned that hers was some sort of singer, which probably explained why the daughter was quite so theatrical. The arts were in her blood, whereas the only thing in his blood was very likely only blood. 'Do you play an instrument, Lord Writtle?'

'Sadly no—I wish I had learned, I certainly wanted to—but my wife and daughters are all accomplished on the pianoforte, so I take great pleasure in that.'

'What prevented you from learning?'

Notes forgotten, she sat forward, giving Piers an unhindered view of her profile and the smattering of freckles that dusted her dainty, slightly upturned nose which she had made no attempt to disguise, no doubt as some sort of statement about her intention to march to the beat of her own drum. She was that sort of woman, exactly the sort which, unfortunately, had always appealed to him.

Heaven help him.

So much for being once bitten, twice shy. It didn't matter that he had been bitten so badly, huge gaping chunks of himself were now missing and would likely never grow back, his idiotic hand still tingled from where it had shaken hers over an hour ago, and no amount of fisting the thing behind his back was doing anything to make the damn appendage forget.

'I was the heir. My father insisted I had to learn more important things that he considered appropriate for my future as the Earl—accountancy, stocks and bonds, estate management...'

'Dull things then.' She beamed and Piers found himself strangely jealous of his father. She certainly hadn't beamed at him—even when they had first been introduced and some feigned beaming was expected.

To give her some credit, she hadn't baulked either or looked horrified as so many had since his divorce, before they scurried away as if such a scandalous catastrophe were contagious. Instead she had stared him boldly in the eye as she had shaken his hand. And while he reeled as his nerve endings bounced all over the shop at the brief contact, she had been assessing him unsubtly like a specimen in a jar before she rendered him speechless with her forthrightness.

I've read so much about you. I do hope, for your sake at least, some of it is untrue.

A comment which, though at least honest, had completely knocked the wind out of his sails.

Or at least that was what he wanted to convince himself had left him stuttering something which he was fairly certain wasn't even a recognised word in the English language, before his mother had stepped in and rescued him by assuring the forthright Miss Brookes emphatically that the newspapers had told nothing but grievous lies.

If he'd had his wits about him, he would have had to contradict his mother in the spirit of mutual honesty because, of his many unfortunate character traits, he was always predictably honest first and foremost.

The press hadn't told a complete pack of lies.

They had twisted several uncomfortable truths, omitted several pertinent facts and failed to acknowledge, even slightly, that there were always two sides to every story. In this case, the other side of the story had been safely ensconced in Lisbon with her lover, eagerly awaiting the birth of their first child, happily ignorant of the complete implosion of Piers's life while he had moved heaven and earth to set her free. Not that he had expected his former wife to give him a passing thought then. Why would she when he had barely registered in her thoughts when they had lived under the same roof?

'Yes, Miss Brookes! Very dull things indeed— but eminently useful as it turned out else we'd all be living on the streets. What my spendthrift father passed down wouldn't have lasted, I can tell you!' And now she had his father bragging to impress her, when the Writtle men never bragged as a point of principle. 'It was my canny talent at speculation which rebuilt the family's fortunes.'

'What a great achievement, my lord!' His father's chest puffed out at the compliment and once again her eyes flicked briefly to him before she hastily dragged them back. 'And if I may also say, jolly well done. For both saving the family fortunes and for having the fortitude to do something to fix them in the first place. Between you and me...' As she leaned forward conspiratorially, the old man did too, almost as if he were a besotted puppy and she his adored master. 'I've never had much time for those spoiled aristocrats who rest on their laurels and bemoan the hand life has dealt them. I much prefer men of substance and action.' His father seemed to grow several inches at that. 'Do you speculate still?'

'Of course I do!' Because he was now a man of substance and action, ridiculously keen to impress the vixen who had bewitched him. 'Speculating is much more exciting than the dull day-to-day estate matters which take up so much of my time.'

'Once the dull things are done, what else do

you enjoy?' She picked up her pencil again and Piers noticed her hands. Long, elegant fingers which absolutely refused to remain still. No sign of any wedding ring either, although why that seemed such a huge relief, he had no earthly idea. From her pained glances his way, the judgemental Miss Brookes had already formed an intense dislike of him which was obviously so ingrained she wouldn't sway from that opinion even if Piers managed to find the wherewithal and the words to defend himself.

Her disgust was inevitable, he supposed.

If these last six months had taught him anything, it was that gossip and scandal always trumped the truth and people always preferred to believe the worst. And the most tragic thing of all was he couldn't blame them. Gossip and scandal were exciting and the absolute truth, in this case at least, was entirely depressing. For him anyway. His only consolation was that the other party in the sorry mess which had once been his marriage had been able to move on.

And that was another predictably dreary set of traits he wished he didn't possess!

Piers was always gallingly gracious in defeat and irritatingly noble to his core, even when he was well within his rights not to be either. To such an extent, even he preferred the completely fictitious version of himself he read in the news-papers. If nothing else, that heartless villain was interesting and would have had no trouble spitting out a perfectly brisk and acerbic response to her daring question which told her in no uncertain terms to mind her own damn business.

True villains didn't stutter and flounder and reel when they shook a hand. Nearly an hour on and he still couldn't make head nor tail of his body's immediate and unwelcome response. It had been a great deal like lust—but lust tinged with something else. Something more potent yet strangely profound at the same time.

Whatever it was, it was most peculiar that lust had suddenly decided to show up again after its prolonged and protracted absence. Especially as he had sworn himself off the sort of women who always inspired it. The sort who crackled with life and individuality and intelligence like the siren currently enchanting his father. Usually so sensible and level-headed, the old fool was hanging on her every word.

'I love to ride… Cross-country steeplechases at our estate in Surrey rather than the sedate and sensible kind one has to do in Hyde Park.' More bragging—but this time about his vigour. His poor father had been completely seduced. 'I love to feel the wind on my face and the thunder of hooves beneath me as I eat up the ground.' Good grief! Now his father was waxing lyrical. Thunder of hooves indeed. Flowery words which had never been heard in the Writtle drawing room in the history of for ever.

'So you have a reckless streak, my lord?' The vixen smiled in obvious approval as she noted that titbit down. 'Who do you race against?'

'Usually Piers. Most Sundays you'll find the pair of us galloping around Richmond Park. Although as age advances, I suspect he pulls his punches to save my foolish pride and to make me feel as though I've still got what it takes to give him a good thrashing.'

'Really?' Those curious almond eyes suddenly slanted to his and his mouth dried as his tongue apparently grew thicker under her scrutiny. Like the rest of her, those inquisitive eyes were an unusual shade. Not quite blue, not quite violet, but the lashes which framed them were long and her eyebrows were expressive.

'And because I am a vain and shallow old man, Miss Brookes, I like to think I can still give him a good run for his money.'

'I don't doubt that for a second, my lord.' She thankfully glanced away allowing Piers to let out the breath he had not realised he was holding. 'Age is but a number.'

He made the fatal mistake of taking a calming gulp of his tea and almost spat it out when she suddenly addressed him directly out of the blue, skewering him with her stare.

'What about you, Lord Eastwood? Aside from racing your father, how do you fill your leisure time?'

'A better question would be when does he allow himself leisure time!' His mother's frustrated voice filled the void he couldn't seem to muster the ability to fill himself. 'My son works too hard, Miss Brookes. Every waking hour seems to be taken up with his responsibilities in Whitehall. Either he is working at the ministry or he brings the ministry home here to work on in his study. I keep telling him it is not healthy to work every waking hour God sends, but sadly my heartfelt pleas fall on stubbornly deaf ears.'

The vixen tilted her head as she assessed him thoroughly this time and his toes began to curl inside his boots. 'You work for the government, do you not, Lord Eastwood?'

'Yes.' Thanks to his uncooperative tongue, that lone syllable took far more effort than a mere syllable warranted, which really wouldn't do at all when he was apparently going to be stuck with her disapproving presence for the next few months. Unless he gave up bringing work home to finish in his study and simply slept in his office for the duration. The idea had merit… 'I work with the Secretary of State for War and the Colonies, although in the current climate, war rather than diplomacy takes up most of our efforts.' And nearly every waking hour.

'I have a former student who works in Whitehall.' Augustus Brookes joined the fray. 'Lord Rayne—do you know him?' Piers nodded, hoping his lack of enthusiasm for the wastrel didn't show.

'Yes. We've collided a time or two.' Usually when Piers bumped into him in a corridor because he hadn't been quick enough to turn and walk the other way. Rayne was one of those peers who toadied around Whitehall trying to be important, and to ingratiate himself with the most powerful, but did nothing of any substance. But as the son-in-law of a cabinet member who failed to see his flaws, or saw them but didn't want to upset his daughter, he'd been foisted from one department to the next. Last he'd heard, Rayne was doing something mundane at the Board of Trade—probably twiddling his thumbs in between all his glad handing, as that was all the fellow was good for.

'He had some potential as an artist.' Augustus Brookes smiled wistfully at the memory.

'But perhaps not the dedication, although for a while he showed promise. A nice chap as I recall.' They would have to agree to disagree on that score. 'But alas he gave up his lessons in the summer of 1809 when he married. Or was it 1810, Faith? I can never remember.'

'It was 1808.' Miss Brookes now looked as though she had just sucked a lemon as she briskly skewered Piers with another glare before she interrogated him again. 'Do you enjoy working for the ministry, Lord Eastwood?'

'It is important work.'

'I don't doubt that, sir.' She smiled as if he were a child, clearly amused by his stuffy answer. 'But I asked if you enjoyed it?'

Good lord, he felt stupid.

And irrationally irritated that he felt that way. What was it about her that turned him into a blithering idiot? The way he was behaving, anyone would think he was shy rather than terminally uninteresting.

'I am not entirely sure one can ever enjoy trying to manage a war, Miss Brookes—but it is challenging and occasionally rewarding.' And now he sounded crusty and staid. Old beyond his years. Exactly as Constança had always lamented. So terminally predictable, buttoned up and English it made him dreadfully dull. 'It keeps me very busy.'

Dull! Dull! So blasted dull!

'I am sure it does.' She turned her attention back to his father again, clearly as bored by his pitiful attempt at conversation as he was. And who, in their right mind, could blame her? He was dull. Depressingly dull, but now also a despised social pariah to boot. Not the most attractive combination of attributes for a man in his apparent prime.

However, Miss Faith Brookes, damn her, was the complete opposite of dull and, from her easy way with everybody present but him, would be the sort of effortless social butterfly who lit up a room simply by entering it.

Of course she was, else his long-buried lust wouldn't have slammed into him without warning upon her mere arrival. His staid eyes had always been drawn to the extraordinary—more was the pity because Piers was only too aware the only way he ever lit up a room nowadays was by leaving it.

From the top of her artfully curly, copper head to the toes of the brightly patterned slippers poking out from the hem of her vivid gown she oozed sparkling charisma. The dress alone spoke volumes about her character. Emerald green trimmed in gawdy cerise-pink brocade should never go together, but on her, not only did those vibrant colours look like a match made in heaven, they suited her pale complexion perfectly.

She was extraordinary and unconventional and delightfully erudite—and therefore just about as dangerous as a pride of starving lions as far as he was concerned. Already he could hear the loud, clanging alarm bells ringing, donging out the familiar chimes of impending doom. See the bright beacon of the lighthouse warning him of treacherous rocks just off the shore, signalling that effervescent women like her weren't compatible with dreary, dull, predictable men like him so he should steer well clear.

He'd learned that lesson the hard way and had no intention of ever repeating his biggest mistake. So why was he already so thoroughly seduced by the minx he could barely speak?

Clearly he was a glutton for punishment.

Or an idiot.

Or, more likely, both.

Especially as she kept glancing at him as if she had something unpleasant stuck to the bottom of her shoe.

'I think, at this juncture, it would be useful for Faith to see the proposed space for the tableau.'

Augustus Brookes waved a dainty scone in the air, addressing nobody in particular and everybody in general. 'She likes to see the light and get a feel for the atmosphere and mood of a room before she considers the concept.'

More artistic nonsense. As if an empty room could have an atmosphere, or bricks, plaster and furniture were capable of expressing moods. He scoffed internally, wishing he was back at work, then immediately willed the floor to open up when every eye suddenly swivelled in his direction and he realised he had snorted his obvious disdain out loud.

His mother shot him a warning look. 'Do forgive my son. You have caught him on an off day. He's not normally so curmudgeonly. In fact, he can be quite personable when he puts his mind to it.'

'Can he?' Miss Brookes seemed entirely dubious this could possibly be the case and he was sure she looked down her perfect nose at him as she blandly sipped her tea.

'Oh, indeed he can, dear,' said his mother as she proffered around the cake plate forcefully, as if cake alone might erase his rude outburst and smooth any ruffled artistic feathers it might have caused. 'He can be thoroughly *charming* when he puts his mind to it, but he has always been better at showing his affable side in individual conversations rather than as part of a crowd, where much to my consternation, he prefers to disappear.'

Then she got that calculated expression she always got when she was about to do something petty but ultimately hideous to punish one of her children when they disappointed her. 'Indulge me, Miss Brookes, and allow him to prove it.' Two traitorous maternal eyeballs rolled leisurely to him and she smiled her most sickly smile.

'Piers, darling—kindly escort Miss Brookes to the ballroom and show her the wall. There's a good boy.'

Chapter Three

'The ballroom.'

After making her trail after him while he marched down the hallway, Lord Beastly threw open the double doors and strode across the dance floor, the heels of his boots clicking impatiently on the polished parquet.

In an attempt to look nonplussed rather than extremely unsettled to be all alone with him so soon after she had promised her mother she never would be, Faith clutched her notebook to her chest like a shield and forced herself to glide across the threshold. Although it wasn't just his dreadful scandal, or his proximity she found unnerving. She was still trying to make sense of her peculiar reaction to their innocuous handshake over an hour ago. Because surely a simple handshake shouldn't have caused her flesh to tingle or her pulse to bounce so erratically—and not with fear. She recognised attraction when she felt it and still could not fathom why her usually sensible and supremely selective female body had decided to feel an overwhelming attraction towards his!

London's most notorious divorcee! And another earl-in-waiting to boot, exactly like Rayne! When she had convinced herself she now preferred men of substance and intelligence. Men who had made something of themselves, rather than those who were born with it all laid out on a platter, and men who valued those same qualities in others irrespective of rank. Yet her traitorous, foolish pulse still fluttered for another callous, titled scoundrel! She was positively livid at herself for the unpalatable slip, as well as reeling at the unwelcome realisation she was still capable of one.

To calm her nerves and reclaim her missing equilibrium, she spun a slow circle and took in the room. 'What a lovely space.'

The truth. Despite the slate-grey February skies outside, the room was bright and airy, thanks to the wall of French doors which separated the house from the garden and the high vaulted ceiling which was painted in stark white. The biggest chandelier she had ever seen hung suspended from its centre, composed of thousands of sparkling crystal teardrops which would be magnificent once lit and the pale striped-silk-covered walls would reflect that light everywhere. The stark, effortless simplicity reeked both class and affluence. Proof, if proof were needed, that the Writtles had money.

As if pointing was too much effort, he gestured to the right with a curt flick of his dark head. 'That's the wall.'

It was the biggest wall in the room and the only one unbroken by windows, doors or fireplaces. 'Gracious! That is enormous.' Much bigger than she had anticipated despite her father's careful measurements. No wonder he desperately needed her assistance.

He had planned a canvas of five by six feet, which necessitated painting the picture in situ as neither of them cared for separate butting panels because the finish was never quite right. But seeing the space now, she realised he had grossly underestimated. To do this room and this wall justice, it would need to be at least two feet larger either way, which would make the Writtle tableau the biggest picture they had ever created. Suddenly, the four-month timeline felt inadequate too—but, oh, what a picture it would make!

Already she could imagine it. Rolling parkland filled with trees, pasture and acres of sky. Her Ladyship sat on a picnic blanket to one side, surrounded by her daughters while the children flew kites with their fathers closer to the centre. His Lordship on the other side, sat astride a horse, smiling at a ghostly steeple in the distance. One inscrutable, sinfully handsome dark-haired man hovering detached somewhere on the periphery, staring at the proceedings with disdain from afar...

Exactly as he was now.

'It's quite a wall, Lord Eastwood!' Ridiculous words no sensible woman should ever utter, but words at least when just his presence seemed to have the power to completely scramble her wits.

He gave it a cursory glance. 'As walls go, I suppose it is.'

He had a nice voice, drat him. Deep. Manly. Too deep and manly because the sound of certain consonants apparently had the power to create goose pimples—which really would not do at all when she was supposed to loathe him on principle. 'I get the impression you lack enthusiasm for this project, my lord.'

'My mother has decreed we must have a Brookes masterpiece, so apparently a Brookes is what we must have.'

'But you couldn't care less?' She smiled professionally, unoffended, and because staring directly at him was disconcerting, turned to face the huge wall again just so that she did not have to look at him. 'Are you not a fan of art, Lord Eastwood?'

'I am not a fan of disruption or invasion, Miss Brookes.'

Out of the corner of her eye she could see he had folded his arms. It made him look arrogant and ever so slightly intimidating because the stance emphasised both his height and breadth. By her best estimation he was a few inches over six feet and had the dimensions of a labourer or a pugilist rather than the spare frame of an aristocrat. There was muscle on those big bones which suggested he did—or had done—much more than sit behind a desk and waste his life with idle pursuits like the presumptive Earl she'd misguidedly plighted her troth for. It irritated her immensely that she noticed all those things, and worse, wholeheartedly approved of them, and that irritation leaked into her tone.

'Because of your *important* work? Which I am told you like to bring home with you.' It was especially irritating that Lord Eastwood was *not* a dedicated man of leisure. It was galling to have to give him points for anything substantial when she would much prefer him to have no substance at all.

'England is at war with Napoleon and America

simultaneously, Miss Brookes—there is much to do and not enough hours in the day to do it.' It was the longest sentence he had uttered thus far and by his expression he wasn't happy to have strung so many words together solely for her entertainment. Those expressive green eyes were irritated. It was obvious he held her and her work in little esteem. How typical he would look down his nose at her. Almost-earls were all the same.

'I am curious, my lord...' More unpalatable truth which she couldn't quite believe, although she slowly opened her notebook rather than stare at him like she wanted to, and began to jot down the new dimensions for the canvas to let him know he wasn't that riveting and she wasn't at all bothered by his censure or his presence, nor was she the least bit impressed with his title. 'How does one fight a war abroad from the comfort of one's armchair in Mayfair?'

At his absolute best, he was a bureaucrat, not a soldier. One who likely made life-or-death decisions from a distance with the impersonal stroke of a pen—just as he had impersonally disposed of his wife. A cruel fact her silly pulse could well do with remembering. Whatever he did in Whitehall, he likely only did it to feather his own nest. If he had aspirations of political power to go alongside that which already came from his wealth and status, as the newspapers had hinted at time and time again, then the inconvenience of an apprenticeship in a ministry was par for the course. An important rung on the ladder. A token show of commitment before he manoeuvred his annoyingly taut behind into a seat in the government alongside the other hereditary lords who ran the country without any serious thought for the millions they supposedly ran it for. 'Aren't you a tad withdrawn from the action to be of any *real* use?' She slanted him a glance and was pleased to see her well-aimed barb had made his compelling green eyes narrow, while something hot and dangerously human swirled molten within them.

'Armies march on their stomachs and cannot fight without bullets. It is one of my responsibilities to ensure they receive the necessary supplies to do their jobs properly.' As if anticipating her disappointment in his explanation, his chin lifted defiantly. 'It is not the most exciting of occupations, Miss Brookes, but I can assure you it is one that is most essential for the war effort.'

'I suppose that makes you a strategist, Lord Eastwood.' Her gaze resolutely still on her notes because his unyielding gaze was just too unnerving, Faith shifted her position slightly so she could surreptitiously study him better in her peripheral vision. Would calling him a Whitehall warrior be a step too far? Probably. 'I should imagine such a *Herculean* task involves a great deal of strategising *and* planning.' Which doubtless involved more nudges, winks and pompous, self-aggrandising backslapping in White's or Brooks's than actual work. In the *ton*, it wasn't what you knew which garnered the most reward, it was who. And if you weren't a *who*, you were ultimately inconsequential and therefore disposable.

'It does.' His handsome features rearranged themselves back to severely put upon rather than defensive. 'Two things which require order and quiet, Miss Brookes.'

She could tell already working near Lord Beastly was going to be a delight. 'Well, unless you have the sudden urge to strategise here in this ballroom, I think you can be assured of both, sir. Is your private study close by?' Because hell would have to freeze over before she ventured near that part of the house.

'Unfortunately, it is just along the hall. We are to be neighbours, Miss Brookes.' This was accompanied by another curt head jerk to the left, causing Faith to stifle a smile. She couldn't help it. He was as stodgy as a treacle pudding and more self-important than any man she had ever met—no mean feat when she had encountered quite a few. If it weren't for his eyes, which spoiled his attempts at calm inscrutability completely, she would have assumed him entirely emotionless and stiff. But those eyes were anything but.

They were dangerously compelling.

'You have my solemn pledge I shall never darken that door under any circumstances.' A promise she was suddenly relieved to make. She had never been so physically aware of a man in her life.

'See that you don't.'

She should have left it at that.

Should have but didn't. It was the flicker of triumph on his expression which did it. The sanctimonious, entitled arrogance that felt too painfully familiar, which in turn made her rebellious nature and stubborn pride chafe at his brusque order.

'Is this the fabled affable side of your character which you are supposed to be showing me, Lord Eastwood?'

She watched his jaw clench as his dark eyebrows furrowed. 'I have just the one side, Miss Brookes.' Arms still stubbornly crossed over his chest, he drew himself up to his impressive full height. 'What you see is what you get.'

'How disappointing.' Even though she knew baiting him was not the best course of action, and despite her promise to her father to behave professionally, she couldn't appear to help herself. As expected, he was beyond insufferable and in dire need of knocking down a peg or two with his dismissive, superior and surly attitude, never mind that something about him set her wildly off-kilter. 'And there I was hoping you would make some effort to make me at least *try* to find something to like about you.'

The dark head tilted, those intelligent, hypnotic and suddenly stormy eyes holding hers unbending. 'And what, pray tell, would be the point of that, Miss Brookes? When you, like everyone else, have already prejudged me in the lofty court of public opinion, and have already concluded that there is absolutely nothing about me to like?'

He had her there and that truth, so honestly and plainly spoken, left her momentarily speechless. And bizarrely ashamed, although she couldn't fathom why. She had prejudged him. Of course she had, and with good reason—but the whole of London had also done the same. In view of his callous behaviour towards a helpless woman, how could they not? Yet she knew how it felt to be prejudged and knew too, it wasn't pleasant. Especially if the prejudgement was entirely unfair.

He watched her pause and mistook her momentary doubt as confirmation. 'Admit it, madam. I have been duly weighed, measured and found wanting.' That steady gaze was now daring her to agree—or perhaps hoping she might not. 'Let us not pretend it could possibly be otherwise.'

'Are you suggesting *all* the reports about you are untrue, Lord Eastwood?' Because they both knew there had been a great many, and some of them quite atrocious. You could fool some of the people all of the time after all, but not all of them, and there was no denying he and his unsuitable wife were now definitely quite divorced.

'I am not suggesting anything, Miss Brookes— merely stating the facts. You came here today with firm opinions which you are absolutely entitled to have, based on a glut of irrefutable evidence I confess I cannot be bothered to read, let alone attempt to redress.' A fact, she realised with a start, which was entirely true. In all the time she had devoured those *irrefutable* newspaper reports, it had never occurred to her before now that Lord Eastwood, despite his powerful connections, hadn't once made the effort to refute any of them. At least not that she had seen.

Nor had anybody else for that matter. Why had he remained silent?

Either he knew there was no defending the indefensible or he was just too arrogant and really did not care, or he was astute enough to have known there was no point in even attempting to put forward a defence because nobody really cared to hear it.

The scandal was just too delicious, the news so shocking, the papers had relentlessly pursued it because they knew it would sell. Yet she also knew the truth was often by the by as far as the press were concerned. Knew that through intensely personal experience too. How many times had they printed balderdash about her and her family in the past? Just this morning they were filled with more rumours about her impending engagement to Edward based on yesterday's innocuous, brief and unplanned collision at the British Museum. Nonsense grounded only tenuously in truth for which they were wholly unrepentant and all because the Brookes family lived among the forward-thinking, fashionable, artistic and decadent types in Bloomsbury, so therefore must be wholly decadent themselves as a matter of course. All so laughable they had laughed about it around the dining table—even when at times the wild accusations weren't particularly funny at all—because Papa was a firm believer in only fighting the fights you could win rather than adding fuel to a fire which would inevitably burn itself out if ignored.

Had Lord Beastly been similarly maligned? Was he that pragmatic? That fatalistic?

That misunderstood?

Her sudden and surprising flash of sympathy *had* to be misguided.

It wasn't as if she were comparing like with like when their situations were entirely different. The gossip about her family was born out of rumour and speculation which usually came after something innocuous witnessed at a social gathering, then amplified and misconstrued as it spread around the drawing rooms of the *ton* who routinely looked down on those who lived on the periphery. It was tenuous and flimsy and, like smoke without a decent fire beneath it, swiftly disappeared.

His came from a very different route—the irrefutable divorce petition which he put before Parliament and the subsequent proceedings which had been cast into law for all to see.

His was fact, *not* gossip. A man as well connected as he, from a family as esteemed as his, and a future earl no less, would surely move heaven and earth to protect that reputation if he were able?

'Even in the lofty court of public opinion, my lord, you have the right to rebuttal.'

He stared at her then as if she had gone quite mad before he slowly shook his head. 'No, Miss Brookes, I do not.'

Was that an admission of guilt? For all his standoffishness, and much to her consternation, he didn't strike her as particularly malevolent irrespective of what had been written to the contrary. She had encountered it a time or two, when one lived on the fringes of society it was impossible not to because all the flotsam and jetsam of society tended to gather there alongside the creative, the individual and the academic. Malevolent had always raised her well-honed hackles but had never made her pulse quicken quite so fervently before. 'Should I take you as entirely guilty as charged then, Lord Eastwood?'

'You will undoubtedly take me exactly as you see fit, Miss Brookes.'

'That is an infuriating answer, my lord.'

'I am told I am an infuriating man, Miss Brookes.'

Faith stared back at him, searching his face for any clue to the truth of his character until she became transfixed on his eyes once again. It was obvious there was something hidden in those un-fathomable mossy depths. But was it really disdain? Or simply defeat? Or even disappointment with the world in general? She couldn't say—but it intrigued her. He intrigued her. Undoubtedly a great deal more than a complete blackguard should.

They stared at each other for several strangely loaded seconds until the storm in his unusual eyes calmed and his expression became annoyingly bland once more. 'As scintillating as our conversation has been, Miss Brookes, I have neglected my work long enough and my *armchair* awaits.'

He bowed curtly and turned to leave, then thought better of it. There was no mistaking the emotion on his face this time.

It was contempt.

'I would say it has been a pleasure meeting you, Miss Brookes, but for all my many, many, *many* well-documented flaws, lying isn't one of them.'

Then without further ado and with a thunderous expression, and before she could articulate a suitably pithy response, her new nemesis stalked to the door and, to her complete horror, straight into her father.

Chapter Four

Invitations went out this morning for the Earl and Countess of Writtle's Annual May Ball. Doubtless we can expect a veritable exodus of society from town on the first of May, or thereabouts, as all those not worthy enough to have received one pretend they are otherwise engaged...

Whispers from Behind the Fan
February 1814

Distracted by the continued sounds of hammering in the ballroom from the battalion of workmen who were apparently necessary to build a mere structure for the canvas, Piers huffed again. 'While I will admit it wasn't my finest hour, in my defence I was provoked. The sanctimonious Miss Brookes had been looking down her nose at me all morning and something snapped.'

'That doesn't excuse it. And to be fair to her, you were in a foul mood long before she arrived.'

'And surely that's the point? I was in a *bad* mood before she arrived, Isobel, which got worse because of her haughty, judgemental behaviour and was then only made truly *foul* when my dear mother decided to try her hand at matchmaking and forced Miss Brookes upon me.' Piers felt his toes curl involuntarily at the memory, knowing his wily mother must have noticed he had been wildly attracted to her in the first place. 'You know acute embarrassment always brings out the worst in me.'

'Your mother asked you to show Miss Brookes a wall—not marry her.'

He rolled his eyes. 'Even my mother is not that unsubtle! But I can assure you, in suggesting I showed that artist my *affable* side, the implication was implicit.'

'I don't think it was. If you read more into it, then perhaps that is because you rather fancied the look of Miss Brookes yourself but are too stubborn to admit it—even to yourself. Therefore, once you were alone with her you panicked and made a royal hash of things.'

'That's ridiculous!' It would be a cold day in hell before he admitted he had rather fancied the look of her and that *had* made him panic. Which in turn had made him angry. Which had resulted in the most shocking display of rudeness towards a lady he had ever perpetrated.

I would say it has been a pleasure meeting you, but for all my many, many, many well-documented flaws, lying isn't one of them.

He was still cringing over those words and couldn't for the life of him explain what had come over him to say them when he was always polite, even in the face of the most extreme provocation. In fact, he prided himself on his ability to remain calm and reasoned in a crisis, yet she had brought out the worst in him after less than five minutes with a few fairly inane veiled insults which were nowhere near as bad as the majority he had been subjected to since his scandal. Why did they hurt more coming from her? And instead of wasting his valuable time mulling over that futile question, he would do better to consider the wider implications of his slip, because ultimately, what use was a diplomat who could no longer be diplomatic? He should probably note that down to ruminate on later if the vixen remained lodged in his head.

'In your mother's defence, I did notice you watching her on more than one occasion when you thought nobody else was watching. Don't you dare try to deny that.'

Hoisted royally by his own petard, and when he had thought he was being so subtle in his frequent perusals. 'Of course I was watching her. She was speaking. She didn't stop speaking. It is basic good manners to look at somebody when they are speaking.'

'If you say so.'

'I do!' He glared down at his tormentor sat in a puddle of chalk and paper in her favoured camp beneath his giant desk. 'And what could you possibly know about anything anyway? You are only nine.'

'I will be ten next week, Uncle Piers, and as Miss Brookes quite rightly said to Grandpapa, age is but a number.' His precocious eldest niece regarded him with patronising pity. 'Even at nine I know that the right thing to do is to go and apologise to her for being so boorish. That is *also* basic good manners. That you haven't, when she has been here for two hours already, smacks of cowardice.'

'I have important work to do this morning.' None of which he had so much as glanced at.

'So I can see...coward.'

'Brat.'

The sharp, unexpected knock at the door in the midst of such an awkward conversation caused him to guiltily jump out of his skin so his hastily barked *come in* came out a tad high-pitched. To his complete horror, when the door slowly swung open, it framed a rather wary but gorgeous-looking Miss Brookes dressed in a paint-splattered smock, which caused him to almost trip over his big feet in his hurry to stand up.

'I am sorry to disturb you, Lord Eastwood, especially after I gave you my solemn pledge never to darken your door but...' She edged in and closed the door quietly behind her then stood as prim as a nun on the threshold. 'I felt I owed you an apology for yesterday.'

'You...er...' Thanks to his now strangled blasted vocal cords, he was still speaking in a tone several octaves higher than any man worth his salt should speak in, so tried to cover it with a cough before he tried again. Thankfully that seemed to do the trick even if it did make him look like a crusty old schoolmaster. 'You do?'

'I was impolite and confrontational when neither were deserved.' She stared down at her elegant hands which were clasped tightly in front of her. 'As a guest in your home, I had no right to cast aspersions on your character, nor to talk to you with such a disregard for both your status or your feelings. I wholeheartedly apologise.'

At a loss for words, he could feel himself blinking. If she had come in and performed a fan dance on the Persian he couldn't have been more surprised and if his niece hadn't punched him hard on the foot to galvanise him into action, he likely would have done nothing but blink for hours. 'Er...your apology is accepted.'

Miss Brookes's delicate shoulders slumped in relief. 'Thank you... You are too kind, my lord. I barely slept a wink last night recalling all the awful things I said—all quite unprovoked. My father was furious and rightly so.' She had been sent here then, which rather diminished it. 'But thank you for listening to my apology and for being so gracious in accepting it.' She turned to leave just as Isobel tugged hard on his coat-tails, then thrust a piece of paper out of her hiding place which only he could see into.

In garish pink chalk and a large font were written two words in capital letters.

APOLOGISE BACK!!!

Then her small fist punched him in the shin for good measure in case he was too dim-witted to take heed.

'I should...um...' Another, quite unnecessary punch landed just below his right knee. 'I should probably apologise in return, Miss Brookes.' He sidestepped his niece's small fist this time and attempted a smile the moment his vivacious visitor turned back. A smile which he feared resembled more of a grimace. 'For I too was rude and confrontational. I am not normally so quick to temper.' He usually avoided confrontation and swallowed his anger, a tactic which he had used ineffectually throughout his turbulent marriage and which never failed to give him indigestion later in the day, but which had uncharacteristically deserted him when faced with Miss Brookes.

She beamed at him and it did odd things to his insides. 'Hardly a surprise when my Papa says I would try the patience of a saint. He is quite correct—I am too outspoken, my lord, and need to learn when to keep my own counsel. It is apparently my worst character flaw.'

'And according to my mother, I am infuriatingly tight-lipped about everything. That is mine.'

She smiled again and he found himself smiling inanely back, until he saw another chalk-written placard waving frantically out of the hidden confines of Camp Isobel.

Pay her a compliment—idiot!

'That is a very nice…um…smock you are wearing, Miss Brookes.'

A sentence so terrible, he wished he could claw

the wretched thing back the second it escaped. He was going to strangle his niece as soon as he had her alone, and then he was going to have some stern words with himself for blithely following the advice of a tyrannical almost-ten-year-old. Because surely stuttering and looking like a fool was better than blurting out blithering idiocy and confirming it for certain.

She clearly thought the same as it was now her turn to blink back at him in outright disbelief. Before he could fill the dreadful silence, things got much worse because beneath the desk his niece slapped her forehead then groaned aloud at his total ineptitude.

'Is somebody *under* your desk, Lord Eastwood?'

Before he could stop her, Miss Brookes had darted around to see for herself and he watched in mortification as her lovely eyes took in the now cheerfully waving Isobel, who was still grasping her damning chalk instruction to pay a compliment while the other, the one instructing him to apologise back in capitals, complete with its triple exclamation marks, lay face up on the floor.

There wasn't a chance in hell the vixen hadn't seen it, but in case she hadn't and while he powerlessly felt the tips of his ears glow crimson,

Isobel snatched it up and tossed it behind her before she scrambled out of her den and curtsied.

'Good morning, Miss Brookes. You look very pretty this morning.' The traitor shot him a smug *that is how you pay a compliment* look. 'I love how you have arranged your hair. I wish I had natural curls like yours. Hasn't she got lovely hair, Uncle Piers?'

She did, it was quite beautiful, but there was not a chance he could admit as much now without blushing all over like a beetroot when already his ears were on fire. 'Have you met my precocious niece Isobel?'

'Good morning, Miss Isobel...' Those not quite blue, not quite violet eyes slanted to his in amusement. 'I most certainly did not expect to see you under your uncle's desk this morning.'

'It has only been his desk for two years, Miss Brookes, it has been my camp for seven, so technically we have agreed to share it.'

'By technically, Miss Brookes, my niece means she refuses to leave despite numerous evictions and for the sake of peace we have agreed I will ignore her as long as she remains silent. Sadly, we are still trying to establish exactly what silence means because the difference between Isobel's definition and mine leaves a lot to be desired.'

'No order and quiet for you then, Lord Eastwood?' Amusement danced in her beguiling violet eyes as she quoted his harsh words from yesterday back. 'Even though you require plenty of both for your exceedingly *important* work?'

'Are you listening to this, Isobel?' Piers took the playful barb in the spirit it was intended, supremely grateful she hadn't mentioned the chalk placards or his obviously glowing ears. 'Miss Brookes has been here for less than a minute and already she has acknowledged that I am much too important to be inconvenienced by your continued and unwelcome presence in my study.'

'Miss Brookes most certainly did not say that, Uncle Piers, did you, Miss Brookes?'

'I most certainly did not, Miss Isobel, as I had absolutely no intention of taking sides in this private family dispute.' Her lovely gaze held his as she feigned annoyance for his niece's benefit. 'However, I've a good mind to ally myself with Miss Isobel on principle now that I have been so shamelessly misquoted, my lord.'

His niece beamed up at her angelically, as if butter wouldn't melt in her mouth. 'Seeing as you are now on my side, Miss Brookes, then perhaps you can intercede? As I fail to see why I should be the one to relinquish my claim upon the desk, when I was plainly here first.'

'Even though it was technically my desk before it was your desk, brat?'

Miss Brookes winked at Isobel. 'In my family, any sentence which includes the word *technically* is considered fundamentally problematic, my lord, as it wouldn't stand up in court.'

Piers found himself smiling. 'Then here is a fact which is fundamentally unproblematic and which no judge or magistrate could possibly argue. Seeing as you live next door, Isobel, you *technically* have no legal claim to *any* of the furniture in this house.'

'Miss Isobel lives next door?' This news seemed to surprise Miss Brookes and charm her in equal measure. 'It's so lovely that your sister purchased a house so near just to be close to your parents.'

'It was worse than that I'm afraid. Much to my father's consternation, my sister fell in love with our neighbour and within two mere months of clandestine courtship, upped and married him, so we have never properly got rid of her. Although both she and my vile niece are here so much, I constantly wonder why they haven't yet demolished the wall between us to make my misery complete.'

'That's even lovelier... Romantic even.' She

made an odd face as if the word *romantic* surprised her. 'If you like such things.'

'But so very inconvenient for those of us continually invaded.'

'Grandmama and Grandpapa do not feel invaded—nor have they ever minded me using this desk, so there!' Keen to prove she held the moral high ground, Isobel crawled back under the desk and decisively selected a new stick of chalk to resume her drawing. 'Besides, you abandoned it to go and live in Portugal, Uncle Piers, and so any prior legal claim you might have had to it is now null and void too.'

Miss Brookes's copper head tilted in curiosity and he decided there and then he was going to strangle his talkative niece. Any mention of his past invariably led to things best left there. 'How long did you live in Portugal for, Lord Eastwood?'

As long as it took Constança to tire of him and replace him with a more exciting man. 'Three years. I worked with the British Ambassador there ensuring our Portuguese trade routes remained open.' Why did he always feel compelled to justify his work with the dullest possible examples? Yesterday, he had blathered on about feeding soldiers and now he was boring her with shipping lanes. She would think he was just a delivery boy or a pen pusher, when the truth was the government employed him for his mind, his unique talent with languages and his unflinching ability to think logically in the most fraught and challenging circumstances.

Not that he would mention any of those things because they smacked of bragging, and bragging was another thing his annoyingly noble character did not do. 'I returned two years ago. Before Portugal I was stationed at the consulate in Tripoli.' Where he had also been involved in all manner of exciting and unpredictable things. None of which he felt comfortable discussing.

'But still, for three whole years you were not safely here at home while the war raged across the Peninsula directly around you. That must have been difficult.' Miss Brookes clearly read more than just the gossip columns.

'I haven't spent the entire war in my armchair, Miss Brookes.' There had been times when there had been no sign of any chairs at all, or even walls for that matter, after the returning French cannons had worked their magic. Those had certainly been a trying few weeks until the British retook the city.

'I should probably apologise for that comment too…'

'No need.' Piers smiled as he waved it away.

'Occasionally things were difficult, I cannot deny.' Although largely thanks more to Constança than Napoleon's rampaging army. There was a predictability about the Emperor's ceaseless hostilities which had been sadly lacking in his volatile wife. 'But by the time I arrived in Portugal, Wellington had already kicked most of Boney's army out of the region and thankfully most of the battles thereafter took place in the south and central regions, while myself and my trusty armchair were stationed predominantly in the north. In Porto to be exact—overseeing the dense concentration of British interests there.'

Her unusual eyes held his narrowed, but plainly amused. He liked the way it made them sparkle. 'You are never going to allow me to forget the armchair comment, are you, Lord Eastwood?'

'Probably not, Miss Brookes.'

She smiled, then rested her hip on the corner of his desk while her fingertips idly traced the shape of the heavy crystal inkwell he had inherited from his grandfather. It was an unconscious action. Informal. And he liked that too. 'Why were the British interests concentrated in Porto when I thought Lisbon was both the capital and the country's major shipping port?'

'Because of a much more important kind of port—the drinking kind. The wine is produced in the Douro Valley and shipped here via Porto. Even during wartime, the aristocracy must have its wine, Miss Brookes. That work was *crucial*.'

'Very important work then indeed, Lord Eastwood.' She offered him another smile, a more awkward one this time because she had also realised she had picked up his inkwell and hastily returned it to its silver tray before she stood. 'And on the subject of important work, we doubtless both have plenty to get on with so I shall leave you in peace—both figuratively and literally. I am glad we cleared the air, my lord.'

'As am I.'

She dipped her head to peek at his niece under his desk. 'And thank you for your lovely compliments about my hair, Miss Isobel. It was a vast improvement on your uncle's lacklustre praise of my tatty old painting smock—but as I insulted his trusty armchair I shall let it slide. It was lovely to meet you again.'

'You too, Miss Brookes.'

'Good day to you both.' She had opened the door again before she turned around one last time, all contriteness now replaced with the bold confidence which had first called to him yesterday. 'Your mother was right, Lord Eastwood. You are much more affable in an individual conversation. To my utmost surprise, you are almost tolerable this morning.'

His heart seemed to swell at the compliment. 'And you have been an unexpected pleasure yourself this morning too, Miss Brookes...good day.'

And all at once, as far as he was concerned, it suddenly was.

Chapter Five

While her father continued his preliminary sketches and the workmen prepared the huge canvas in Mayfair, and her mother went for yet another costume fitting at the theatre, Faith decided to take advantage of their unusually silent house in Bloomsbury to throw herself into her own work. As much as she was tempted to use the time scouring through the old newspapers at the Minerva Lending Library to properly re-read the Eastwood scandal all over again from the beginning, she flatly refused to give in to the sudden and pointless urge to do so. Especially because she only felt compelled to do it because he had made her doubt what she already knew off by heart anyway and, rampant curiosity aside, it certainly did not help her in any way.

With less than two months till the judging, she wanted a decent selection of paintings before she chose the very best to go to the Royal

Academy. This was her third attempt at getting a picture into the academy's prestigious summer exhibition in the hope her talent would finally be seen by the public and garner her some clients of her own. It had been that same exhibition which had launched her father's career, alongside many others including Thomas Lawrence and John Constable, although granted all three of them had also begun as students of the Academy. As a woman, Faith was denied that luxury but considered herself very lucky indeed to have had her father as her teacher. Most female artists weren't that fortunate.

Although that great blessing was also a bit of a curse now that she was seeking recognition, because while the Academy did not exclude women from exhibiting, most managed to get their work past the judges by presenting their painting to the panel using their initials and surname rather than their actual Christian names. But when your surname was Brookes, and the whole world and his wife knew that the great Augustus was cursed with three daughters and no sons, trying to get her gender past the other judges was impossible and some of them were dreadful sticklers. Faith consoled herself over her continued rejections with the knowledge that it had taken her brilliant father five attempts to get a painting into the illustrious exhibition, so it was unlikely she would manage one again this year, but that would not stop her trying her best. If she was ever going to crawl out of her dear Papa's huge shadow and make a name for herself in her own right, she had to persevere. She owed it to herself to succeed.

Faith stared at the seascape again as she mixed more linseed oil into her paint, promising herself she would not let it dry too much again with her wool-gathering, then immediately forgot that lofty promise once more to gaze off into space. She had been in an odd mood since yesterday and it was playing havoc with her concentration. She blamed Lord Eastwood entirely, because it seemed to be him who kept occupying her thoughts. She had gone to Grosvenor Square two days ago, fully expecting to meet a monster and had left yesterday not quite knowing what to think of him.

On that first day, they had argued. With the benefit of hindsight, she realised all those harsh words were entirely down to her. At first, she did not want to acknowledge it, and only agreed to apologise to him the next morning because her livid father had forced her to. Papa had rightly pointed out she had been spoiling for a fight from the first moment she had met Lord Eastwood, and after a huge argument which thoroughly ruined dinner, when Faith was finally all alone with her thoughts and unable to sleep, she couldn't deny that was true.

She had dragged prejudices into the Writtles' drawing room, assumptions which very well might be correct, but with no provocation whatsoever, she had allowed them to influence her behaviour towards him. Whatever dreadful things Lord Eastwood might have done to his wife, he certainly hadn't done them to Faith. Therefore, her apology yesterday had been genuine, if not still a little begrudging.

However, that brief meeting in his study had challenged all her preconceptions still further, and frustratingly left her in two minds now. Completely torn. Partly convinced he was still a monster and partly intrigued by the prospect he wasn't. Because yesterday, he hadn't only come across as eminently likeable, he had also left her thoroughly charmed. A state she was extremely uncomfortable with.

But how could she not be charmed when he allowed his niece to make camp under his desk, and spoke to the child with such obvious familial affection she could not fail to like him a little bit? She knew from her own father's excellent example in comparison with the relationships her childhood friends had had with their fathers, few men had such natural patience and rapport with a little one. Less still if the little one happened to be a girl. Yet Lord Eastwood and the incorrigible Isobel clearly adored one another. Monsters weren't supposed to be good with children.

They weren't supposed to be attractive either.

The way her pulse had fluttered when he had first shaken her hand had been peculiar in the extreme and most unlike her, the strange way her nerves had danced each time she glanced at him, the indescribable, strange stirrings of awareness she had instantly experienced when she had had no intention of being attracted and most certainly not by him. Yet the odd effect he'd had on her had resolutely lingered through both of their brief encounters and both left her feeling thoroughly out of sorts since. None of it made sense.

She sighed at the vexing conundrum, then groaned as she glanced at her forgotten palette and realised she had mixed so much oil with the Prussian blue that it was no longer fit for purpose.

As she reached for a cloth to scrape it all off, she heard her sisters in the hallway and scant moments later their feet heading her way, and knew her unproductive stretch of peace and quiet was now unequivocally at an end.

It was the youngest Brookes, Charity, who barrelled in first, closely followed by a more subdued Hope. 'We weren't expecting you to be home! Aren't you supposed to be assisting Papa?'

'His men are sizing the canvas today. It's considerably bigger than we originally planned and will need longer to prepare, so I cannot lay the base coat until it dries.' There was no rhyme or reason to the way a canvas behaved, and the larger the canvas, the more temperamental it could be. It could be a week before she could get to work on it. 'How was Whitstable?' The pair of them had spent the past week visiting their maternal grandparents in Kent, a regular trip Faith would have accompanied them on had it not been for the Writtle commission.

'Whitstable was Whitstable, as it always is.' Charity flapped the question away before grabbing Faith by the arms. 'Who cares about Whitstable when Hope and I might burst unless you thoroughly apprise us of all your dealings with the infamous Lord Eastwood.'

'Well, first of all, you should probably know that Mama has decreed he is to be called Lord Beastly henceforth in her presence and not Lord Eastwood.'

'Why? What did he do?' Hope made herself comfortable on the old tatty sofa in the corner of

Faith's small studio next to the kitchen, throwing a cushion behind her head and stretching out.

'Nothing really, but you know Mama.'

'"Nothing really" suggests he did something.' Not much ever got past Hope.

'He was a tad obnoxious.' After she had practically goaded him into it. 'And generally unlikeable.' In an oddly likeable sort of way. 'To be completely honest with you, I haven't really worked him out.' Which was probably why he had taken up too much space in her thoughts.

'Was he as horrid as the newspapers say? Could you smell the evil coming out of his pores?'

Hope rolled her eyes at the youngest. 'I'm not sure evil has a smell, Charity.'

'Well, that shows how wrong you are, because it does. Fire and brimstone. Or so it says in the Bible at any rate, and you cannot argue with that.'

Faith smiled. She had missed them. They were three entirely different characters but despite their wildly conflicting personalities, they still managed to be the best of friends. 'No fire or brimstone. No sign of any horns or cloven hooves either—I checked. Not even the faintest whiff of sulphur. Just the customary arrogance and aloofness which pompous peers tend to wear like cologne.' Although he did smell rather nice, now that she recalled it. Clean, fresh, subtly spicy...

'If he was arrogant and obnoxious perhaps you read him completely correctly. Perhaps there really was nothing else to see?' Charity shrugged, clearly disappointed. 'Lord Beastly is as beastly as we expected and that's the end to it.'

Except it hadn't been. Yes, he had been rude... eventually. But initially he had been... Faith still couldn't put her finger on what exactly he had been beyond compelling. Whatever he was, something about him called to her and refused to shut up. 'Mostly, he was reserved—polite— almost shy in his bearing. Taciturn and even, dare I say it, slightly awkward in his own skin.' Or so he had initially seemed around her until she had gone out of her way to bait him. Even then he had been calm and measured, stoic even in his rudeness, and she couldn't help but admire that when any normal person would have torn her off a strip for her unprovoked impertinence—let alone a peer of the realm. Her first question had been downright insulting and it had gone rapidly downhill from there, to such an extent her father had been furious at her in the carriage on the way home for her comments in the Writtle drawing room, but he had thankfully not been in the ballroom to witness her crowning glory.

Is this the fabled affable side of your character which you are supposed to be showing me?

Just thinking about those combative, tart words made her cringe. She had been spoiling for the fight and, very calmly and politely all things considered, he had given her one.

Then there was the endearing way he had cringed and stumbled over his words when she had gone to his study to apologise, so mortified that she had seen his niece's chalk pointers telling him to pay Faith a compliment that she had not had the heart to mention it.

'Not at all like the newspapers described actually.' Which really bothered her. She huffed out a sigh. 'He has intelligent eyes.' Very nice, intelligent eyes truth be told. Deep and green and, she was sure at times, perhaps even a little bit lost. She found herself constantly drawn to them and wondering why that was while she interviewed his mother and father and tried to appear oblivious to him stood so quietly in the corner.

Only she hadn't been oblivious.

Far from it, in fact.

'Intelligence can be a dangerous weapon in the villain's arsenal.' Hope liked to write dark and suspenseful Gothic novels. Her imagination was as vivid as her trademark red hair. 'You should probably be especially careful around him if he's cleverer than average. The most ruthless and malicious men are often geniuses. Villains are rarely two dimensional. They are as complex and as adaptable as a changeling. What you see on the surface is rarely what lurks beneath.'

Never a truer word was spoken and a timely reminder to maintain her guard irrespective of her indecisive feelings towards him. Lord Rayne had seemed lovely and genuine on the surface, as hopelessly besotted with her as she had been with him, until he went off to visit his family's estate and within days she read about the snake's engagement in *The Times*.

It still made her queasy to think of that. That same bile had bubbled when her clueless father had innocently brought the snake up in conversation in the Writtles' drawing room, and all at once she had been that stupid, green and humiliated girl again. Hideously ashamed of her monumental lack of propriety and furious at her blindly naive foray into passion with a man who was rotten to the core.

Some of that had, with hindsight, also leaked into her dealings with Lord Eastwood, who had undoubtedly borne the brunt of her disgust. As a result, she had been waspish, confrontational, and downright obnoxious herself.

Not her finest hour.

'He was curt—not malicious.' Nor did she sense any malice in him, which was probably not a reliable measure when she had been so thoroughly duped before. It was humbling to realise she was a generally poor judge of character, but knowing it was useful because it now forced her to question everything. 'Ruthless perhaps as the papers say but...' Did ruthless men indulge their mothers? Or allow their fathers to win steeplechases to spare their pride? Or clearly love their nieces to distraction? Or accept a strange woman's censure calmly and unflinchingly, and with more stoicism and patience than her combative comments and questions deserved, let alone graciously accept an apology without using his rank to make her beg and squirm for it first?

'But he does possess a sense of humour and can be rather charming too, when he puts his mind to it. He's very tolerant of his niece who clearly adores him. He allows her to play under his desk while he works and talks to her as if he listens, which is surprising when one considers the callousness with which he offloaded his poor wife.' Faith shrugged at the quandary. 'Which I suppose perfectly illustrates Hope's point. Villains are rarely two dimensional.'

'Was he at least as sinfully handsome as they say he is?' Charity perched on the arm of the sofa grinning. 'Only I've never caught sight of him at any social functions...'

Hope interrupted. 'That is because he never attends social functions. Because he knows full well if he did, he would be thoroughly shunned at them. And that's if he is allowed through the door to begin with. I've heard the patronesses have banned him from ever attending Almack's, therefore he is officially a social outcast.'

Faith felt compelled to defend that. 'Those same patronesses have always denied us vouchers to Almack's too, Hope, so I hardly think they are the most reliable gauge of a person's character.' Although theirs had been denied because of the circumstances of their birth rather than their behaviour, which made the petty prejudice even more galling. As did the friendly conversations those same ladies frequently had with the Brookes girls at all the other society engagements they were invited to, the polite how do you dos and believable smiles which always served to highlight the fickle double standards of the aristocracy in general.

'Anyway,' said the youngest undeterred. 'Dorothy Philpot said she saw him in Jermyn Street last month with his father and that just the sight of him made her want to swoon.' Charity batted her eyelashes for effect as she sighed. 'But then Dorothy is a silly dolt with fluff for brains, so I doubt it would take much for her to swoon. Did he make *you* swoon, Faith?'

Hope glared exasperated at their youngest and most wayward sibling. 'Surely even you have learned by now that a Brookes girl never swoons. Not only is it a sign of weakness—it's a mark of stupidity.' Thankfully, neither sister was aware of Faith's short but unfortunate bout of swooning over the snake.

'Well, I've certainly been tempted to swoon a time or two and am entirely convinced that when we meet the right gentlemen, swooning will be inevitable—or at least I hope it will.' Charity clutched her hands to her chest dramatically purely to vex the most serious of the three of them. 'To be perfectly frank, Hope, the idea of marrying a man who doesn't send me all aquiver fills me completely with dread. I want passion and emotion from my marriage, like Juliet felt for Romeo or Isolde had with Tristan, and I am quite determined never to settle for less.'

'Because obviously both those emotional and passionate love stories ended so well?' Hope did not possess a romantic bone in her body. 'You spend far too much time at the theatre with Mama if you believe all that nonsense.' Charity was training to be a soprano too and had enough foolish optimism for the three of them. Like their mother, she still believed in fairy tales, especially if they involved handsome men.

'And you spend too much time with the villains and macabre demons you make up in your odd head, that you imagine every man is intrinsically bad and will likely end up dying as an embittered old maid as a result.'

Oblivious of the petty argument about to erupt just feet away, Faith was still pondering Lord Eastwood and the concept of swooning. 'He was handsome—but not overtly so.' But certainly enough for her to have noticed and to keep noticing. She remembered every minute but perfect angle of his face even now. Not that she would admit that either to her sisters when they all knew the scandalous lord was not the sort of man any sensible young lady would deign to look at twice. And Hope was right, as a sensible and well-educated Brookes, it would be inconceivable to imagine she would have deigned to look once. All three of them had been brought up to have more substance than that. 'He was tall and dark and a bit brooding perhaps.'

Very tall.

Very dark.

Undeniably brooding.

'Did you just sigh?' Charity grinned and pointed her finger in accusation. 'You did, didn't you? You just *sighed* over Lord Eastwood! Sighing is practically swooning!'

Flustered, she snatched the tube of Prussian blue from her paint box and squeezed a blob on her palette. 'If I did sigh, it was because he is an enigma—and not in a romantic sort of way either, Charity, before you get any ideas.'

'A handsome and brooding enigma—a promising start.'

'To what, Charity?'

'To redemption of course!' Her sister sighed theatrically. 'Lord Beastly certainly sounds like the perfect candidate for it because if he is good with children he plainly has a soft heart.' Which was a huge part of the dichotomy Faith was struggling with. 'A soft heart he keeps hidden from the world behind layers of tortured complexity but which he will only reveal to the perfect, insightful woman who finally steals it.'

'Assuming he has a heart in the first place.' Hope echoed the other part. The pragmatic, sensible and battle-hardened part of Faith. 'And so far, tolerating his niece does not make up for the selfish and heartless way he treated the poor, un-fortunate woman who married him. You need to remember that, Faith, when he turns on the charm around you again.'

'Oh, for goodness sake! I am well aware that a gentleman can seem to be pleasant on the out-side but hideous beneath.' Only too aware. The scars left behind were permanent and deep. 'But no amount of pleasantness on his part detracts from the hideous way he treated his poor wife. It takes more than charming to charm me.'

A mantra Faith decided she probably needed to repeat as often as it took to completely believe it.

Chapter Six

'It is too soon, *senhor.*' And it was too damn early to attempt to manoeuvre seven separate and stubborn nations in one direction. Or too damn late if you still considered five o'clock in the morning very much the territory of the night before, which on this dreary Saturday morning, Piers was inclined to think it was. 'While we understand the Conde do Funchal is eager to report to your government that our attack of Toulouse is imminent, now would be the wrong time.'

Two months of unprecedented torrential rain had made Wellington's advance through southern France slow going, and while they certainly had the manpower and with the recent victories at Nive and Orthez under their belt, Soult's troops in the south of France were still too scattered for a battle now to achieve anything decisive. Despondent, ill-disciplined and ill-equipped, the reluctant French conscripts were also on the cusp of revolting. Something which was also happening along the volatile front in the north of the country, as the Russian, Prussian, Austrian and Bavarian allies rapidly converged on an increasingly weak and desperate Napoleon and the capital, Paris.

British High Command were keen to allow that dissension in the ranks to keep festering in the dreadful weather for as long as possible, reasoning that it would be easier to beat an uncommitted and unfocused enemy in one organised, conclusive battle once Paris had fallen, than a riled one still clinging to the hope of victory and baying for allied blood in a prolonged series of skirmishes.

Piers had spent the better part of the last hour explaining that logic to the men around the table, painstakingly repeating the highlights of Wellington's latest dispatch in three different languages, yet true to form, the representatives of the Sixth Coalition to the Palace of St James were as uneasy in one another's company as the troublesome alliance was flimsy. They all came to these meetings with varying agendas, they always had, stubbornly ignoring that only one truly mattered—and that was defeating blasted Napoleon.

Russia, Prussia, Austria and Bavaria were fairly

aligned on their purpose once more, although that had been a close-run thing after an unexpected flurry of French victories had almost caused the changeable Austrian and Bavarian leaders to retreat completely. Both had once been aligned with Napoleon, so for a while it had not been inconceivable to imagine they would fall back behind him again. Fortunately, the Tsar had talked them around, but his growing power within the uncomfortable alliance was a major concern for the British who did not trust the Russians to leave France when the war was done. And the Portuguese were, understandably, sick to the back teeth with the never-ending battles which had raged for years either directly on their doorstep or on neighbouring Spain's, and were all done with the dithering and could not fathom why Wellington was dragging his feet when they were raring to go.

'Leaving Marshal Soult to regroup in Toulouse is pure folly.' The Portuguese diplomat was a troublesome character at the best of times because he preferred to react to unsubstantiated rumours rather than waiting for the cold, hard facts which only came from diligent reconnaissance, and in this case, even with those facts now in his possession, preferred to scaremonger. 'We have it on good authority they have amassed another half a million conscripts who are preparing for a mammoth assault within days. We have also heard...' Piers politely raised his hand to stay the litany, using the excuse of translating all this to his own superiors as a way of calming the fellow down.

'Oh, good grief...' The Foreign Secretary, Lord Castlereagh, had only barely managed not to roll his eyes as he whispered through gritted teeth. The ink was barely dry on the Treaty of Chaumont, a negotiation which had tested all Piers's skills to the limit but had guaranteed the coalition would continue to fight the war until all of Napoleon's troops were beaten and France retreated back to within its original borders. But already, trying to maintain that agreement for solidarity among the allies a mere few weeks on, was proving problematic. 'We've been over this. Twice at least.'

'And clearly we are going to have to go over it again.' Lord Bathurst, the Secretary of State for War, was always more patient than his fiery counterpart at the Foreign Office. Subtly, he glanced at the clock on the mantelpiece, pretended to nod sagely as if giving the sabre rattling from the Portuguese Ambassador's most annoying lackey some serious consideration, then also whispered in case any of the men around the table had a much better grasp of the English language than they were prepared to let on. 'Unruffle the idiot's feathers, Eastwood, without promising him anything of course, and then perhaps we can all escape in time for breakfast.' A near impossible task under the best of circumstances. 'And then look into finding a new harbour for our message ships. It's dashed inconvenient to keep having these meetings in the small hours.' Inconvenient but inevitable when all the untrusting allies had a network of spies carefully watching each other's every move in case they were being duped. Hence as soon as this message arrived from Dover they had all been raised from their beds at an ungodly hour to argue in circles with their allies like they always did. The only difference being that now the end really was in sight, relations between the six nations were deteriorating because they were all impatiently determined to get to that final destination in their own way.

Instead of groaning his frustration with the pettiness of it all out loud, Piers offered his most reassuring smile before attempting to achieve the impossible in fluent Portuguese. 'Senhor Melo, France is in utter turmoil and Bonaparte has lost the goodwill of most of his people. Those he has managed to recently press-gang into his army

are a ragtag bunch of angry farmers and peas-
ants and children who have been given such little training they barely know one end of a gun
from another. And let us not forget Marshal Soult
isn't the only French General seeking reinforce-
ments. They all are. I have fresh maps and charts
I can show you.'

'I should like to see those documents.' The
Portuguese official seemed placated.

'We all would.' The Russian Ambassador
spoke in his native tongue despite his obvious
understanding of Portuguese and his own translator sat right beside him. 'That we haven't yet
seen them when we have been here for an hour
is a grave concern, gentlemen.' The Russians
might well be closest to Paris, but British intelligence and communication lines across northern
France were far superior and, thanks to the navy,
arrived much quicker in London than to the allied commanders of the coalition. If those armies
or Napoleon's advanced six inches, Whitehall
knew about it within a few days. It was sending
that intelligence speedily back to Wellington in
the south which was more problematic. 'If you
have kept vital French troop movements a secret,
what else have we been kept in the dark about?
And more importantly *why*?'

At this, the Bavarian, Austrian and Prussian

representatives pricked up their ears, all equally as suspicious of the potential superiority of the others as the map of Europe was slowly being redrawn, all wondering if the British had designs on filling the void which would be left by Napoleon. Land meant power and the British knew that better than most—they had been amassing it for centuries.

Piers kicked himself for not articulating it better, knowing lack of sleep was not an excuse which would cut the mustard with the Prime Minster if he inadvertently caused another war because of an ill-thought-out sentence. There was no denying he wasn't as sharp as he should be thanks to the scant hour of rest he had managed last night in between a particularly vivid and lusty dream involving Miss Brookes, himself and a wingback armchair, and the government messenger who hammered on his door sometime around two. That was three nights in a row he had dreamt of her, fuelling his newly awoken lust which refused to subside no matter how much he willed it to. He had only met the siren twice, briefly, and hadn't seen hide nor hair of her in five days, so couldn't understand why she already had such a hold on his urges or occupied so many of his thoughts.

As his exhausted mind tried to wander to her,

he dragged it kicking and screaming back to the table. 'The maps I am referring to came overnight with the latest dispatch.' Piers hated speaking Russian. At best he had a schoolboy's grasp of the language, at worst, because he was still learning it, his accent made him sound like a complete amateur. He much preferred German, or French, or even Italian despite it being a little too dramatic for his staid character. 'Copies are being made as we speak, which we will have delivered to your legations within the hour. We are in this together, Your Illustrious Highness.' Another reason why he loathed speaking Russian. Their aristocracy had an overinflated sense of their own importance and the Ambassador Count von Lieven was a stickler for such details. 'And only by working together, with mutual trust and complete transparency, will we *all* defeat Napoleon.'

Before that answer was dissected and purposely misinterpreted, he hastily brought the meeting to a close. One by one the diplomats filed out of the room, leaving Piers alone with Castlereagh and Bathurst.

'Is it just me or is this getting harder.' Castlereagh was never one to beat around the bush. 'It's like herding cats in fog.'

'It's been a difficult couple of months. Every-one is battle weary.' Including Piers.

'It worries me.' Bathurst frowned. 'We have all come so far, and victory feels so close, yet I fear it could all go to hell in a handcart if the al-liance crumbles.'

'I miss the old days.' Castlereagh huffed out a sigh. 'Diplomacy was so much easier when we did it over cigars and port. Everyone is always more agreeable when they are three sheets to the wind. Nowadays, we're all so suspicious of one another.'

'We could have a pipe of port delivered to the next dreary meeting. It would certainly make it more bearable.' Piers began to gather his papers, trying to ignore his rumbling tummy because there was no chance of any breakfast for him for at least the next three hours. Once the trans-lations of the latest dispatch and now also those blasted maps and charts were done, he had a mountain of other things which urgently needed his attention, not least Isobel's birthday present. His life wouldn't be worth living if he didn't make the time to buy her something. Birthdays in the Writtle household were sacrosanct, and not even a war was a valid excuse for not mark-ing one.

'Port would certainly make the Russians more

bearable. At least for me it would.' Castlereagh sighed wistfully. 'Perhaps we should have two pipes of port delivered.'

'That would at least make Portugal feel a little more loved. They are *very* proud of their port.' Bathurst's flippant comment irritated.

'Since Chaumont, they feel like the poor relation. With hindsight, we probably should have included them in those negotiations rather than assuming they would simply go along with whatever we wanted regardless.' They hadn't because Portugal was the poor relation. It had always fought alongside Britain because that was traditionally where their interests lay, but there was no denying they now took the Portuguese, their army and their unflinching support for granted. 'Melo is flexing his muscles because he wants it to appear to the others as if they do have a say, even though we all know they really do not. We really should treat them with more respect. They deserve it.'

'You make a good point, Eastwood.' Castlereagh frowned as he nodded. 'We could have played that better. Perhaps we should do something to make them feel special and keep them onboard? They are our most stalwart allies after all.'

They were and had been right from the very

beginning. They had also suffered more than the other allies. 'Perhaps we should wheel out the Regent to make a gushing speech over a nice dinner?' It was a throwaway comment, meant to be as glib and dismissive as the Secretary of War's had been, but Bathurst's eyes lit up.

'That's actually not a bad idea. A bit of pomp and pampering might be just the thing to make them feel loved.' Castlereagh stared at the Secretary for War and shrugged. 'It is an easy solution to a spiralling problem. We could paper over the cracks with a state banquet.'

'Then I think we should do it. And the sooner the better.' Bathurst didn't appear to need any more convincing. 'Contact the Master of the Household and see if we can secure a date within the month.' Both men stared at Piers as if they were expecting him to jot that down on his already enormous list of things to do. As the silence stretched, the alarms bells began to ring.

'Surely you're not expecting *me* to organise it?'

'We have to run it past the Prime Minister and cabinet first.' Bathurst never even blinked as he deftly avoided the question. 'But before we put it to him, we need to investigate if it's even viable in such a short timeframe. Only the palace will know that, so speak to them today and report back as soon as you can.'

'And if it is?'

'Then we extend an invitation to His Royal Highness Dom João, and if he accepts, we decide the best course of action and choose the best person to lead it.' A true politician's answer. Never confirm or deny anything until the last possible moment, and no comfort whatsoever to Piers. 'This isn't any old party, Eastwood, it's a potential diplomatic disaster unless handled correctly. It will require someone who understands the delicate balance of power, the different egos, the fluctuating politics and the ever-changing situation and is adept at manoeuvring around it. Besides, whomever that person is would *oversee it*, rather than organise it. The capable staff at St James's Palace will do all the menial work.'

It already sounded dangerously like a hideous fait accompli. 'I am most assuredly the wrong man for the job.'

'I disagree.' Castlereagh tucked in his chair and leaned heavily on the back of it. 'Nobody knows the Portuguese better than you do, Eastwood. You've attended their Royal Court, you know their customs and speak their language like a native.'

'But I don't know the first thing about banquets!' Or any other sort of fancy social gathering for that matter. Piers normally avoided them all like the plague. Always had. 'Which surely is the most important prerequisite for somebody put in charge of one.'

'What's there to know?' Castlereagh had the gall to smirk at his comment. 'If the palace can accommodate us, you liaise with them and the Portuguese, send out a few choice invitations to the great and the good, placate the other allies, glance at the seating plans to make sure we don't inadvertently upset anyone and make sure His Royal Highness makes a suitably gushing speech which flatters the Portuguese without jeopardising the status quo.' He slapped Piers on the back. 'It's a simple enough job and nothing a fellow of your intelligence and experience can't do in his sleep.'

Deflated, put upon but horribly and nobly resigned, Piers gathered up his never-ending pile of work before glancing wistfully out of the window at the beginnings of the sunset. It was barely dawn, it wasn't even six o'clock and already he knew, without a shadow of a doubt, it was going to be one hell of a bad day.

'Good afternoon, Miss Brookes.' Milton, the Writtles' butler, met her at the door and relieved her of her coat and warm bonnet. 'Your father has been asking about you.'

'Doubtless only in between sitters when he remembers I exist.' Dear Papa did tend to get absorbed in his work, losing all track of time and place. Five days into what would likely be a month of preliminary sketches, he had commandeered the music room as his studio and now ruled there like an unreasonable despot who only cared about the art he was creating. It was a familiar pattern which she was well used to but which always came as a shock to the unsuspecting clients who, not unreasonably, assumed the same sane and personable man they had commissioned to paint their portraits would be the one to do the painting.

'Which poor family member is he torturing now?'

She had made a point, on the first day, of quietly apprising everyone in the household of his demanding methods to forewarn them, just in case one of them strangled him after an hour of standing as still as a statue in the total and unreasonable silence her father insisted upon. Already, the poor Writtles had accepted that the Augustus Brookes behind the easel was a very different character from the one they had taken tea with last week.

'I believe it is a very reluctant Lord Eastwood at present.'

Who had, to her father's great consternation, thus far deftly managed to avoid being sketched by holing himself up in Whitehall and pleading work.

'He ran out of excuses?'

'No, Miss Brookes.' The butler grinned. 'He inadvertently ran into his mother while attempting to sneak in unnoticed an hour ago and was promptly frogmarched to the music room before he had time to remove his coat. I wouldn't be at all surprised if she has locked him in to force His Lordship to comply.' A prospect too entertaining not to investigate.

After a cursory glance in the ballroom which confirmed the many layers of size on the canvas were finally dry, Faith hurried to the music room. She slipped inside, knowing her usually sane father was always at his most unpredictable if he was interrupted, and quietly took in the scene.

Poor Lord Eastwood was sat uncomfortably upright astride a saddle strapped to a trestle table while her father fervently sketched. As Milton had claimed, both his greatcoat and hat had been hastily tossed on one of the striped silk sofas and even with his broad back to her, she could picture his expression. His face might well be static and arranged just so for Papa, but those eyes—those stormy, expressive, mesmerising eyes—would tell a completely different story.

When her father glanced up and acknowledged her with a curt nod, Lord Eastwood's dark head whipped around and the message in them was clear. He was royally fed up, thought the whole thing daft and was plainly desperate for any just cause to escape.

'Good afternoon, my lord.'

'Hello, Miss Brookes.' His deep, velvety voice sounded so despondent; she barely stifled the laugh as her father bellowed his disapproval.

'How many times do I have to tell you *not* to move, my lord? I cannot draw a fidget! I need stillness!' Like a shot Papa was then off his stool and manhandling his unwitting victim, grabbing his chin and impatiently rearranging it forward, then tilting it up, then down, then roughly to the side as he sought the correct angles. 'Absolute stillness!'

To his credit, Lord Eastwood bore it all with surprising good humour, only his eyes tilted to hers when she moved to peek at the sketch. Although forcing her gaze to focus on the drawing was near impossible when it decided it would much prefer settling on him.

'How is it going?'

'As you can plainly see...' He managed to

speak with the minimum movement of his mouth to appease her father. 'It is pure, unmitigated torture.'

She chuckled. 'That bad?'

'Perhaps not as torturous as the rest of my interminable day has been, or heaven forbid a dreadful society party—but most definitely a close third.'

'Interminable? But it's only two.'

'Which means I have already been up for twelve hours and probably will be for another twelve more at this rate. My mistake here was coming home to eat and believe me, I am kicking myself for it.'

'And I also need silence, Lord Eastwood!' For good measure, her father shot her a furious look. 'You too, missy! Stop distracting my muse.' A comment which widened poor Lord Eastwood's eyes.

She did openly laugh at that. She couldn't help it. His appalled thoughts were so loud, she could practically hear him thinking them.

'By muse...' She waved her arms expansively in the ether theatrically to encompass the entire universe. 'He means his *artistic* muse, my lord, and not that you have suddenly become it and must therefore sit for him for all eternity or he will never be able to paint again.'

Those wonderfully broad shoulders relaxed at the welcome clarification, which earned him another prod from her father.

'Straighter, my lord! Slightly arch the neck and stare forward like I showed you. Hold the reins higher.' Papa flapped his palms upwards. 'A tad more...'

He did as he was instructed, Lord Eastwood's now amused eyes locking with Faith's once more and something about the way they twinkled caused her stupid pulse to quicken with gay abandon when it had thus far behaved itself. Off-kilter, she stared resolutely at the drawing to cover her discomfort and instantly frowned— and not just at her wayward and unwelcome reaction to him.

The picture was all wrong.

Despite being a preliminary and exploratory drawing, and therefore expected to be rough around the edges, it still fell woefully wide of the mark.

That was unlike her father. He normally had a way of uncovering the real essence of a person behind the public façade swiftly, often in minutes, capturing the subtle nuances of body language and expression perfectly. Effortlessly, in fact. That was what made his portraits so desirable. They were usually so natural, fluid and yet still intensely personal. But this charcoal Lord Eastwood was more like the one she had just read about in the newspapers rather than the man who worked with his niece playing beneath his desk. Instead of quiet confidence and cheerful stoicism, she saw surly arrogance, and his expressive eyes were flat, almost as if there was nothing at all behind them. Never mind that the pose was all wrong. It was too noisy and aggressive, too regal, too pompous and lacked the real man's innate subtlety.

'I can sense your disapproval, Faith!' Her father's delicate stick of charcoal snapped between his fingers as he bristled. 'Admit it! You do not like it, do you?'

Chapter Seven

'It's not so much that I don't like it as...' As Faith struggled to temper her words, her father swivelled around on the stool to stare belligerently, arms crossed and jaw set stubbornly. Behind him, Lord Eastwood took the opportunity to roll the tension out of his shoulders and sit more casually. Instantly, it suited him. 'What I meant is, this is supposed to be an *informal* family portrait, yet your depiction of Lord Eastwood is a little too formal for the composition, don't you think? Does he need to sit so rigidly in the saddle?'

Her father gazed back at his drawing and shrugged defensively. 'Lord Eastwood enjoys riding in his spare time, so putting him on a horse *is* informal.'

'Of course it is...under all normal circumstances...' She pointed to the scowl he had drawn and the resolutely furrowed dark brows. She had witnessed his actual scowl, caused it even, and it was nowhere near as evil as the one her father had drawn. 'However, here he looks as though he is about to charge into battle.'

'Nonsense!' Her insulted father refused to see it. 'He is *nonchalantly* sitting in the saddle.'

'While clearly contemplating dastardly and murderous deeds.' She traced the harsh line of the eyebrows in the air to avoid smudging the paper. 'Those are angry eyes, Papa, and while I will grant you Lord Eastwood is largely unenthusiastic about this portrait and prone to a little surliness from time to time...' She couldn't resist looking up and seeing the amused twinkle in the real eyes. 'I am not convinced he deserves to be captured for posterity with a face like thunder. And the least said about the fearsome horse you have sketched the better. It looks so thoroughly sinister, even one of the four horsemen of the apocalypse would have second thoughts about riding it.'

Unsurprisingly, her father took instant umbrage at her words and she wanted to kick herself for being so forthright when she knew how fragile the artistic ego could be—especially her supremely talented father's. 'And I suppose you could do better, daughter?'

Normally, she would dismiss that comment

out of hand, knowing he might initially chafe at her criticism, but he would swiftly see for himself exactly what she was talking about once his temper had cooled. But this time, she wasn't certain. Papa might know Lord Eastwood liked to ride, but that knowledge came alongside a huge swathe of evidence from the court of public opinion which had obviously clouded his vision—just as it clouded hers. Yet if she could see there was plainly more to Lord Eastwood than the newspapers had reported, when she had more reason than Papa to distrust this almost-Earl, then she owed it to the portrait to help her father see those complex layers too.

'I could give it a try, Papa...' An answer which surprised them both. While she could draw faces well enough, he was the master of the portrait and she normally respected that distinction.

'Then please...' He stood, clearly very put out, and expansively gestured to the stool before brusquely removing his drawing to reveal a fresh sheet of paper underneath. 'Be my guest. I cannot wait to be taught a valuable lesson in the complicated art of portraiture.'

For the briefest moment, she considered backing down rather than stepping on his sensitive toes, then rejected it. This was such an important commission and she wanted it to be the triumph her father deserved. Lord Eastwood's expression, the pose and the tone were entirely wrong and if Papa stubbornly refused to see that then she needed to show him.

Trying to ignore dear Papa's pinched expression of blatant annoyance, she sat down and selected a piece of charcoal from the box on the floor and instead smiled at the man she felt compelled to smile at to put him at his ease.

'Why have you been awake since two?' Papa might well prefer silence while he sketched, but she did not.

'I've been saddled with the chore of organising a state banquet.'

'And for that you were roused from your bed at such an ungodly hour?'

'Not exactly. That chore was foisted upon me at dawn after I stupidly suggested it. Now, for my sins, I am stuck with it.'

'That still doesn't explain why you had to get up at two, my lord.'

'Unfortunately, the war doesn't confine itself to town hours.'

'That's a very cryptic answer.'

He smiled wryly. 'Yet it is all I can give you, Miss Brookes. Infuriating, I know, but there it is. Sharing state secrets is a treasonable offence.' The wryness was replaced by a mock serious expression which completely missed his eyes. 'And for all I know you could be a French spy.'

'Very true.' Faith liked his dry sense of humour. It was subtle but intelligent, much like the man himself. 'Then while I work out another, more devious way to prise those valuable secrets out of you, I shall disarm you using the distraction of another topic instead. How is Isobel today?'

'Still precocious.'

'Yet you love that about her.'

'I wouldn't go that far.' He offered her an ironic half-smile which did nothing to hide his deep affection for his eldest niece. 'At best, I tolerate it for a quiet life.' As she had hoped, talking about a safe topic he cared about, like Isobel, instantly lowered his guard and he started to forget to feel awkward. 'It is her birthday in two days, and I have no earthly idea what to get the brat. Now that she is turning ten, she claims she is too old for dolls, so that's my first idea blown to smithereens.'

She sketched some bold lines on the paper, trying to capture both the economy of expression alongside the dry humour. 'And the second idea?'

'There isn't a second idea. That's the problem. And not for the want of searching either. On the way home, I visited Noah's Ark in Holborn for the second time to hunt for something and left, for the second time, depressingly empty-handed.'

'But Mr Hamley's emporium is the best toy shop in London. Surely they had something.'

'Nothing which screamed Isobel... It is so frustrating. Especially as time is rapidly running out and I shall have to head back there again tomorrow, with no earthly clue what for. A gift should always be special rather than make do...' He sighed, his gaze wandering to the window for a second before he caught himself and remembered the situation. 'Should I be sitting straighter?' He wiggled the fake reins he was still holding. 'And where do you want my hands?'

'Just relax them. Sit how you feel comfortable.'

'I am sat on a saddle, on a trestle table in my mother's music room, in the middle of the day— under duress, Miss Brookes. What, pray tell, is comfortable about that?'

'Absolutely nothing at all, my lord, but try.' She peered at him haughtily over the easel. 'Or, as a ruthless disciple of Napoleon, I shall make you pretend to gallop and then you'll be sorry. A fake gallop is brutal on the leg muscles.'

He grinned at that and his features softened, showing her a glimpse of an altogether different Lord Eastwood again. A man who didn't take himself too seriously or take easy offence when mocked, which was a rare attribute for a man of his ilk. As was caring so very much over a child's birthday.

Which made Faith wonder again about his character. Would a man who believed a gift should always be special and who agonised over the selection for days really be the same sort of man who could ruthlessly detach himself from a disadvantageous marriage purely to pursue his own lofty ambitions? He did not seem preoccupied with rank or come across as particularly cutthroat. If anything, and to her complete surprise, he came across as extremely likeable now that they had called a truce. 'Then my poor leg muscles thank you for your benevolence, Miss Brookes, and I shall endeavour to relax, even though I look entirely ridiculous on this bizarre contraption. But I am still not going to tell you any state secrets.'

'Another fiendish plan foiled.'

He grinned again. 'You were a little girl once, surely you have a suggestion for a present?'

Faith paused to give it some thought. 'I have two sisters, my lord, and growing up we all liked to play with different toys. To properly advise you, I would need to know what sort of things Miss Isobel likes to do instead of playing with dolls.'

He let go of the reins with one hand so that he could run it impatiently through his hair, completely destroying the harsh neatness he, or more likely his mother, had prepared for the sitting. It suited him, a little too much. 'Besides get under my feet?' There it was again, that feigned air of being vastly put upon when she suspected, where his family were concerned, he was anything but. It was obvious he adored the child. She could see the love shining in his green eyes whenever he mentioned her. 'She's always drawing something and covering my study floor with chalk dust in the process.'

Faith focused on his eyes, trying to emulate the animation and emotion in them on the paper without being distracted by the urge to drink in his face. 'She is a budding artist then?'

'I doubt the poor maids see it that way when they have to pick the daily dust rainbow out of the parquet.'

'Chalk is messy.' She could feel her father's assessing stare as she quickly tried to convey all that she saw into the sketch, and tried not to allow it to put her off even though he would likely rip her efforts to shreds with his inevitable criticisms. 'Is it her preferred medium?'

Lord Eastwood's dark head tilted while he considered it. 'I think it is her only medium, to be honest. There was a set of paints once, but they were confiscated when she decided to redecorate the drawing room and recolour her sister.' He chuckled at the memory, managing to look thoroughly sinful in the process as those distracting eyes danced. 'I believe a moratorium was declared on all paint then by my mother.'

'How old was she then?'

'Six...no...wait...' As his brows furrowed, a tiny, endearing crinkle formed between them. 'It was before I left for Tripoli, so she had to have been four. I remember now because Elspeth was still in leading strings and the colour she was caked in was such a vivid shade of green that it took a week of baths to get it all out of her skin.' Faith could tell he particularly enjoyed that memory.

'A moratorium is not an outright ban, so *technically* it could be lifted.' She found her eyes shamelessly seeking his again. 'I sincerely doubt Isobel would paint her sister now, or the drawing room either for that matter. Maybe it is time the family forgave her for her regrettable early green period and entrusted her with some new paints. If she is a budding artist, then the limitations of chalk will stifle her talent.'

He laughed at that, a low, deep, rumble which came from somewhere deep in his chest but which she felt everywhere. 'I said she liked to draw. At no point did I say she had any talent for it.'

'Even so, I think she might appreciate some grown-up paints for her birthday.'

He took a moment to ponder it then offered her a smile so devastating she almost sighed aloud. 'That is actually not a bad idea...thank you. I shall visit the Ark again tomorrow and get some.'

'Those will be basic children's paints, my lord.' In case her father sensed her pulse was bouncing erratically all over the place, Faith forced her focus back to her sketch. 'For a mature young lady like Isobel, Ackermann's on the Strand is the best place to go, and if it were me choosing them, I would start her on watercolours first. Oil is a tricky medium and needs some practice. She will tire of it and become frustrated before she gets the hang of it unless she has achieved some success beforehand. Watercolours are much more forgiving and garner quicker results. I could also give her some lessons if you think she would like some?'

He pulled a face. 'Be very careful what you offer, Miss Brookes, and be quite specific in the parameters if you do, because my niece is a manipulative hellion of the first order and she will make a pest of herself otherwise. Trust me, if you give her an inch, she will invariably take a mile and before you know it, she will have made a new camp in the ballroom and you'll never be rid of her.' Then mischief shimmered as their gazes locked again. 'Which I shall, of course, make no effort to dissuade her from. Because at least I'll be shot of her.'

'You'd miss her.'

'Miss her? I am already considering having some bunting made in celebration of her imminent departure.'

Faith grinned, added one final flourish to her hasty composition, then sat back so her father could scrutinise her work, quietly pleased with the quick sketch.

'What do you think, Papa?'

To her complete surprise, his long pause was followed by an impressed nod as all sign of her father's previous bad mood seemed to have evaporated.

'I think you did a much better job than I did, Faith, and you were right to dispense with the saddle. What say you, my lord?' He unclipped her picture and held it up alongside his for comparison. 'Which do you prefer?'

Those intelligent, mossy eyes studied them both and she saw his expression change with obvious approval at hers, then they narrowed in mock affront as they took in her whole composition.

'I cannot help but notice you have eschewed my noble steed to sit me in an armchair, Miss Brookes.'

'I did indeed, Lord Eastwood.' Her lips twitched as she failed to suppress her laughter. 'I know how wedded to it you are.'

Chapter Eight

*If my sources are correct, gentle reader, then
the infamous Lord E. is finally stepping out of
the shadows to grace the Renshaw Ball with
his maleficent presence...*

Whispers from Behind the Fan
March 1814

'I know I agreed to it.' After a great deal of
browbeating. 'But I still fail to see why I absolutely have to come tonight?' The carriage door
closed decisively behind him like the lid of his
coffin, signalling he was doomed regardless, yet
a tiny part of him still clung to the faint hope of
a reprieve.

'Because you were expressly invited, Piers.
Because the Renshaws have been our friends for
years. Because they have stuck by us through
thick and thin and because the Marquis bent over
backwards to aid your cause with Parliament.'

All depressingly good reasons to attend. 'They *still* want to help, Piers, and both your father and I agree this will be good for you.'

By good for him, they meant they wanted him to venture into society again to begin to repair his shattered reputation, convinced that once he did he could move on, put the dreadful past completely behind him, find another woman and trust her enough with his bludgeoned heart to blithely live happily ever after. As if blithely trusting anyone was even an option on the table when he and his poor heart could personally think of nothing worse.

He wasn't the same optimistic and idealistic young man who had rushed headlong into marriage, convinced the giddy strength of his love was enough to conquer all. It hadn't. Leaving him too jaded, too wounded, too cautious and only too aware of the awful consequences of rushing headlong into anything any more. Love, it turned out, hadn't conquered all, nor had it endured. It had quickly fizzled, died and abandoned him after reality had rampaged over the horizon and trampled it all to death.

'I've always loathed balls.' Especially nowadays. It was one thing to have his private heartbreak gossiped about openly behind your back whenever you ventured out, another entirely to have to stand in a room of couples stood all alone. He was almost used to being a social pariah, but being forced to display the crushing loneliness in front of a hundred judgemental people... Well, that was another matter entirely.

His mother reached across and squeezed his hand. 'It has been two years since you came home, darling. You cannot hide from society for ever.'

Yet Piers was prepared to give it a jolly good go! When even extended family gatherings left him feeling raw and uncharacteristically maudlin, exactly as Isobel's birthday party had only yesterday. There was nothing better for reminding you of all your failures in life than the cheerful presence of your two happily married sisters, one complete with two adorable grandchildren already for his parents to coo over and the other, the youngest of the three of them, on the cusp of giving birth to her first. While he was delighted for both his sisters, he also envied them their happiness and their families. Things he should have had now too had it not been for his own blind stupidity. 'As far as the outside world is concerned, it has been just six months.' When he had reluctantly emerged from the blessed obscurity of his sanctuary at Whitehall to set Constança free.

He missed that obscurity and craved it now more than anything. After months of hell, the newspapers had only just left him alone, a state of affairs which would rapidly change in tomorrow's scandal rags if he couldn't continue to lie low. 'My reappearance tonight will doubtless cause rife speculation in the gossip columns. You know already what the stories will say. Now that I have successfully offloaded the first unfortunate wife, I am blithely on the hunt for a replacement...' *Good grief, he didn't need that too!* 'They will assume I am an eager bachelor about town—and that will only make things more awkward.' Because Piers might well be a bachelor again, if he pushed his unwelcome and overwhelming new obsession with Miss Brookes to one side, but he certainly wasn't eager. He had never been one for society before his marriage. Being reserved, dull and staid in nature, he had always found large gatherings hard work. But now—divorced and vilified—they felt more daunting than ever. A feeling not helped by almost two years of determined avoidance.

'And those that know you and respect you are well aware of the truth of the matter and will pay none of those scurrilous reports any mind. The Renshaws are dear family friends and our attendance at their annual ball is a tradition.'

His father's tone was kind, but like his mother, they were both ready to take the next tentative steps, believing reintroducing him to society in a friendly environment was the beginning of the inevitable restoration of his good name and reputation, as it would surely remind everyone of who he really was. Over time—an overly optimistic time frame in his humble opinion—they were convinced society would forget the scandal and those unfortunate years in purgatory would all disappear from memory. Piers sincerely doubted it was going to be that easy. Scandals faded eventually, but they never fully disappeared, and his had been so momentous it would always follow him around. But they wanted him to be happy and he didn't have the energy to tell them they were wasting their time.

'There is also an argument for giving them something positive to write about, don't you think?' His mother had that innocent, butter-wouldn't-melt-in-her-mouth expression again. 'Because who cares what they print as long as it is good news for a change.'

'And me attending a ball is good news?'

'Your meeting a nice young lady tonight might...'

'Oh, for pity's sake! Not this again.'

Even his father rolled his eyes. 'Leave the boy

alone, Margaret! How many times does he have to tell you he isn't ready for that? After that witch Constança, it should hardly come as a surprise he is unenthusiastic, and who could blame him either? That woman was enough to put any sane fellow off all women for life!'

A sad truth Piers couldn't deny. Especially women who came from that same mould. Vibrant, exciting, unconventional women who were absolutely nothing like him. Free spirits—like Miss Brookes. Oil and water could never mix. He understood that now. There was no point in yearning for the exceptional, yet no matter how much he willed it, he couldn't envisage ever being able to settle for the mundane.

'Piers is dipping his toe back into society again. Nothing more. Let the boy ease in gently, Margaret.'

His mother turned away stubbornly to stare out of the window. 'I am merely saying, in the most general of terms, that if one *does* happen to take his fancy, he shouldn't allow one mistake to hold him back for ever, that is all.'

Piers would have argued, but knew it was ultimately pointless. His mother wouldn't be swayed from her belief that it would all come out in the wash any more than he would be swayed from his belief that the stain he carried was just too ingrained. Instead, because he was a predictably dull diplomat to his core, he stared despondently out of his own window and changed the subject. 'The queue of carriages is ridiculous. They are already snaking down Davies Street. We could be here awhile.'

Which suited Piers perfectly.

'Didn't I say taking the carriage to a destination just around the corner was a stupid idea, Margaret?' His father wasn't hampered by a constant need for diplomacy. 'We shall be sat here for a good hour now, when Berkeley Square is less than a five-minute walk from our own house! Why do we always have to bring the carriage to travel around the corner?'

'Because that is what people *do*, Henry, never mind that it looks like rain.'

'Well, I'd much rather walk!' Before anyone could argue, his father was up and out of the door like a shot. 'Come along, the pair of you!' He glanced skywards and rolled his eyes at the distinct lack of storm clouds. 'I dare say we can manage the hundred yards before the heavens open.' A depressing fact which couldn't be argued with when he would much prefer an hour stuck in the carriage to an extra hour of hideousness at the Renshaws' blasted ball.

Piers trailed behind his parents, wondering

how soon he could leave without appearing impolite or offending his parents' oldest friends. He was too pessimistic to hope for an hour of pure torture, knowing he'd be lucky if he could escape within two. Unless Napoleon did something and he was called away. As he silently prayed for the arrival of such an urgent missive, they arrived outside the Renshaws' just as another of the waiting carriages lurched forward and its passengers spilled on to the pavement, making his misery complete.

Because the first person out of the shiny black conveyance was none other than Augustus Brookes.

'Good evening!' His parents rushed forward as a handsome woman of around his mother's age stepped out, sporting an impressive headdress of dyed turquoise ostrich feathers.

'Lord and Lady Writtle! What a lovely surprise. I haven't seen you in ages.'

'Christmas and New Year was hectic, so we have not been out much—but we are looking forward to seeing your performance next week.' His father kissed her gloved hand just as a taller, younger woman with vivid red hair alighted from the carriage, followed by a slightly shorter blonde.

'Of course, you must have already met my

daughters.' Mrs Brookes beamed with pride as she gestured to the young ladies.

Both daughters were clearly beauties in their own right—but nowhere in their sister's league. Vigorous hands were shaken and inane pleasantries swapped while he watched unnoticed from the periphery, unaware he was holding his breath in anticipation, until one perfectly turned silk-clad ankle emerged tipped with a scarlet slipper and it all came out in a whoosh.

She noticed his mother and father first.

'Good evening, my lord, my lady!' Her evening cape was black, but with a typical flamboyant Miss Brookes flourish, the lining of the hood was also scarlet, as were the ribbons woven into her loose curls. 'How ironic to see you when only moments ago Father and I were apprising my sisters of our plans for your portrait.' Then she turned, those not quite blue, not quite violet eyes searching for him before smiling. 'And I see you managed to persuade Lord Eastwood to come too.' Her gloved hand briefly grasped his as she curtsied and sent a waft of something exotic and seductive up his nostrils. 'I most certainly did not expect to see you here, my lord. I thought you loathed parties?'

'I do.' He slanted an accusing glance at his mother and rolled his eyes, enjoying the way

Miss Brookes smiled in understanding. 'Yet here I am.'

'Lord Eastwood?'

'Oh, yes! You haven't yet met our son, have you, Mrs Brookes? Although that's hardly a surprise when I usually have to drag him kicking and screaming to any social function.' Perhaps it was his imagination, but Mrs Brookes now suddenly appeared to have sucked a tart lemon and was struggling to smile on the back of it. 'Piers, darling, this is Mrs Roberta Brookes the famous soprano—and Augustus's lovely wife.'

'How do you do.' He hadn't imagined it. The singer offered him her limpest handshake and her coldest stare before looking hopefully elsewhere. If his mother noticed her obvious lack of enthusiasm at the introduction, she did not show it.

'And these lovely ladies are Miss Hope Brookes and Miss Charity Brookes—Miss Faith's younger sisters.' Charity eyed him with barely disguised interest as she curtsied, Hope with outright suspicion.

'Ladies.' Piers had barely straightened from his polite bow when the mother began to herd her daughters like a sheepdog. 'Well, it has been lovely to meet you, Lord Eastwood—but we must relieve ourselves of these heavy capes and the girls are eager to collect their dance cards. You know how it is.'

Augustus smiled, his pained eyes the only clue he was alarmed by his wife's haste to be rid of them, while the eldest Miss Brookes appeared thoroughly appalled but tried to cover it with conversation. 'What convinced you to attend this *torturous* ball, my lord?'

'My mother has a life-long friendship with the Renshaws which she used mercilessly to make me feel guilty about...'

'Come along, Faith! Stop dallying.' Mrs Brookes pulled her by the arm before he had finished his sentence, her apologetic smile as chilly as her frozen glare. 'Kindly excuse us, Lord Eastwood, but we have friends awaiting us inside and we are already much later than we originally assured them we would be.'

Miss Brookes shot him a mortified glance of apology before she was practically dragged up the front steps. Then it was his mother's turn to paste on a false smile. 'Mrs Brookes was...um... clearly...'

'She was downright rude, Mother, the very second she met me.'

'I was going to say she was clearly eager to attend the ball. If she was anything, she was a tad brusque rather than rude, which hardly comes as a great surprise in view of the huge queue of carriages.' She flapped a hand behind. 'Five people crammed in a coach for an hour would try anyone's patience and a prolonged conversation out here when it is about to rain isn't ideal when dressed in one's finery.'

'You don't need to make excuses for her. I dare say she is merely the first of a long line of people who are about to do much the same.' And Piers would have to suitably steel himself for all of them. 'Society's opinions aren't going to change overnight. Their acceptance of me isn't going to come easily and their forgiveness might never be forthcoming. Please, for the love of God let us not pretend otherwise or this evening is destined to be more unbearable than it needs to be. I am braced for the censure.' Because frankly, he couldn't ride in Hyde Park without witnessing it everywhere. 'And expect to be avoided like the plague—but for the sake of the Renshaws and for you, I shall make the best of it.'

She opened her mouth to argue, then promptly closed it again when his father squeezed her arm. 'Piers is right, darling. His first proper foray back into society is unlikely to be pleasant, so we shall all make the best of it. But most importantly, we will show them all a resolute, proud and united front which shouts to everyone we have nothing to feel ashamed about.'

Although still Piers did and likely always would. How could he not when he bore at least half of the blame?

They joined the long line of people waiting to be relieved of their coats, ignoring the stares and the whispers around them by pretending to be engrossed in their own conversation, until Lord Renshaw himself broke away from his own receiving line to join them. That single action of unfailing support and friendship made Piers glad he had come, even though he was already racking his brains for a suitable excuse to leave just as soon as he was politely able.

As the old friends caught up and swapped stories about their respective grandchildren, his gaze wandered to the front of the line at the same moment as Miss Brookes unclipped her evening cape, and the sight of her stunning scarlet evening gown left him breathless all over again.

Good lord she was something! If you appreciated the unconventional, which of course he still apparently did despite working hard to suppress that unfortunate and self-destructive character trait.

The cut of the heavy velvet gown was simple, but that simplicity in a ballroom full of the fashionably fussy made her unique. The bold, passionate red was a stark and alluring contrast against her pale alabaster skin and copper-toned hair. The way she held herself, so typically confident, made her stand out even more. She wore no jewellery, which meant nothing obstructed the splendid view of her graceful neck and shoulders, while the daring scooped neckline showed enough of her curves to make his mouth water and covered enough to be decent. Then of course, there was the hair. An inviting confection of loose copper curls which shimmered beneath the chandeliers, the only adornments a few scarlet ribbons to apparently hold the style in place and one single fat hothouse red rose secured just above her right ear. A touch, he knew, that the artist would have insisted upon herself. The delectable Miss Faith Brookes had a style all of her own.

Wishing she did not appeal to him with quite the force which she did, Piers surreptitiously looked his fill before a swarm of eager gentlemen crowded around her asking for her dance card. But while she smiled politely as she scribbled down the names, he couldn't help but notice she didn't beam. Or at least she didn't until an unfamiliar golden Adonis with a profusion of fussy lace at his collar and cuffs suddenly strode across the ballroom towards her, the clambering beaus instantly parting like the Red Sea to let him through before he took her hand and possessively wrapped it around his arm before leading her away.

While they disappeared into the crush, he bent to whisper something into her ear and she laughed, clearly delighted by whatever charming on dit the perfect, dandified specimen of manhood had uttered. Piers had no idea who the flamboyant fellow was, nor did he particularly care what it was he had said, but he knew one thing without a doubt.

He had never irrationally hated a stranger more.

Chapter Nine

'I knew I would find you hiding somewhere.'

He turned, surprised, then straightened, stepping a little away from the remote pillar he had been leaning upon for at least the last half an hour while he watched the dancers from afar. 'And there I was thinking I had hidden myself well.'

'No mean feat in a room this crowded.'

But Faith had seen him.

It had been difficult not to when she seemed constantly aware of him no matter where she happened to be in the ballroom. Even during the first waltz, while her talkative partner had rattled on and on, she sensed him and found her gaze actively seeking him out. Not that he was hard to find. With his height, unusual, hypnotic eyes and quietly brooding presence, he was far and away the handsomest man in the room.

Not that that was why she had been searching for him. She was on a different mission, or so she was frantically trying to convince herself—a mercy mission. One which had absolutely nothing whatsoever to do with the way she was drawn to the intriguing conundrum that was Lord Eastwood like a veritable moth to a flame which had pulled her to this alcove. 'I am impressed that you managed it.' But not surprised. Exactly as his mother had stated upon their first meeting, her son undeniably preferred to disappear in a crowd. And disappear he had, almost as soon as they arrived.

He shrugged and suppressed a smile. 'Hardly a feat at all for a lofty armchair strategist like myself, when even the common-garden variety would be able to clearly discern that this particular spot is the furthest possible distance from the dance floor and thus the least likely to be populated.' Then he glanced pointedly at the card dangling from her wrist. 'Speaking of which, why aren't you dancing still, or are you in hiding yourself? Perhaps from one of your battalion of overeager young bucks, in case the besotted fool proposes to you for the thirty-seventh time in as many minutes?'

'And what is that supposed to mean?' Bizarrely, a rogue part of her hoped he was jealous, which came as a bit of a surprise when she still couldn't quite get over the fact that she liked him in the first place. For a scandalous, callous almost-earl, he had a few too many redeeming qualities for comfort.

'I saw them all clambering around you when you arrived. It reminded me of the feeding frenzy at the Menagerie.'

'What can I say, Lord Eastwood?' She flapped her fan coquettishly for effect. 'I cannot help being popular.'

She resisted the urge to add that she did nothing to encourage them and certainly wasn't interested in any of them either. Instead, Faith gestured to the bank of ladies nearest to them, all holding themselves in the doubtless well-rehearsed pose to show off their figures and faces to the best advantage. 'But why aren't you dancing, my lord, when tonight there is a positive glut of eager ladies in dire need of a partner?'

'While there may well be a glut, Miss Brookes, I doubt their need is dire enough to consider dancing with London's most infamous social pariah.' His expression was suddenly ironic—amused even—but was it her imagination or had the light in his eyes dimmed? 'The poor things would doubtless run screaming from the room if I even attempted to approach, let alone ask. Never mind how the chaperons and parents would react. I'd likely have to fight six duels before dawn for bringing a family's good name into disrepute.' Then all at once he was all dry irony again as he shrugged, seemingly unperturbed by his infamy. 'What can I say, Miss Brookes? I cannot help being *un*popular.'

She was tempted to ask how he felt about that but didn't. It was too personal a question when they barely knew one another, and she was basically an employee—albeit a highly paid one and their cordial relationship was still polite but resolutely distant. She had consciously maintained that distance, not trusting herself to spend any more time with him than was necessary in case he charmed her some more. She would be maintaining it still were it not for the fact she felt compelled to apologise for her mother. But while she plucked up the courage to broach the subject, he thankfully filled the void.

'Thank you for suggesting watercolours for Isobel, by the way. They went down a storm—with Isobel at least. My mother and sister were quite horrified…' His eyes were dancing as they stared at the crowded dance floor again. 'And stark warnings and strict parameters were issued regarding the exact use of the paints. But a tentative accord has been reached as my niece has sworn an oath the dreaded paints will only be used for good rather than evil, and I have had to make myself the guarantor to see that is the case. If so much as one spot of lurid green is found on the wallpaper, it has been decreed I will have to redecorate the whole room alone, myself as penance.'

'Ahh...'

He turned back to her and the warmth in his smile made her want to sigh and grin sloppily back until she reminded herself she never did that on principle and certainly wouldn't with a man of his ilk and reputation, no matter how much she was tempted. Liking him was one thing, but extending anything beyond an occasional and wary olive branch of professional friendship was entirely out of the question. He was still an aristocrat and she was not, and never the twain would truly meet, even as friends.

'Anyway, the brat is thrilled and declared my present the best present she received so...'

'So you are secretly thrilled too.' Which in turn delighted Faith disproportionately—simply because she had made him happy. 'I am glad my suggestion came up trumps.'

'It is always nice when a gift is well-received.'

'How are the plans for your banquet coming along?'

His face fell. 'It's all hideous, as I am sure you

can imagine. I had to sit through a two-hour lecture today by the Master of the King's Household discussing menus and china patterns. He lost me in the first twenty minutes, although I do seem to recall agreeing to beef and something peculiar sounding involving salmon. Our next meeting is destined to be longer because we have to discuss the seating arrangements, although thankfully, I can postpone that indefinitely until I hear back from the Portuguese Royal Court. If they decline the invitation there will be no point in having a banquet in their honour and I will be spared.'

'Then, for your sake, I shall pray that they have a prior engagement.'

'That would be much appreciated, Miss Brookes. Thank you.' He leaned his back against the pillar, tilting his head as he watched her. 'So... Faith, Hope and Charity Brookes? You are named after the Virtues?' She could tell that undeniable fact amused him.

'Sadly yes. Those names are a lot to live up to and unfortunately are all misplaced. I doubt everything, Charity is much too selfish, and Hope is a confirmed pessimist. If there had been more of us, there would have been a Patience and a Chastity too, which are far worse, don't you think? But thankfully fate felt it was too cruel to saddle any babe with such hideously pious names and limited my parents to just the three precocious offspring. But Mama and Papa are all for symbolism and my mother, especially, has quite puritanical views…about everything.'

It was probably better to soften the ground before apologising about her mother's shocking rudeness, in the hope he also understood that though crass and heavy-footed, it had been instinctual rather than meant maliciously. 'Her grandfather was a Quaker and…well…she tends to think the entire world is evil which makes her a tad overprotective.' And of the firm belief Lord Eastwood was soundly without morals because she didn't know him beyond the gossip she had read. Just as Faith had believed she had his full measure until she had met him in the flesh and the overwhelming but persistent doubt had crept in. 'Especially of her daughters. Which was why she…'

He flicked the words away before she could apologise properly, astutely pre-empting exactly what she had come to say. 'You do not need to explain or apologise. She is a mother and they all tend to be overprotective even of the most innocuous of gentlemen, let alone a heartless scoundrel like me.' The dismissive expression seemed false, but quickly disappeared before she could be sure. 'I am curious, what would you all have been named if your parents had had boys?'

He wanted to change the subject, and because she feared knowing him better would make her like him more, she made an immediate, conscious and unsatisfying decision not to probe further. 'As my mother disapproves of most men as a matter of principle, and not just you, my lord, I've always suspected any male offspring would have been named after the Seven Deadly Sins, although she has always denied that. But I think Gluttony Brookes has a ring to it, don't you?' Despite knowing now was the opportune time to leave seeing as her mission to apologise was complete, Faith felt compelled to stay.

'Excluding me, of course, because we both know her reasons for thinking the absolute worst of me—' And there it was again, that fleeting flash of hurt in his eyes which was gone so fast she already questioned if she had either imagined it or projected it, trying to see what she wanted to see in those fathomless mossy depths to justify why he intrigued her. 'What does your mother have against all other men?'

'She has three daughters...' Faith raised her eyebrows, leaving the implication to hang while her mind whirred.

She wanted to stay. Here, chatting to him. Because he did intrigue her.

What on earth was the matter with her? Of all the men in this ballroom, all the handsome and less scandalous men in this ballroom, why was she so inexplicably suddenly drawn to him? Why was she so hell-bent on liking him when all she was basing that on was a feeling the rest of the world might have got him all wrong, when she knew it was misguided? When she knew, without a shadow of a doubt, where attractive men were concerned she was a very poor judge of character. Automatically, her gaze flicked to where Lord Rayne and his suitably aristocratic wife were stood across the ballroom, and she absorbed every bit of the anger and shame just the sight of him caused in the hope it would fortify her.

'Ah...yes. Having three daughters must be awful for your mother *and* your father.' Unconsciously, Lord Eastwood's eyes wandered to where his parents stood laughing with friends and instantly they softened, making her wonder if he had abandoned them on purpose at the first available opportunity so they could still have a good time without having to suffer more unsubtle and rude behaviour like her mother's. Which was an altogether too selfless and too self-aware gesture from a man who selfishly thought only of himself first, last and always. 'My father used to worry all the time about my sisters. I recall all unrelated men were considered potential de-spoilers before they were safely married and out of harm's way.'

He leaned a little closer, dropping his voice conspiratorially, completely unaware that the whispered tone raised goose pimples on her flesh. 'Between you and I, I am not entirely sure he's entirely taken to my two brothers-in-law de-spite them both proving themselves to be thoroughly worthy men.' He smelled positively sinful too, the subtle blend of his spicy cologne making her want to move closer so she could sniff it directly from his skin.

Being all alone in the quiet alcove suddenly felt deliciously intimate. Unnervingly so.

'He's beginning to warm to my elder sister's husband...' As the dancers clapped their appreciation at the end of the set, he briefly leaned closer still so he could be heard over the cacophony, his warm breath caressing the sensitive skin of her neck. Something which had the most unexpected and wholly improper effect on her. An improper effect which brought her up short. For a level-headed, not easily impressed and usually cynical young lady who had been duped before, she was certainly not behaving like herself around him.

She had always been far too inquisitive. Too nosy and determined to understand everything. That had to explain why she had purposely avoided her waiting dance partner and determinedly sought Lord Eastwood out instead. That she enjoyed his company as much as she enjoyed looking at him was by the by.

'But they have been married almost eleven years, so it is long past time. The younger is only two years in so has yet to prove his mettle. It'll be years before the poor fellow is fully accepted—if at all—what with Melissa being the baby of the family, and therefore much too young to have a husband in my father's eyes despite her four and twenty years.'

'Did your father feel the same way towards your wife?' Faith winced at her crassness, blaming the way his proximity kept distracting her for saying aloud exactly what she was thinking. 'I'm sorry—that was insensitive of me and is entirely none of my business.'

Myriad complex emotions skittered across his features before he sighed. 'In all honesty, they barely knew her. We met during my first weeks in Portugal and married there within a month.' A fast courtship by anybody's standards. Had he stumbled blindly into a marriage, married rashly in haste before he realised it had been a huge mistake then...

Annoyed at her continued habit of always trying to see the good in him when she had nothing but her own gut instinct to go on, Faith decided to focus on his face rather than speculating on the whys and wherefores, then regretted it the second she thought she saw another brief flicker of pain in those seductively hypnotic eyes. 'They only met once when I brought her on a brief visit to London for our honeymoon and we stayed with them for a few days. The next time I returned home, I came alone and then...well... I stayed alone thereafter.'

He stiffened then, and looked momentarily horrified by his frank admission before that telling expression vanished too. 'But enough of that depressing story... Let us talk about something more interesting.' His gaze swept the room until it latched on to her youngest sister who was dancing a cotillion. 'For example, are Hope and Charity cut from the same cloth as you, Miss Brookes?'

She wanted to ask him why he remained alone thereafter. Wanted to know why his marriage came to such a swift and decisive end. Needed to know how he felt about that and why he, a mild-mannered diplomat who appeared to have avoided the gossip columns before his marriage, sought to legally terminate it when he clearly would have loathed all the fuss and scandal such an unusual action created. She already knew him well enough to know that without a doubt. But there was a glint of panic in his expressive eyes now which belied his carefully schooled expression and she did not have the heart to put him through that turmoil too, when just being here at this ball was quite obviously hideous enough for him to be avoiding it so thoroughly.

'Are we cut from the same cloth?' She tapped her lip and pretended to ponder it, watched the utter relief in his gaze to have been granted such a timely reprieve and wished she could take him by the hand, lead him into the privacy of the night outside and encourage him to let it all out. He was clearly still in pain because she felt it viscerally, even though she really did not want to, and he clearly was in dire need of a friend here in this ballroom.

'If my sisters follow me in anything, it is only in that they are as outspoken and as unfashionably overeducated as I am. Outdated puritanical values aside, my parents brought us up to be independent and freethinking individuals... although between you and I...' It was her turn to lean forward conspiratorially and she did it to show him she might be able to be that friend she thought he needed so very much, which came as a huge surprise when the sensible part of her still wanted to hate him.

'I suspect they regret that expensive, liberal education now as we all drive them to distraction and never do as we are told. I suppose I favour Papa the most, as I am the only one to inherit his flair for drawing and despite my love of music and annoying tendency to sing to myself all of the time, I have not inherited *any* of my mother's talent for it. It's dreadfully unfair as both my sisters can sing. Charity intends to pursue it professionally like Mama, so I don't begrudge her the talent in the slightest, but Hope doesn't particularly even like music so the gift is completely wasted on her.'

He was smiling again and that warmed her. 'What does she do instead?'

'She writes.' Faith pulled a horrified face. 'Intensely dark, Gothic novels filled with trauma, villains, ghosts and chaos. She's desperately trying to get them published but is struggling because she flatly refuses to take on a male pseudonym and publishers baulk at the shocking prospect of printing anything written by a female. Not that I blame her for her continued and stubborn persistence, as I doubt I would either.'

'Yet you paint half of some of your father's pictures and only his name appears on the bottom. Doesn't it gall a little that he gets *all* the credit?'

'It does sometimes.' Especially when people raved about the whimsical landscapes on the giant tableaus which she created, but neglected to mention her hand in them even though they had seen her paint them, albeit in her father's style to his exact specification. But Lord Eastwood was the first person who had ever asked that question. Most people assumed women had no ambition of their own and that she would be happy with always playing second fiddle. 'But it is not uncommon for great artists to use apprentices to assist them on large compositions. Michelangelo and Raphael famously allowed students to practise their skills on portions of their bigger canvases. It is the best way to learn and I am learning from the best after all.' Although of late, she had felt herself straining at the bit, yearning to paint things her way.

She loved her father's work, had once been only too happy to emulate it, but their styles and even their methods were different. He liked to rigidly plan, whereas Faith preferred to let the muse take her, which meant that she often felt hemmed in by his clear vision. She also, although she would never admit it aloud to another living soul, frequently felt some of his group portraits erred too much on the traditional formal side for her taste. Tried and tested poses. Classically toned palettes. Still always brilliant of course, because nobody painted a likeness better than him, but a tad safe. Something her reckless streak rebelled against. When she eventually branched out on her own, her pictures would be very different. But she quashed all that to answer Lord Eastwood.

'The truth is, my lord, until somebody deigns to buy one of *my* compositions, I consider myself lucky to be his apprentice. Any budding artist would give their eye teeth for the honour of working with my father and there is a waiting list for his classes at the Royal Academy. He is a brilliant teacher and a generous one. He has always been my strongest advocate who actively encourages my own ambitions.' A fact which couldn't be denied. 'So when I assist with one of his commissions, like I am with your family's, I like to think what emerges on the finished canvas is an amalgamation of the both of us.'

He folded his arms as he regarded her, drawing her gaze briefly to the muscles in them where the fabric was pulled taut and making her wayward artist's eye consider he would be a good specimen to paint. He was tall, broad, classically handsome. Perfectly proportioned. Shirtless perhaps.

Or completely nude...

Her pulse quickened at the illicit and improper thought.

Not that her father would countenance such a study. In all her years of training, with all the various sitters she had honed her craft on, not one had ever been anywhere close to naked! She glanced guiltily back at Lord Eastwood, only to find him staring at her amused and for one horrible moment she was convinced he had read her mind.

'I said, are you never tempted to swap, Miss Brookes? Let your father paint the landscapes for a change while you tackle the faces?'

Of course she was. All the time. She itched to spread her wings and explore the entire gamut of her talent. To try new things and experiment with different and radical ideas and methods. Except nobody had yet asked for a uniquely Faith Brookes picture of anything—let alone a portrait. Nude or otherwise. 'Why would we do that?'

'Because—and you must excuse my language here, Miss Brookes—it hasn't escaped my notice you draw a damn good portrait yourself. The one you did of me was excellent. It ran rings around your father's.'

The compliment warmed her while making her feel disloyal at the same time. 'My father was merely having an off day. I am no match for his talent.'

'If you say so...' The knowing look seemed to see straight through her, perhaps even to the scandalously nude image of him her mind adamantly refused to relinquish. 'But if you don't mind, I have a faith in you, Miss *Faith* Brookes, and I believe you are *as* talented, if not more so, than your brilliant father, and I for one would like to see what you will accomplish when you decide to come out from behind his shadow.'

'I...' She was touched. Momentarily speechless. Thoroughly charmed and scandalously attracted to a man she shouldn't even be talking to in public, let alone smiling at. 'I have no plans to...' She had never admitted her own ambition outside the safe confines of her family, assuming they would inevitably scoff because of her sex, but for some reason she wanted to tell him because she felt he would understand. 'That's not true. I do have plans. Huge lofty plans of setting up my own studio and painting things all my way. Vast landscapes and seascapes mainly because the raw intensity of the ocean and nature fascinates me, but I would like to dabble in portraiture too just…' She paused, feeling disloyal.

'Different to your father's?'

'Yes…a little *less* traditional. I know the fashion for portraits is close up and demure, and some, like my father's, are less formal, but I should like to paint people doing things rather than staring out of the canvas. I suppose that is why I prefer to paint nature—I can paint what I see and feel and not what everyone expects.'

His astute green eyes seemed to stare into her soul as he smiled. 'Why am I not surprised by that?'

'It's my wilful streak.'

'No it isn't. It's you. You were born to be different and to shine because of it.' That was the nicest compliment anyone had ever given her and it did something odd to her heart. 'Which begs the question, Miss Brookes, what exactly are you waiting for? If what I have seen is any gauge, you have served your apprenticeship. Paint your pictures, fulfil your destiny and take the world by storm.'

'If only it were that simple.' She sighed and made no attempt to mask her frustration. 'First, to make any headway, I would need to get my work noticed and that requires someone willing to exhibit it. The most prestigious and lucrative route is to get a picture or two into the Royal Academy's annual exhibition, and that is easier said than done. The judges are very particular.'

'And you are very talented.'

'Perhaps...' She shrugged, wanting to believe him, to cast out her own crushing doubts about her talent, and then huffed out a frustrated sigh. 'But I am also a woman, which automatically puts me at a disadvantage even though they might claim it doesn't, and then I am also the daughter of Augustus Brookes, which bothers them more.'

'Why? Isn't he one of them?'

'That's the problem. While he isn't a judge, he is an Academician, and to avoid any accusations of nepotism on their part, I suppose they cannot accept one of my pictures unless it truly is one of the best put forward. The bar is set ridiculously high and so far, I have failed to meet it.' Deep down she suspected that might be because she too played things safe when submitting to them. Offering a canvas which she thought might appeal to them instead of risking one of the paintings she had poured her heart and soul into.

'You will.'

'Because you have *faith*?'

He smiled at her reuse of his pun. 'I do. When is the next exhibition?'

'June. Submissions need to be in next month as they need a long time to deliberate, and I have a few paintings which I might enter, and one I am still working on which I might finish in time.' The one her heart and soul wasn't in but that nagging voice of doubt thought the judges might understand better.

'I'd love to see them.'

And bizarrely, she was tempted to show him them, which came as a total shock when she ferociously guarded her truest art by making sure it never left the sanctuary of her studio. 'I thought you had no interest in art?'

'I have no interest in my mother's family portrait, largely because she insists on putting me in it, which involves your father forcing me to sit for hours bored stiff while he shouts at me. Is he always so...'

'Unreasonable? Temperamental? Downright impossible with a brush in his hand?'

'I was going to say tetchy, but then I am a diplomat and I do have an uncanny knack of bringing out the worst in people nowadays so...'

'There you are, Faith!' Her next dance partner suddenly strode into their private little oasis. 'I was beginning to despair of ever finding you. Have you forgotten you promised me the last waltz?'

'Is it that time already, Edward?' Because she now wished she could turn back time a little or will the hands of the clock to move slower. Obvious reservations aside, she now had so many unanswered questions about Lord Eastwood, she would happily chat away to him all night. He was surprisingly easy to talk to.

'It is about to start.' Two blue eyes, nowhere near as compelling and expressive as the suddenly stormy green ones, glared at Lord Eastwood with downright hostility. 'If you will excuse us?'

'Of course.'

Edward offered Faith his arm and reluctantly, she took it, not liking the way everyone initially treated this conundrum of a man like the worst sort of scoundrel—herself included. He immediately covered her hand with his possessively, but as he started to lead her away, he turned.

'Forgive me, but I do not believe we have been formally introduced, my lord—although, *of course*, I know you by reputation.' He held out his hand in challenge, the implied insult as clear as a gauntlet being thrown down, almost as if he was waiting for any flimsy excuse to be aggressive. 'I am Edward Tate. A particular friend of Faith's and indeed of her entire family.' He still held her firm like a prized possession. 'You have doubtless heard of me.'

Appalled at both the lack of manners, the presumptuous proprietorial claim upon her and the haughty prejudgement of a gentleman who had been nothing but polite, she wanted to slap Edward away, then rail at him for his rudeness. Instead, mindful of both a potentially hideous scene and causing Lord Eastwood yet more undeserved embarrassment, she let go of Edward's arm as a mark of protest and stepped aside. Hell would have to freeze over before she danced the waltz, or any other dance, with Edward Tate tonight! If he was going to be petty and small-minded, she wanted no part of it or him and tried to tell Lord Eastwood as much with the power of her outraged glare and the yard's worth of frigid distance she had put between them.

'The poet?' Being the bigger man in every way, Lord Eastwood politely took the proffered hand and shook it, seemingly oblivious to the unwarranted slight he had just been dealt.

'Among other things—but it is indeed my poetry I am most famous for.' As much as she liked him, she had always thought Edward a bit too confident, but she had never noticed the smugness before. Or the shallowness—which suddenly made sense of her reluctance each time he

had pressed his suit despite her mother's continued encouragement of it.

It was staggeringly unattractive.

'Only, of course, by reputation.' In that one
sentence Lord Eastwood managed to convey that
he had the full measure of Edward Tate while
still behaving like a complete gentleman. 'But
I am keeping you from your charming partner,
sir, and that will not do.' He inclined his head
politely then turned to smile at her. 'Goodnight,
Miss Brookes. Once again, it has been a pleasure.' Then with the quiet dignity her dance partner would never possess, he slowly sauntered
away.

It was the quiet dignity which was her undoing, because it was wrong on every level.

It did not matter what crimes he had or hadn't
committed in the past; he hadn't committed any
today and certainly not to either her or to Edward. If anything, he had been minding his own
business from the periphery—as usual—and
she had unintentionally brought trouble to him.
She couldn't stand by and watch such despicable, unprovoked treatment and do nothing. As
a Brookes through and through, she had more
substance than that!

'Lord Eastwood…?'

He turned, his expression as bland as bland

could be but his clever eyes locked with hers warily as if he knew she was about to do something wilful and impetuous and was cautioning her against it. 'Yes, Miss Brookes?'

Her mother was going to have a fit but it couldn't be helped. She owed him and was too outspoken not to take a firm stand against Edward's unjustifiable challenge. 'As I have danced with Edward already this evening, I am sure he will not mind in the slightest if you take his waltz.'

Chapter Ten

A strange quiet settled over the ballroom as Piers led her to the floor. It amplified the sound of his wild hammering heartbeat in his spinning head.

This was a very bad idea, for so many reasons he couldn't begin to count them. He had tried to talk her out of it in the scant few moments she had given him to answer, but she was adamant, and as a gaggle of wallflowers had seen her take his hand and tug him towards the floor, nobly digging his heels in would only cause a scene.

Although how this was going to cause less of one was beyond him, especially as the blond Adonis had reacted to her bombshell with noisy petulance, at first forbidding her to dance and then storming off in a belligerent huff when she quietly told him to she did not answer to him or anyone.

Already he could picture the frenzied paragraphs of rot and speculation in tomorrow's newspapers and wished he knew how to spare her from it.

'It's not too late…simply dither for a moment then have a very public change of heart.' That was certainly safest for both of them. It was bad enough he kept imagining what she would feel like in his arms, he did not need either confirmation or the experience to torment him further, and certainly not when he had been rigidly adhering to his perfectly excellent plan to avoid her at all costs all week until tonight. 'I promise you, not a soul in here would blame you for it.'

'No—they will blame you and that wouldn't be fair.'

Piers did not need her to be decent because decent made her too damn likeable when he wanted to believe she was exactly like Constança beneath the beautiful exterior, even though he already suspected she wasn't. She was brilliant, intelligent, talented, insightful and kind.

How the blazes was he supposed to remain impervious to the siren if she wasn't shallow and selfish?

'*I* wouldn't blame you, Miss Brookes. *I* understand what a precarious—and potentially distasteful and awkward situation this puts you in.'

'Why? Because you are worried I might feature in the gossip columns, Lord Eastwood?'

'I think I can guarantee you will feature in them if you dance with me. You would become the source of much unfair and unwarranted speculation.'

'I am afraid that ship has long sailed, and all without your assistance.' She smiled unperturbed as she gracefully manoeuvred them to the very centre of the floor, then dipped into an exaggerated curtsy which drew every covetous male eye in the room. 'Clearly you do not read them often enough or thoroughly enough yourself, my lord, else you'd know we Brookes girls tend to feature in them with alarming regularity without even trying. They have printed some shocking things about all three of us over the years, so I am well used to it. Gossip is merely gossip, and it passes soon enough.'

As the orchestra played the first chords, she gave him no option but to take her in hold, which did absolutely nothing to ease his galloping heart while simultaneously assaulting all his senses regardless of his resolve not to be seduced.

She felt divine beneath his fingers. The gentle flare of her waist, the soft skin of her hand clasped in his. This close, he could see exactly why the precise colour of her eyes always eluded him because the irises were ringed with an intense dark blue on the outer edges before they melted into the flecked violet which framed the pupils. He could also count every pretty freckle which dusted her perfect nose. And then of course, there was the hair and the single loose curl which bounced next to her cheek, the one his index finger itched to twirl itself within. Fearing he might, he concentrated on the steps instead, and prayed the dance would be short.

'For a man who claims to loathe balls, you dance divinely, Lord Eastwood.'

With every eye in the room suddenly riveted to them and the sublime, heady scent of her perfume playing havoc with his senses while common sense raged a losing battle in his head, it was nothing short of a blasted miracle his big feet were able to move at all, let alone in synchronisation with hers.

'I have two sisters who forced me to practise with them.' A nuisance he had hated growing up but was ridiculously grateful he had been bullied into tonight. They might well be causing a fresh scandal in front of a hundred or more people, but thanks to those interminable hours he'd spent twirling around under protest, at least he didn't look ungainly and stupid while he did it. That was something.

God help him.

'You might try smiling at me though…at least pretend to be enjoying it.'

It was near impossible to smile when he was sure that parts of him were enjoying holding her in his arms a little too much. Tonight's fevered dream was already a fait accompli, and doubtless the next months' worth were too. Although to be fair to her, that was a done deal when she had started talking to him and he had watched the excitement in her eyes when she had talked about her art, or perhaps even before that. His fate had likely already been sealed the moment she peeled off that beguiling scarlet-lined cape and he had seen her gown. Now she was so close he could smell the seductive rose in her hair.

'Everybody is watching us.'

Good grief! He sounded so stiff and ungrateful, when despite knowing this was absolute folly in every possible way, he was actually supremely touched by her sacrifice. It had been a long time since a virtual stranger had been this kind to him.

'I know…all the more reason to smile or they will think we are both here under duress. Try to ignore them, Lord Eastwood. For me…' Her gaze locked with his and the flagrant amusement in her eyes did the trick. The rest of the room seemed to evaporate in a puff of smoke, alongside the remnants of his plans to remain detached and unmoved by this new and dangerous temptation who had invaded his life. Much to his complete surprise, Piers found himself genuinely smiling back.

'That's much better.'

And it was.

Which was a worry.

'You know they are all going to think there is something going on between us. You should brace yourself for an avalanche of nonsense tomorrow.' If he maintained a flow of rational conversation about all the negatives, then perhaps he might still be able to crawl away from this foolhardy, intimate waltz relatively unscathed. His head intact and his heart untouched.

She tilted her chin defiantly. 'My mother is an opera singer, my father a painter. We live in Bloomsbury among the rest of the disreputability—believe me, I am used to being used as cannon fodder for the titillation of my betters here in blue-blooded Mayfair. I asked you to dance, Lord Eastwood, knowing full well the implications. I have no doubts this one short waltz will be splashed all over the scandal sheets tomorrow. That is as inevitable as night following day.'

That she understood that awful ramification

made him feel a little better—until her next words thoroughly spoiled it. 'But you should brace yourself for some nonsense too, my lord, for you are about to be unwittingly press-ganged into the ranks of a long list of supposed suitors who have apparently knocked at my door—but not in the acceptable and proper way if you catch my meaning.'

'I am not sure I do?'

She sighed, the half-smile failing to cover the tired resignation and the anger. 'Then forgive me for speaking plainly, my lord, but it is better you are prepared also rather than ambushed on the morrow. Because almost every blue-blooded aristocrat currently watching us with interest, very likely also views me as fair game for a fellow aristocrat such as yourself. Wholly acceptable mistress material—but nowhere near worthy enough to ever join their illustrious ranks.' There was sadness in her eyes now. Deep-rooted and, for Piers, unbearable. 'In truth, a great many of those supposed suitors *have* proposed things to me over the years and none of them has been marriage.' A staggering revelation which baffled him when she was hands down the most beautiful, vibrant and fascinating woman in the room.

'They may well assume I have procured myself a new benefactor, or might even suggest I have seized a golden opportunity to use your current predicament as the *ton*'s favourite social pariah to better myself, and therefore intend to entrap you into a more permanent attachment, using my well-practised and well-used wiles.' She tilted her chin defiantly and beamed for the benefit of their audience. 'You might be a scandal, Lord Eastwood, but you will one day be an earl. Whereas an upstart from Bloomsbury like me would obviously stop at nothing to be a countess.'

He heard the note of irritation over the casual matter-of-fact tone. Heard it and felt for her because he knew she was right. As unfair as it was, that was exactly what they might think just as they assumed he had parted ways with Constança because she wasn't of noble blood. Even when things weren't about rank and reputation, London society made it about them. Procuring a future earl, even one as sullied in reputation as him, would be seen as a massive social achievement for her. There was every chance, in being kind and charitable, the intrepid Miss Brookes would come off looking much worse from this than him.

'I'm sorry.' It seemed like such a lacklustre response to such a well-intentioned good deed.

'Don't be.' She smiled stoically and it made

him want to slay dragons for her. 'If this *shocking* waltz achieves nothing else, at least it will put paid to the persistent and annoying rumours concerning me and Edward Tate.'

His foolish heart soared at the way her expression soured at the mere mention of the poet. 'But I thought he was your *particular friend*?'

'Recently he has intimated that he would like to be and there is no denying my mother would like him to be, and it is true we have been the best of friends for years, but…' She huffed out an irritated sigh. 'After tonight's churlish performance, I think it is safe to say any chance he might have had is now well and truly gone.'

Ridiculously, and more alarmingly, he possessively hoped that was true. 'Don't be too harsh on him.' Good grief! Sometimes he loathed his diplomatic streak, but it wouldn't be fair to allow her to throw all caution to the wind simply because he selfishly wanted her to. 'It is obvious he cares about you a great deal, else he wouldn't have charged in to save you from my evil clutches. Jealousy can do odd things to a man and I'm sure he meant well. If your mother approves of him, he can't be all bad.' Piers had seen Roberta Brookes laughing with the poet earlier, sat cosied together behind the refreshment table like the closest of friends. 'And with his talent for words, his apology is bound to be very pretty, and his ill temper is understandable when I did technically steal his dance.'

She stared at him, smiled then shook her head as if his response amused her. 'It is very noble of you to be so forgiving, Lord Eastwood, but the truth is, in a strange sort of way I'm actually rather relieved he was so boorish. I've always enjoyed his company, and he can be very funny and undoubtedly charming, but despite my mother's sudden keenness for the match, I've never felt *that* way about him...' She glanced away, embarrassed to have brought *that* up. 'I have tried to tell him as much, but...'

'Your mother's obvious approval has given him false hope you will miraculously develop feelings which you don't have, and you have been caught in the middle. I have a mother too, Miss Brookes, and when a mother gets that matchmaking bee in her bonnet...'

He felt the tension leave her body. 'Yes—that is exactly it. My mother thinks I am being fickle and is convinced if she keeps thrusting Edward at me, I'll eventually change my mind, when I know I won't. He is a friend, nothing more. This has given me the perfect excuse to stop pretending that might change.'

'My mother thinks that if she keeps thrusting me into society, I shall miraculously grow to enjoy it.' Although at this precise moment he wasn't exactly hating it for once. Waltzing with the most beautiful woman in the ballroom was hardly a chore. 'But I've never enjoyed it. Not even when I wasn't a social pariah. Yet my mother still thinks she knows best, so I sympathise.'

As she smiled, she stepped closer, and the urge to tug her closer still was overwhelming. 'My mother has always been one for flowery words and romanticised sentiment, whereas my over-protective father—much like yours—has strong opinions about all his precious daughters' potential suitors, including Edward. Much to her chagrin of course.'

'And what does the great Augustus Brookes think of your poet?'

'He thinks Edward wears too much lace for his liking.'

'He does.' Piers couldn't help smiling down at her. He was so relieved he wouldn't ever have to suffer the tortured image of her wrapped in the arms of the golden Adonis in the midst of one of his fevered dreams, he couldn't help it. 'All that froth is a sure sign the fellow is unworthy. Trust me, as an armchair diplomat, I know these things. Napoleon likes a lace cravat so I would never trust a gentleman so frilly.'

He felt her spontaneous giggle everywhere, and God help him he liked it. 'I thought you were an armchair strategist, sir, not a diplomat.'

'There are no ends to the things one can achieve from the comfort of a well-upholstered chair, Miss Brookes.' And doubtless he'd be dreaming about that again tonight for sure. But she laughed again and he revelled in it. Then, as he realised he was actually enjoying himself irrespective of all the many reasons that he shouldn't, Piers came to a staggering and well-reasoned conclusion. One even he couldn't argue with. What was the harm in enjoying just this one, unexpected waltz? It wasn't as if they would ever share another—especially after the newspapers eviscerated them on the morrow.

This was it.

His one dance with the most beautiful woman in the room before he battened down the hatches, hardened his resolve and listened to the wise and noisy warnings in his head to avoid her at all costs going forward. He already liked her too much as it was, which was too dangerous a gamble for someone as understandably cautious and wary as he was. Besides, in an uncharacteristically undiplomatic moment, he also reasoned that if he was going to be hanged for a sheep instead of a lamb regardless, he might as well blasted enjoy it. They were here anyway, in front of everyone, and that damage could not be undone.

So he did. For the next few minutes he banished his marriage, his divorce and his fears from his mind, and he adored every single second of having her for the duration.

But when the music stopped and as he bowed towards her final curtsy, reality descended again like smog as he became aware of two hundred hungry stares boring into his skin and making improper and unfair assumptions. Among them an incensed poet with his nose badly out of joint, his delighted mother who assumed he had taken her advice and, directly opposite on the other side of the dance floor, Mrs Brookes's clearly horrified one.

As he led her back through the sea of unsubtle, nosy onlookers to her parents, the incensed soprano looked ready to tear him limb from limb and probably would have if one of her other daughters hadn't gripped her by the arm to stop her.

'I should probably stay with you and explain how we came to be dancing...'

'I really wouldn't.' She managed to say this

without moving her smiling lips. 'Despite her Quaker roots, Mama's temper is legendary. Look at her. Does she look rational or reasonable to you?'

Piers did and she didn't. 'She looks like she wants me dead.'

'That is because right now she does, and she will need at least a day or two to cool down before I dare risk her near your person without sturdy restraints. Please leave her to me and Papa. I know he has been an absolute tyrant this last week, but when he isn't being the slightly deranged and obsessive painter, he is actually the most reasonable man on the planet. Once I explain things to him, he will be able to smooth it all over.'

'If you are sure...' Leaving her to face the music alone felt cowardly and wrong.

'I most definitely am.' She stopped several yards short of her family, giving him ample room to escape and curtsied solemnly once again before ruining it completely with a thoroughly rebellious glint shimmering in her lovely eyes. 'Thank you for the dance and the impending scandal, Lord Eastwood, although I fear one will prove to be much more enjoyable than the other.'

He inclined his head politely as was expected but dropped his voice so that only she could hear.

'Thank you, Miss Brookes, both for asking me and for causing it. If nothing else, it will make a refreshing change to have a fellow cellmate in purgatory.'

As she grinned, something odd happened somewhere in the vicinity of his battered, hardened heart and despite knowing it was only going to make everything considerably worse in the scandal sheets in the morning, he succumbed to temptation and recklessly kissed her hand.

Chapter Eleven

In a staggering and unexpected turn of events, Miss B. from Bloomsbury has publicly parted ways with her gentle poet after apparently enticing a significantly bigger fish to her hook...

Whispers from Behind the Fan
March 1814

'This is the best one!' An absolutely delighted Charity smoothed the *Morning Chronicle* open on the breakfast table before theatrically clearing her throat. 'The highlight of the Renshaw Ball was surely the spectacle of a certain Miss B. twirling *breathless* in the arms of the infamous Lord E.'

Their mother's teacup clattered into its saucer.

'Oh, good heavens! They are getting worse!' She began to rhythmically massage the bridge of her nose in the faint hope it would iron flat the enormous indent currently ploughed deep between her furrowed eyebrows. 'I cannot fathom what you were thinking, Faith! After all my stark warnings...'

'It was difficult to discern which of the pair appeared more smitten by the encounter,' continued Charity unrepentant. 'Suffice to say it appeared both were thoroughly seduced by the intoxicating power of the once forbidden dance of *love*.' She slanted Faith a glance and raised her golden eyebrows suggestively. 'We await with bated breath, dear reader, to discover if there is significantly more to come, as we have it on good authority that this pair will be spending a great deal of time together over the coming months while the smitten young lady assists the nation's premier painter at none other than the scandalous aforementioned gentleman's well-appointed Mayfair abode.'

Hope shook her head in disgust. 'What a poorly constructed and verbose sentence.' A comment which earned her a snarling glare from their mother.

'Your sister is likely ruined, and the only thing you can find to comment upon is the grammar?'

'Well, it is a dreadful sentence, Mama. These people are paid good money to write, yet fail to understand the importance of simple punctuation, let alone cadence.' She took a nonplussed sip of her chocolate. 'It makes my blood boil that such pathetic penmanship is allowed in a national newspaper when an illiterate could construct better.'

Their mother's incensed eyes began to bulge. 'What makes my blood boil, Hope, is that my eldest daughter decided to toss away her good reputation to dance a *breathless* waltz with Lord Beastly! In front of everyone!'

'She is hardly ruined, Roberta.' Their father tried to lay calming oil on troubled water. 'It is just a bit of silly gossip, nowhere near as bad as some of the nonsense they have printed about our girls over the years. Like all those, it will disappear as quickly as it began—just as it always does. Lord Eastwood isn't the first gentleman one of our daughters has been erroneously linked to and I sincerely doubt he shall be the last. Next week they'll print some other nonsense about Hope or Charity or the pair of us and Faith's waltz will be forgotten. Let us not forget, that same paper claimed you were about to run off with a Spanish tenor last year, my dear. Yet here you still are and there has been no mention of it since.'

The tenor in question had dined with them at least thrice with his wife, who had taken the gossip so badly she had marched to Bloomsbury and had a screaming fit on their doorstep. That had made the papers too. It had been a much more scandalous story in the long run than one paltry waltz.

'And it was hardly breathless, Mama.' Although for several alarming moments as Faith had drowned in his hypnotic green eyes it had been, yet it seemed prudent to clarify in case her sisters picked up on that damning comment and bludgeoned her mercilessly with it. 'It was a single dance, that is all, which only came about after Edward behaved like a total cad without the slightest provocation.'

'Edward wouldn't have had to be a cad if you hadn't been huddled unchaperoned in that alcove!' Her mother's finger prodded in accusation. 'Do not try to deny it because I saw you! Chatting amiably away with him as if he wasn't the D-E-V-I-L incarnate.'

'Faith was in an alcove all alone with Lord Beastly?' Charity was enjoying this a little too much. 'The plot thickens...'

'Indeed it does!' Her mother's finger now wagged in perfect time with the pendulum on the mantel clock. 'I sent him there specifically to extract you from that monster's clutches, terrified he had already S-E-D-U-C-E-D you with his silver tongue.'

'Oh, for goodness sake!' Faith stared heavenwards and prayed for strength. This was all ridiculous. 'Lord Eastwood has the least silver tongue of anyone I have ever known, Mother. If you had taken the trouble to talk to him last night when you had the opportunity, instead of treating him like a leper, you might have discovered as much for yourself.' He was often charmingly tongue-tied and when he wasn't, he was dry and sardonic, not effortlessly charming—although she found that subtle wit quite charming enough in combination with his other attractions.

Like the solid feel of those artistically pleasing broad shoulders beneath her palms or those expressive eyes which continually held hers captive. All a very dangerous combination which she had henceforth decided to avoid anyway, which in turn made this entire conversation moot. She would never have her head turned by a man like him again, and one tiny slip was hardly the end of the world. 'If you hadn't been so unspeakably rude to both him and his perfectly lovely parents, I would not have had to seek him out to apologise for it and I would have left straight after had *you* not sent Edward.'

She was stretching the truth a bit there, as she

had not been in a hurry to leave him. He had looked so lost and lonely, it had called to something within her and she had been powerless to do anything but answer. 'If you wanted to subtly extricate me from Lord Eastwood, what possessed you to send Edward Tate anyway? Of all the people in our acquaintance, he is the least subtle. He thrives on drama and adores being the centre of attention. He charged in like the cavalry and behaved like a bully, and didn't seem to care who saw him do it.'

'Are you saying this is my fault?' Dear Mama's face was now so hot it was a miracle steam didn't shoot out of her ears. 'That I should have ignored the fact my eldest daughter was in deep, intimate and unmonitored conversation with a morally moribund, callous, manipulative and despicable S-C-O-U-N-D-R-E-L?' Two palms slapped the table with such force the last slice of toast vibrated out of the silver toast rack and flopped belly up on the crisp linen cloth. 'If I am guilty of anything in this shameful debacle, daughter, then it is of trying to rescue you as any decent mother would! Had I known you would respond to poor Edward's offer to intervene with your customary pig-headedness, I would have fetched you myself and that awful dance wouldn't have happened!'

'It was hardly awful.' Hope fished the last piece of toast from the tablecloth then began to smear it with jam. 'I thought Lord Beastly danced very well for such a big man and the pair of you certainly looked very striking.' Her sister's typical flippant comment wasn't helping.

'They looked scandalous! The whole waltz was scandalous! Faith's complete lack of judgement was scandalous!'

'Oh, it was.' The last of the toast disappeared into Hope's mouth. 'I am merely stating that if one is going to be a scandal, one might as well look magnificent while doing it and she did.' Her sister turned to her. 'Would you mind if I borrowed that red gown for Mama's opening, Faith? I sincerely doubt anyone will notice it is the same gown—everyone had better things to be staring at.'

'Like Miss B.'s smitten expression while she *twirled breathless* in the arms of the infamous Lord E.' The dark art of subtle innuendo was lost on Charity, who clutched her hands to her heart. 'I thought that was a particularly good sentence. It was certainly the best one I have read this morning.'

'Enough!' Her father snatched the paper out of Charity's hand and waved a furious finger at all of them. 'Or I'll have the lot of you dispatched to a nunnery!' His glare rested on Faith. 'That waltz was ill-considered and foolish, irrespective of the provocation, and has caused a flurry of unnecessary gossip for this family! Again! Let alone the poor Writtles, who have suffered more than their fair share of press attention these last few months. At least have the decency to acknowledge it.'

'I *am* sorry, Papa.' But more for the way the papers were treating poor Lord Eastwood than for anyone else, but she wasn't stupid enough to admit that out loud. 'It will not happen again, Mama.'

'Be sure that it doesn't.' Her father gave her one last hard stare, then his eyes skewered his wife. 'And you were unforgivably rude to both the Writtles and Lord Eastwood, Roberta. I cannot fathom what you were thinking to be so unsubtle.'

'I was curt, not rude, Augustus.'

'You used a mallet to crush a walnut, Roberta, and have put me in a very uncomfortable position with a perfectly respectable and decent family! They are paying me to paint them, remember! Yet today I shall have to go there and repair the damage you have done! And that is assuming they want me back to paint them. I could be issued my marching orders on the doorstep and lose that valuable commission to any one of the hundreds of portrait painters in the capital. And what would that do to my reputation, madam? Did you consider that when you grievously insulted their beloved son? Who, I might add, has been nothing but a complete gentleman in my presence since this commission started.'

He too slapped the table. 'There! I've said it. Irrespective of what the press have said, I rather like the fellow and feel dreadfully sorry he has to go through more nonsense because our headstrong daughter decided the best way to put that annoying poet in his place was to drag him into another scandal! But at least Faith meant well! You were unforgivably rude!'

For the first time all morning her mother was contrite. 'I was caught off guard...'

'Had Lord Beastly done anything to you personally to deserve such censure *before* he waltzed with Faith?'

'No, Augustus.' Her mother stared down at her hands.

'Was it Lord Eastwood's fault that that lacy fop Edward Tate charged in like a bull at a gate and behaved abominably at your prompting? And did he, or did he not try to caution our headstrong daughter against dancing with him because he knew an innocent dance would be twisted, misconstrued and smeared over the scandal sheets?' Faith had told them everything except the strange way he made her feel. And perhaps her inexplicable preoccupation with the man. Uncharacteristic behaviours which she hoped were ultimately as transient as they were all-encompassing, even though they still lingered.

As her father continued to glare, her mother's expression dissolved from belligerent to apologetic. 'I owe them all an apology, don't I?'

He finally smiled. 'You do, my dear. But I dare say it's nothing that a brace of the finest seats to your grand opening can't fix, as long as the tickets come with a brief accompanying note which states they caught you at a bad time and you are now mortified you inadvertently took your ill temper out on them. True patrons of the arts are very forgiving of the artistic temperament, and the Writtles have certainly indulged my eccentricities this past week so I am sure they will take your gesture in the right spirit.'

'I shall arrange both to be sent over this morning, Augustus, with some flowers for Lady Writtle.' Apology swiftly turned to theatrical martyrdom. 'I shall even include Lord Beastly in the invitation to be magnanimous.'

'That is very decent of you, my dear.'

Their housekeeper chose that moment to poke

her head around the door. 'The carriage is out front, sir.'

'Splendid.' Eager to escape the madness now that he had calmed the tempest, her father was up like a shot. 'Come along, Faith, I have a busy day ahead and the only hour Lord Writtle has free today begins at nine.'

'You cannot mean to take her with you, Augustus!' Her mother's expression was now one of utter astonishment coloured with a healthy dollop of betrayal to make him feel guilty. 'Not back to the lion's D-E-N... Surely?'

'Like me, Faith has work to do. A great deal of it. I cannot get this commission finished without her.'

'But she is at risk, Augustus. Can you not see that?'

'She really isn't, my dear.' He strode towards the door like a man in a desperate hurry. 'As usual you are worrying unnecessarily. I have heard Faith's explanation of what happened, and I am satisfied by it. With the benefit of hindsight, it perhaps was not the most sensible course of action, but I can see no real harm was done.'

'But the papers...'

'Will print rot regardless and always have. Giving this latest gossip more credence than all those equally ridiculous stories which we have suffered in the past is silly and we have never enjoyed unblemished reputations anyway. That is exactly why blue-blooded society secretly adores us mere mortals who exist on the fringes—we enrich their staid, upright lives with fascinating titillation.'

'Did you not see the way he looked her? The way she looked at him?'

His feet paused, as Faith felt the weight of her sisters' twin stares at the outrageous comment which was a little too close to the truth for comfort.

'Augustus...for a while there, it was just the two of them on that dance floor...nothing else existed. Don't you remember what that felt like?'

'This is all nonsense!' Faith's outrage was more to do with her panic than fury, because there had been a moment when there had been only him and it hadn't been anywhere near as fleeting as she had desperately tried to convince herself since. Yet undeniably, there was something about Lord Eastwood which made her feel...odd. 'I cannot believe we are even having this conversation when all of us, Mother included, have been romantically linked both scurrilously and erroneously to all manner of gentlemen over the years and we have always laughed it off. We have always seen it for exactly what it is! Utter absurdity. Complete claptrap!'

That she had been that transparent, that unguarded was mortifying. If her mother had seen it from the edge of the floor, had Lord Eastwood seen it too? Had everyone else?

Twirling breathless.

Of course they had. And it had been sublime. Magical.

Breathtaking.

An odd look passed between her parents. One which clearly said more than the two words which came out of her mother's mouth.

'Augustus…please…'

An eerie quiet settled over the table while they all waited for his judgement, and Faith willed him to dismiss her mother's ludicrous comment out of hand with his customary chuckle whenever she was being dramatic and overly fanciful. Instead, he sighed.

'She will be with me, Roberta, under my watchful eye and therefore I can assure you no harm will come to her.' His gaze then fixed on Faith and she saw his concern unbelievably mirrored his wife's before he masked it with a smile. 'This is all a storm in a teacup. Mark my words.'

Chapter Twelve

It was just a thank-you.

One which really did not require this level of overthinking or debate. A polite acknowledgement that her kindness towards him yesterday was appreciated alongside an apology for the unfounded furore her generosity had inadvertently caused in the press this morning. It was the very least he could do after she had had her name splashed all over the newspapers.

There was absolutely nothing anybody could read into a simple thank-you.

Not even his mother could read more into it than common decency and good manners demanded. In fact, it would be jolly poor form if he did not seek her out and mention it after she had made such a public stand on his behalf. They *should* commiserate it briefly together.

So why the blazes was he still dithering outside the blasted ballroom a full five minutes after arriving there, rehearsing the damn words in his head when the whole thing should be done and dusted by now?

Unfortunately, Piers knew exactly why.

He was procrastinating because he wanted to have more to say once the necessary thanking and commiserating was done.

Something erudite and amusing which she might find interesting. Something which might spark another sparring conversation and which gave him an excuse to linger in her company a little longer than a quick, efficient and polite acknowledgement afforded—because clearly, despite his better judgement and thanks entirely to one short, foolhardy waltz, he had gone completely stark, staring mad!

Especially when there was nothing wrong with his sensible strategy to steer well clear of the vixen for evermore. As much as everything about her called to him—from the bright gowns she favoured to the attractive outspokenness and witty sarcasm which highlighted her intelligence, or the selfless bravery which had led her to make a public stand against the sort of unfairness he had come to expect from his peers—only a complete fool or a diehard flagellant would consider the possibility that history might not repeat itself if he continued down this pathway to certain doom.

He could privately fantasise all he wanted about the way she fitted so perfectly in his arms, silently lust in complete solitude at the way her lush body had felt against his or the way her eyes had sparkled as he had drowned in them. He could suffer the same fevered dreams as he had all last night for an eternity, but he had to be crystal clear on the pitfalls anything which extended beyond basic politeness would entail.

Women like her weren't for men like him.

He knew that so well he could write a book on the subject. A cautionary tale which might help other mundane and average men from reaching for the extraordinary. Warn them that, like Icarus flying too close to the sun, such foolish aspirations were always destined to fail.

If he did miraculously find himself another woman to share his life with, and he was so wary of that it seemed implausible in the extreme, he needed to find one just like him, cut from the same plain cloth and most definitely not another exotic creature who came from a different species of human being altogether. You only had to observe nature to see the absolute logic in that, because ultimately birds of a feather always flocked together.

194 of The Viscount's Unconventional Lady

At his most scintillating, Piers was a blackbird or a common pigeon, while she was a dazzling peacock. Or perhaps one of those flamboyant pink flamingos he had seen in one of his nieces' picture books about Africa. The kind-hearted Miss Brookes might make do with a pigeon for a while, but just like Constança, she would always crave another peacock. Although Edward Tate was obviously a peacock of the highest order and she had the full measure of him so perhaps...

And clearly he was indeed stark staring mad to even be thinking such rot!

He had wasted the entire morning already on outrageous flights of fancy, barely listening to the briefing on the current state of the Sixth Coalition and their steady advance towards Paris. It did not appear to matter that they appeared to be days away from finally winning the war, or that thanks to the uncharacteristically helpful Master of the King's Household, Piers had to organise a state banquet in honour of the Portuguese in under seven weeks. All he could apparently focus on was the image of a siren in scarlet with a rose in her hair. Her perfume. Her skin. The dusting of freckles on her nose and her mouth-watering and daring neckline which had made him yearn to know what lay beneath it.

Piers needed to concentrate on his mountain of important government work—not fill his valuable hours daydreaming about Miss Brookes's soft freckled skin and fine pert breasts!

It was one thing to compare Miss Brookes to Constança, another entirely to imagine their brief acquaintance stood an iceberg's chance in hell of developing into anything more than what it was.

At least to Constança, for a very short period of time, his sedate Englishness had seemed exotic. That same Englishness was run-of-the-mill mundaneness for a fellow countrywoman like Miss Brookes. His awful new reputation aside, with nothing else but his dull blandness to fall back on, there was no earthly reason a rare jewel like her would look once, let alone twice at him. He might well have been thoroughly seduced by just one waltz, but she had simply been being kind. And he was still procrastinating like an idiot in his own hallway!

Before his brain decided to mull over any more pointless twaddle, he squared his shoulders, tapped briskly on the door before he marched through it, then simply stood and stared while his eyes drank her in.

She had her back to him upon a slightly raised scaffold, her body swaying as she worked. Even the capacious smock which covered two thirds of her vibrant turquoise day dress could not disguise the lush curves beneath. Several stray, heavy curls bounced in time to her movements while her right arm swept in a wide arc as she painted a faint outline of what appeared to be a hill in a dark wash.

It was an arresting sight, one he could have happily stared at for hours, but some sixth sense told him they weren't alone.

'Good morning, Lord Eastwood.'

Augustus Brookes had apparently set up shop in the farthest corner by the French doors. 'What brings you here this morning? I did not think you could spare me any time to pose this week.'

The artist might well be smiling but Piers sensed the undercurrent in the man's tone. Hardly a huge surprise when his daughter was being maligned by the press thanks to him. And he had probably just witnessed him ogling her to boot. To make the situation just that bit more awkward, Miss Brookes had also turned around and there was a tightness to her smile which wasn't there last night either. He recognised bitter regret when he saw it. Constança had worn the same expression near constantly.

'I came to apologise…for all the fuss that I

have inadvertently caused you and your family today.' It was probably better this way, he realised. It drew a decisive line in the sand in his ridiculously spiralling attraction to a woman he categorically did not want to be attracted to. 'All the rumour and speculation… I feel dreadful about it.'

'But not dreadful enough to have refused my daughter's offer last night though?'

'Papa!' Faith hopped down from the platform and moved towards the centre of the room, closer to her father while still maintaining a good distance from him. 'You know I gave him no choice in the matter. If anyone is to blame for the flurry of silly gossip it is I. Lord Eastwood tried to warn me and despite knowing exactly how things would spiral, I practically dragged him on to the floor.' Her eyes flicked to his filled with remorse. 'If anyone should be apologising this morning, my lord, it is I. I allowed my stubborn determination to teach Edward a lesson to embarrass both you and my family.'

There were a great many things he wanted to say, not least of which was the overwhelming desire to take at least half of the blame because the uncomfortable truth was he could have dug his heels in harder. He could have thanked her for the well-meant sentiment, politely declined and then bade her a goodnight before quietly slipping away. But saying as much would only throw more fuel on the fire when her father was quite obviously intent on guarding her like a sentry and would likely see it as the frank admission of guilt it was. Augustus Brookes was no fool and he knew how the male mind worked. In fact, he had just said as much. He, like every other man in the Renshaw ballroom last night, knew without a shadow of a doubt that Piers hadn't dug his heels in far enough for one simple reason— because he had wanted to hold her in his arms.

He had seen an opportunity and he had seized it.

Just as he had been trying to create another opportunity this morning by coming here.

'Even so…' The strategist in him knew his foolhardy campaign was lost before it had started and the diplomat urged him to embrace the status quo. That was not only the safest, but the most sensible option. In fact, it was the only option. 'I am sorry for the embarrassment and hope the gossip subsides quickly. If you would like me to write to the newspapers concerned and refute their unsavoury implications and demand they immediately publish retractions, I am more than happy to do so.'

That offer seemed to impress the artist while entirely flummoxing his daughter.

'That is very decent of you, my lord,' Augustus said, 'but I fear it may only serve to make the situation worse. This nonsense will blow over soon enough, as nonsense always does, and will likely go away much faster if you both avoid doing anything in the future which *unintentionally* might be construed as evidence to the contrary. The absolute last thing we want now is to fan the flames, especially when it truly was just one dance.' Her father's stare was unyielding and spoke volumes.

Stay away from my daughter.

Because he really didn't blame him and knew, for the sake of his own sanity, he had to, Piers couldn't argue with that. 'You have my word, sir.' Even though it pained him to give it, and even though the recently awakened reckless and romantic part of him still wished for more. 'And I thank you for your understanding.' He bowed curtly, wondering why he was already grieving the loss of her when he knew he could never have her. 'Good day.'

Carefully, Piers schooled his features into the blandest expression he could muster before he turned to her, not wanting to give any of his warring, terrifying and outrageous feelings away.

'And good day to you too, Miss Brookes. My apologies again for any embarrassment this has caused—but thank you for your kindness last night. It has restored some of my faith in humanity.'

Chapter Thirteen

The theatre was packed. The stuffy auditorium filled with the excited buzz of patrons waiting expectantly for the lights to finally dim, the heavy velvet curtains to part, the orchestra to play the first notes of the second half of *Così fan Tutte* and for her brilliant mother to step back on to the stage.

Few sopranos could ever hope to attempt the difficult vocal range required to play Fiordiligi, fewer still could ever hope to do it justice, but Roberta Brookes's powerful voice was unique and had left everyone dumbfounded by the end of the first half. Faith too had come to the theatre excited, immensely proud of her dear Mama's achievement and eager to hear her sing the role she had been born to play, and excited too for Charity, who was making her stage debut in the chorus. But thanks to the snake Lord Rayne and his snide and inappropriate comments during the interval, she now felt queasy.

Dangerously so.

At every society function they had collided at in the five years since their short-lived romance ended, although he never directly referenced it he always gave her a knowing look, making sure she was constantly reminded of her own youthful stupidity at her willingness to offer herself to him lock, stock and barrel. With no more than a mere few weeks of heady flirtation, no firm promises and her own wanton, untutored passion, she had assumed her overwhelming love had been reciprocated and she had dived head first into a physical affair. It was, to her most intensely private mortification, the biggest mistake of her life and the snake had never allowed her to forget their brief and shameful dalliance. Even without the smug looks, his presence in the same room always made the bile rise in her, but tonight he decided to take it a step further.

Tonight, he had renewed his offer to rent them a little love nest in Bloomsbury. A place where he could sate his apparently enduring passion for her well away from the prying eyes of his wife or the gossip of the *ton*. And he had proposed it as if he was doing her a huge favour. Even after she had spat that he could go to hell, he had smiled and asked her to at least think upon it. He even named an allowance, as if she could be bought in pounds, shillings and pence, treating her like a common prostitute and making her feel more wretched about her own youthful stupidity than she ever had before.

Which Faith hadn't thought was possible—yet apparently, once again, she was wrong.

Even now, she could still feel him staring at her from his box above, so intense and blatantly lustful that she felt thoroughly violated and dirty by the scrutiny. And hideously nineteen all over again.

To cover it, she stared at her programme rather than attempt to converse normally with her sister sat beside her. Hope would realise something wasn't right and Faith didn't want to have to invent another pack of lies to cover her discomfort whenever Viscount Rayne was close by. As she forced her eyes to focus on the running order of the second half, she sensed another pair of eyes on her too, only these made her flesh tingle with awareness rather than disgust. She did not need to turn towards them to know whose they were, because she knew already they were Lord Eastwood's, but did anyway. Then wished she hadn't when she saw beyond his subtle smile to the sympathy in his astute green gaze. Even from the

204 *The Viscount's Unconventional Lady*

other side of the theatre, he clearly knew something wasn't quite right.

Oddly, his perceptiveness warmed her, and she smiled back, wishing she wasn't always so attuned to him when she had been making such a concerted effort not to be. Since the worryingly charged waltz and the flurry of stories about it in the gossip columns a week ago, they had avoided one another by tacit agreement. But on the rare occasions he was home and they collided in a hallway, or he wandered into the morning room while she was giving Isobel her daily painting lesson as he had yesterday, they said a brief and polite good day and passed like ships in the night.

Yet, each time they did, she instantly regretted the brevity and yearned for more of the meaningful, easy conversation they seemed to share, which in turn hardened her resolve to maintain her distance. Then she had used the snake ruthlessly in that quest, reminding herself they were two men—two well-connected and politically ambitious future Earls—cut from the same cloth despite the fact her silly heart was almost entirely convinced that they weren't.

But tonight, because she needed it, she decided to lose herself in his eyes until the darkness hid her rather than think about the other ones which made her feel ill. Something she almost managed as the auditorium dimmed and, feeling strangely better, she made the mistake of turning away. Which meant she saw Lord Rayne's blatant heated stare once more, then watched him lasciviously and pointedly lick his lips slowly with the tip of his tongue as his box went black.

For several minutes, everything was a blur.

She heard her mother's voice but could not focus on her performance. Her skin grew clammy and hot as her stomach roiled, and then even breathing became difficult. All the while, Faith's mind whirred, frantically trying to fathom why there was such a marked change in his demeanour when she never gave him anything other than short shrift any more. But there had been a change. One which felt like a seismic shift, and it frankly terrified her.

'Are you all right?' Hope's concerned whisper made her panic some more.

'I'm just a bit hot and dizzy.' Very dizzy. 'It's so warm in here.'

'Warm is an understatement. It's an oven. Maybe you need to splash some water on your face? Would you like me to fetch some?'

'No…' But she couldn't ignore the excuse to escape. 'I'll go. The fresh air will do me some good. I shan't be long.' She squeezed her sister's arm in reassurance and quietly slipped out of her seat, thanking her lucky stars she was sat on the aisle.

Only once she had exited the sturdy door to the dress circle did she quicken her pace, taking the stairs downwards almost at a run before she burst out into the near empty foyer below. An usher started towards her, his face a picture of concern at the tears she hadn't been able to prevent, and she stayed him with her hand, then plunged out of the ornate front doors into the night.

Outside, she gulped in several fortifying breaths, welcoming the chilly night air on her fevered skin and the freedom to unleash her emotions. In case any of the late-night passers-by saw her and came to assist in her obvious distress, she hid behind one of the Theatre Royal's four soaring Doric columns and fought for calm. It was a losing battle.

Oh, how she loathed it that Rayne still had this power over her! Loathed too the petrifying realisation that it would only take one spiteful comment from him to the right pair, or pairs, of ears to completely ruin her and scupper any chance she might have to follow in her father's footsteps. While society might well forgive a man for indulging in the sins of the flesh outside of the marriage bed, they might even turn a blind eye to an older, married woman discreetly pursuing her passion elsewhere. But none of them would ever forgive a young and determinedly single woman for it in case such immorality was so contagious she might sully their womenfolk with her wayward badness. Yet there was no denying the snake had seen her naked, kissed parts of her that only a husband ever should and had heard her urgent, mindless words of encouragement as he had plunged into her needy body on more than one occasion.

There had been seven in total.

All fast, reckless, passionate and illicit.

Seven separate memories she could never erase.

Seven permanent stains on her soul.

'Have you changed your mind yet then?' His voice, out of nowhere, made her jump. 'I could *buy* you the house, if that's what you are holding out for. I could have the deeds drawn up in your name so it would always be yours, Faith. No matter what.'

'How dare you!' She tried to storm past, but the snake blocked her way back into the theatre. Because she would rather die than let him see her tears, she turned her back to him and tried to angrily blink them away.

'Come now, Faith, can't we be civilised about this?' She jerked away from his fingers as they grazed her sleeve.

'Civilised!' She wanted to scratch his lying eyes out. 'I doubt you know the meaning of the word!' She strode around the column and down the steps in a wide arc to avoid him, but he followed.

'We used to like one another. We used to *enjoy* one another...' She could feel his breath on her bare shoulder as his long legs quickly caught up with hers. 'A great deal as I recall.' He had the audacity to touch her arm and she tugged it back, then spun to face him allowing every bit of her disgust and hatred to show.

'Stay away from me! I want nothing to do with you! You're nothing but a vile...' A hackney drove past, and she seriously considered hailing it just to escape him, a move he must have guessed because he caught her arm again, roughly this time, and held on tight.

'What, Faith? A vile seducer? When we both know it did not take much seduction on my part to get you to hoist up your petticoats and spread your lovely long...' The fist came out of nowhere, knocking his jaw sideways and sending Rayne tumbling down the remaining three steps to the mucky pavement below. It was closely followed by the large and enraged shape of Lord Eastwood, who loomed over the snake, his face a mask of dark fury as he bent to snarl directly in his face.

'If you ever touch her or speak to her like that again, you will have me to deal with!'

A mewling, bleeding Rayne cowered as he clutched his gushing nose. 'I didn't realise she was yours now! I apologise!' He used his feet to shuffle backwards on his bottom. 'Had I known Faith was already your mistress, I never would have chanced my arm with her tonight.'

It was the wrong thing to say.

'Do not judge me or her by your own filthy standards!' Lord Eastwood roughly dragged him up by his lapels. 'You are an odious, slimy, pathetic excuse for a man, and you will apologise to this lady now for insulting her! Or I swear to God I'll rip out that vile, toadying, sycophantic and lying tongue of yours and I'll make you watch as I feed it to dogs!'

Rayne's eyeballs protruded in his reddened face. 'I am sorry, Faith!'

But her unanticipated rescuer wasn't done, nor did he appear the least bit placated by Lord Rayne's complete and utter capitulation. 'Nowhere near good enough, you contemptible bastard!' He shoved the snake away with such force he landed on his bottom again then jabbed the air near his chest with such calm menace, she had the pleasure of hearing the snake whimper. 'Firstly, she is Miss Brookes to you and you will treat her with the utmost respect! Not that you will ever dare so much as look at her from this night forward, let alone speak—either *to* her or *about* her. Do I make myself clear?'

The snake nodded, clearly terrified. 'I—I'm s-sorry, Miss Brookes.' Then his eyes widened into petrified saucers as Lord Eastwood dragged him up by his elbow this time before proceeding to dust of his lapels with quiet, but frankly terrifying restraint.

'And it won't happen again, will it, Rayne? You'll never look at her again as if she is a piece of prime horseflesh, or make any lewd and un-gentlemanly suggestions, or smear her good character or even dare mention her in a passing comment to another living soul? Including ex-plaining to anyone the real reason how you came to be bleeding all over your shirt.'

The snake looked ready to burst into tears as he frantically nodded like a woodpecker.

'Because if I even hear a faint rumour that you have broken that promise, then I won't just tell your poor wife the truth, I'll also tell your father-in-law and we both know he is unlikely to take it well. There is no telling what he might do to your career to avenge his beloved daughter.'

Faith could tell by the way all the colour drained from the snake's face that that threat had hit the mark. 'You can be assured of my silence.' Then as a pathetic afterthought, he added, 'My lord.'

'Then we are done here.' Lord Eastwood stepped back and for the first time since she had known him, looked every inch the aloof, arrogant and powerful peer. 'Get out of my sight before I change my mind and pummel you to paste just for the sport.'

The snake didn't need to be asked twice. Still clutching his bleeding nose, he scurried back into the theatre as if his breeches were on fire.

Left alone with her gallant rescuer, shock at what had happened took mere moments to turn to utter shame that he had witnessed this. For the life of her, she couldn't think of a single thing to say that would make it all sound better either. Mutely, she blinked up at him until she finally found some words. 'Thank you.' A lacklustre effort but her mind was still whirring. Because now a third person knew of her dirty secret.

'He shouldn't bother you again.' His handsome face was filled with pity. 'I'm so sorry you had to go through that.'

'My own stupid fault as doubtless you heard.' The last vestiges of her pride had her squaring her shoulders. 'Assuming you did hear it all.'

He didn't deny it. 'Would you like me to escort you back via the retiring room so you can fix your face?'

'No...thank you... I would prefer some fresh air.' She offered him her best approximation of a smile, wanting him gone so she could lick her gaping wounds in private. 'I shall go back in shortly.' After she had found a secluded place to curl up into a ball and bawl her eyes out. 'Thank you again.' Decisively she turned, hoping he would take the hint but instead he sighed.

'If you think I am leaving you alone, Faith, you have another think coming.'

'Really, I shall be...' She turned back in time to watch him hail a passing hackney. As it slowed, he opened the door and then gestured inside.

'Come, we'll ride up and down the Strand while you compose yourself. The last thing you need is for one of the journalists in there to witness you in a blubbering state on the theatre steps in the middle of your mother's opening night. Especially if they have already spotted Rayne's nose. They'll put two and two together and make one hundred and sixty-three.'

Because he was right and because she really

couldn't muster an argument, she complied, allowing him to help her up and then staring impotently at her hands as he climbed in and sat opposite.

As the carriage lurched forward, he wafted a handkerchief under her nose. 'It's clean. I promise.'

Faith blew into it as he shrugged out of his coat and wrapped it solicitously around her shoulders, enveloping her in the comforting warmth of his body. Gratefully, she huddled within it, then felt her face crumple as a wave of tears sprung from nowhere, and to her utter disgust, decided to fall in one noisy, soggy rush.

As ashamed of them as she was of her regrettable affair with the snake, she buried her face in his handkerchief and tried to stem the flow.

'Don't hold back on my account. I have two sisters, remember, and I learned a long time ago these things are always better out than in.' He shifted position, and to her mortification, settled in the confined space next to her. She tried to turn her body towards the window, then gave up when his big, solid arm wrapped itself around her quaking shoulders and he gently tugged her to his chest.

Bizarrely, although that simple kindness made her feel better, as she burrowed against him, strangely grateful for both his presence and his strength, it also seemed to unleash all of the five years of hurt she hadn't realised she had stored up inside. But out it all came. Each time she thought she was done, a fresh wave hit her and off she went again. Yet all the while, though heaven only knew how many laps of the Strand they did, he held her close, blessedly silent, and rocked her gently while his comforting hand smoothed her hair.

At some point, the racking sobs must have subsided, because Faith emerged from the fog of pain clutching the sodden front of his shirt, apparently perfectly content to remain wrapped in his arms for ever. In case she did, she dragged herself upright, put as much distance between them on the cramped seat as she could and noisily blew her nose again.

'Feel better?'

She nodded. 'I'm sorry.'

'Don't be. These things happen.'

'How much of those things did you hear?'

'Enough to work out that you and he were once lovers, and enough to assume it ended very badly.' He smiled kindly without judgement. 'Knowing Rayne as I do, I'm inclined to blame him entirely for that.'

He was being nice. A perfect gentleman, though

heaven only knew what he must be thinking. 'I was nineteen. Very young. Very foolish...' Faith shrugged and shook her head at the familiar but bitter taste of regret. 'I thought myself in love.'

'And I presume all this occurred while he was a student of your father's?'

She nodded. 'He was in my house all the time. We often shared the same lessons and then, while Papa left to work on his commissions we practised together and...'

'He took advantage.'

'Only because I let him.' There was no excuse for her youthful stupidity. Her parents had never shielded them from the harsh truths of the world and her mother, especially, had put much emphasis on the importance of morality, virtue and the sanctity of marriage. She would be devasted if she knew Faith hadn't heeded all her wise warnings and had gaily skipped into total ruination without a second thought. 'That makes it all so much worse. Knowing that I encouraged him and he was right, I did not take much seducing all those years ago.' She risked flicking him a glance. 'Not my finest hour, Lord Eastwood, but certainly my bitterest regret.'

'I think now that you have soaked my shirt and ruined my handkerchief, you should probably call me Piers.' He smiled, those intelligent, hypnotic eyes swimming with compassion. 'And I disagree. We all make mistakes, especially when we think ourselves in love. But be in no doubt, he took advantage, so you should blame him more than you castigate yourself.'

'I gave myself to him. Within a scant few weeks of first meeting him, *Piers*.' Mortally ashamed and feeling hideously vulnerable, she dipped her eyes from his astute and compelling gaze.

'You were nineteen. Whereas Rayne is around my age, which means he had at least six years on you, and he used your youth and inexperience to get past your defences.'

'Perhaps but...'

'Did he suggest marriage?'

'Not in so many words.'

'But he made you think he was as giddy about your relationship as you were, didn't he? He alluded to a future.'

She nodded, wishing she didn't feel quite so pathetic and exposed. 'He used to talk about what our life would be like, about how beautiful our children would be...' And like the silliest of dolts, she had lain there in his arms drinking it all in, convinced every single honeyed word was the gospel truth with no concrete assurances whatsoever, nor questioning how he had become so adept at ensuring they didn't also create any children during their brief affair. *Thank God!* 'But I do have to give him some credit in this whole sordid debacle. With hindsight, and as much as it galls me to admit it, he genuinely never, ever mentioned marriage.'

Chapter Fourteen

Piers was instantly sorry that he hadn't pum-
melled Rayne to paste. The temptation to turn
the hackney around, march into the theatre and
drag the bastard out of his seat to finish the job
was so overwhelming, it took all his strength
to sit still and not bellow out the window at the
driver. Instead he settled on grinding his teeth
for a few moments until he could trust himself
to speak calmly. He'd been in an uncharacteristic
state of high agitation since he saw her pale face
in the auditorium and knew, just by the desolate
look in her lovely eyes, that something was very
wrong. Then he saw her warily glance at Rayne,
watched the toad's heated, possessive stare and
his well-honed alarm bells all began to ring.

'Children are usually the result of a marriage,
Faith, therefore it is an entirely reasonable as-
sumption for you to have made, so don't be too
hard on yourself. To err is human after all. Not to

mention that if he was talking about such things, *promising* you such things, within a scant few weeks of meeting you, he was hastening you down his path on purposely false pretences, knowing full well he had no intention of ever making good on them.'

'Clearly you already know him too well.' She laughed without humour, determined to be brave. 'For it turned out the joke was on me and he was already engaged. Not that he told me that of course. He went off, supposedly to visit his family's estate for a few weeks in the spring and no sooner had he left, I learned of his upcoming nuptials in *The Times* one dreadful morning over breakfast.'

'Oh, Faith…' There were no words which would ever make that better, so he took her hand instead in the faint hope it might absorb some of her pain.

She laced her fingers in his gratefully. 'The announcement was apparently just a formality as they had been promised to one another since birth. A fact I might have known had I walked in those same aristocratic circles—but alas, my blood isn't blue enough for Almack's.' The proud, stoic way she tried to minimise what must have been a bitter blow from a cruel and calculated betrayal broke his heart.

'The snake was married by the time he came back to town that autumn and, it turned out, was completely unrepentant for his shoddy behaviour when I called him on it. Future Earls had to marry well, he said, and certainly he could never *ever* consider a woman like me. He pretended to look contrite when he said that he assumed I understood that, he even helpfully outlined how it broke his heart that my dubious parentage and bohemian upbringing would make any sort of legal union with a decent gentleman impossible.

'But to add more insult to injury and to spoil his fake contriteness, he was also quite adamant that he saw no earthly reason why our affair couldn't continue or be able to think why I was angry at the suggestion that it should. He even argued that most married peers kept mistresses, as if that made his inappropriate proposal all the more acceptable. Then he offered to rent me a little house close to my parents in Bloomsbury and had the gall to look insulted when I slapped his face.'

Obviously ashamed and embarrassed by this admission she released her hand from his and turned to stare at the dark street out of the window, her expression so bleak he could hardly bear it. 'An offer he repeated tonight for the first time in five years.'

'Well, he won't be making it again!' The way the scoundrel had spoken to her, the complete lack of respect, had fired Piers's temper on a visceral level he had never experienced before. He had never been one for violence, never understood why some men felt the need for it when he firmly believed that most things could be better sorted through a reasoned debate. All that went out the window when he saw her pain, and when he had felt the crack of Rayne's bone against his fist, he had revelled in it. He still did and sincerely hoped the despicable scoundrel's nose was broken. He deserved all that pain and more for doing what he had done. 'He wouldn't dare!'

'Only because he assumed I am your mistress now instead… Which I suppose makes some sense of it all, so out of the blue.' A deep furrow appeared between her eyebrows. 'At first, I couldn't fathom why he offered it to me again tonight when I've barely been civil to him since he betrayed me and have made no secret of the fact that I loathe him. But I suppose, after all the fevered gossip after *our* waltz, it makes sense. No doubt buoyed by the press's recent unflattering insinuations about the nature of our relationship, he assumed I was in the market for another aristocratic protector—another illustrious viscount—and erroneously thought I'd invite him to warm my bed again if the offer was right.'

He winced at the truth of it. As she had predicted, she had come out of those ridiculous stories worse, while he seemed to have earned some grudging respect from his peers. More than one of his colleagues in Whitehall had attempted to slap him on the back for his excellent taste in his most recent peccadillo, until he had set them straight with a curt denial. He had assumed he had been protecting her reputation by denouncing the rumours as ridiculous. It had never occurred to him that those denials had inadvertently given other predators ideas.

He reached for her hand again, needing the contact. Needing her to know he would always be on her side. 'Oh, Faith, I am so sorry.'

'Don't be. This is hardly your fault.' She was matter of fact, then she smiled as she stared down at their interlocked fingers. She risked looking at him again, needing to see the verdict in his eyes, not sure whether she wanted his absolution or wanted to punish herself with his understandable judgement. 'You must think me such a fool.'

'I think you are gloriously human and flawed as all mere mortals always are. We are all fools at some point in our lives, Faith, and normally because we foolishly allow our hearts to rule our heads.'

'Have you?'

'Yes.' It was his turn to avert his gaze. 'Catastrophically.'

She stared at him for the longest time, her lovely eyes questioning, as if evaluating the sincerity of his words. Then, as the penny dropped, she squeezed his hand. 'You loved your wife, didn't you?'

'Yes.'

'Then why did you divorce her?'

Piers was desperate to change the subject. Discussing anything to do with Constança and his failings as a husband always left him feeling raw, and churned the acid in his stomach so painfully, he had deftly avoided it even with his own family, but he also knew that if he sidestepped her question, then Faith would lose all her new-found trust in him and he realised that would somehow feel worse.

'Because she asked me to.' He huffed out a sigh. 'Portugal is a Catholic country and so her obtaining one there was out of the question.'

'Can I ask why *she* wanted to divorce you?'

Because Piers wasn't anything close to what she wanted in a husband. He was too dull. Too staid. Too occupied by work. Too noble. Too calm. Too English. Too everything and yet never enough. The knot in his throat which had suddenly appeared instantly twisted. 'She wanted to remarry, and time was of the essence.'

'Ahh...' He watched her piece it all together before she glanced at him with pity. 'The child was never yours then? I assume you are absolutely sure of that?'

'As she has remained resolutely in Lisbon and as I have been back here in London for almost two years, I am quite certain. Not that I needed the actual ocean between us to be certain the babe wasn't mine. She was a stranger in my bedchamber long before we separated...but alas, not a stranger in others.' He had never fooled himself her new husband had been her only lover during their turbulent three years together, any more than Constança had tried to hide her desire to seek her pleasures elsewhere almost from the outset when she had quickly tired of him.

'Oh, Piers, I'm so sorry.' Her hand covered his where it rested on his leg. 'I had no idea.'

'Thankfully, next to nobody here does, and pathetically, I prefer to be thought of as a villain than a victim. Not that either label fits me well. I rashly rushed down the aisle with her within weeks of our first meeting. Stupidly fast because I was caught up in the moment and blinded by passion, and I had never felt like that before so I naively assumed that exhilarating and intoxicating first rush of passion was how it would always be between us. But we were never really compatible, and with the clarity which only hindsight brings, I now realise those heady emotions were not enough to sustain us through anything beyond a brief affair.'

Her smile was sad as she squeezed his fingers. 'I know exactly what you mean. I confused passion with love and I blame my inexperience for that. Rayne and I were never truly compatible. Had I spent a little more time talking to him and less time kissing him, I would have realised that from the outset. Whenever I see him now at society events and watch him fawning over the powerful and ignoring the servants, I see how shallow he is as plain as day and kick myself that I did not see it then. Isn't it ironic we both confused lust with love?'

'I console myself that millions of others must have fallen into the same trap over the centuries. History and literature are peppered with stark warnings which are all ignored until it's too late to heed them.' Piers rested his head on the back of the bench while he waited for the bitter taste of bile in his mouth to subside. *'Love comforteth like sunshine after rain, But Lust's effect is tempest after sun; Love's gentle spring doth always fresh remain, Lust's winter comes ere summer half be done; Love surfeits not, Lust like a glutton dies; Love is all truth, Lust full of forged lies.'* He turned to her and sighed, the sight of her calming his stomach more effectively than the deep breaths he usually relied upon. 'Shakespeare—even he apparently learned the hard way. I suppose that is why courtship was invented. To save us from ourselves.'

'The snake and I never even went out for a walk. Everything was so fast. So clandestine.'

'But clandestine is thrilling isn't it? Dangerous but intoxicating.'

'You sound as if you are speaking from experience.'

Piers smiled wryly, dreading kicking the hornet's nest but feeling strangely inclined to suddenly do so. 'Constança's father owned several large and successful quintas deep in the valley miles from Porto. Once a year, she travelled with him and the new harvest of wine to the city where he sold it. He was too strict and she was chomping at the bit to escape and eager to better her station in life, while I was a stranger in a new land desperately struggling to find my feet. We met by chance at one of the wine caves and discovered we also happened to be staying at the same inn. So every night for two weeks we met in secret after her father and her maid went to sleep. The day before she was due to leave, in a rare moment of impulsive madness because she was so upset, I found a clergyman at the British barracks who was willing to marry us for a guinea and considered myself the luckiest man alive.' Those triumphant feelings did not last long. 'It was probably the first and last time I have ever acted entirely on impulse without weighing up all of the pros and the cons.'

'Wisely and slow; they stumble that run fast.' She curved her other hand through his arm as she also leaned her head on the back of the bench next to his. 'You are not the only one who can quote Shakespeare, Piers.'

'I wish I had read more of his wise words before I slipped that ring on her finger, because I soon discovered my new wife was everything I am not—unique, reckless, bold, fiery and vibrant.' Exactly like the woman beside him, whose hand fitted perfectly in his and made him want again despite all his sensible reservations. 'Constança was both breathtakingly beautiful and thoroughly charming to her core. She was a shining light in the centre of any room while I'm one for blending into the panelling. She might have been brought up in the countryside, but her father also brought her up like a princess, catering to her every whim, and she had been trained since birth to one day be a rich aristocrat's wife.' Traits which he might have noticed sooner if they had not married in such haste.

'I suppose she assumed that because I would one day inherit an earldom, then I would share her delight in the spoiled idleness which she had always enjoyed. She craved a life of balls and parties and frivolous entertainments which were denied her in the countryside. She wanted the sort of high society friends who I always thought lacked substance, whereas I prefer work and purpose, as I was brought up to do, and would rather boil my head in a vat of oil than socialise with a room full of popinjays. She loved to argue and I am...'

'An infuriating born diplomat?'

'Yes—as well as being too mundane and boring to hold her attention and too staid and dull to ever hope to change that. Some are born to be unique, Faith, like you, and some of us are doomed for ever to be anything but.' Piers huffed out a sigh of resignation as he shrugged. 'Needless to say, we inevitably grew to loathe one another very quickly once we had realised our grave mistake. Then, when my work took me to Lisbon for a few months liaising with the Royal

Court while our Ambassador was on leave, she begged me to take her. That proved to be the final nail in our coffin.' And he experienced the three most miserable months of his life.

'She embraced every aspect of court life, in fact she took to it like a duck to water, and seemed happier for a while. But while I buried myself in my work, I soon discovered that the real reason for her happiness was a certain duke who shared her perspective on life. And because he was a duke and I was never going to be, she decided to make their arrangement more permanent than her usual transient affairs. Then the Foreign Office called me back to London and she was adamant she would not return with me, it was almost a relief to admit defeat and finally bring the fetid war that was our marriage to a close.'

'But it has left scars, I can tell.'

It had. Big, deep, gaping ones which he feared would never heal. 'Like you, with your vile Viscount, Constança has left me very jaded. I find it near impossible to trust anyone and always expect the worst of them.' Even though he had loathed Constança by the time they went to Lisbon, her affairs, especially the one with the Duke, had left him boiling with uncontrollable jealousy. Not that he was ever jealous of the lover or his cheating wife, it was more that he was jealous he wasn't like them.

All the traits in himself which Constança had abhorred had suddenly frustrated him so much he loathed himself for all of them and hated himself for allowing her callous treatment of him to rob him of all self-esteem. But because he was reserved and staid and instinctively avoided conflict, he buried it all inside behind a mask of indifference. But inside…all that bitterness festered, upset his stomach and caused a knot of nerves so tight in his throat he had frequently feared it would choke him.

Whenever she was mentioned, even now, it seemed to spontaneously flare again, crawling from the dark pit in which it clearly still festered. Then suffocating him in self-loathing and swamping him in shame for being so stupid in the first place. That poison wasn't something which he was prepared drag into another marriage. Not when it ate him from the inside and turned him into a version of himself he not only hated, but did not recognise.

'I know that feeling, Piers—only too well. I am wary of the motives of all men nowadays because I am as jaded as it is possible to be. After my poor judgement with him, I do not trust myself to ever fall in love again.'

'Me either.'

'But you wouldn't settle for less than that either, would you?' It was as if she could see into his soul, through all his defences, to all those futile hopes and dreams which stubbornly refused to die no matter what was thrown at them. He still wanted what his parents had, even though he held out no hope that he would get it.

'Any more than I suspect you would.'

'Then perhaps we will both find true happiness one day?' She sighed wistfully as she stared at the street rushing by. 'That special soulmate who stops us from loathing ourselves and allows us to trust again.'

That truly would be a miracle. To wake up in the morning and look in the mirror and to not be disappointed with what he saw. 'It would have to be after a ridiculously long courtship of course— just to be certain history wasn't repeating itself.'

'Of course.'

'That's if the wariness even allowed either of us to proceed to the courtship stage.'

'Depressing isn't it? To refuse to settle for anything but the deepest and most abiding love but to be too cynical to ever allow it.' She laughed without humour, then, as if noticing their joined hands properly for the first time she gently extricated hers and sat upright again.

'What an odd pair we make, Piers. Both wronged by hedonistic, vain, ambitious and self-ish idiots who didn't appreciate us. Both hiding behind a thin veneer of stubborn pride, both completely misjudged by the world and both made complete fools of by love. And I never expected to have anything in common with you, yet here I am, worryingly predisposed to like you even though, on the surface at least, you are a pompous viscount just like him. In fact, I tried very hard to take an instant dislike to you.'

He couldn't help but laugh at her stark honesty. 'I know that feeling too. The first moment I saw you, saw the vibrant clothes, heard your bold outspokenness, saw the way you lit up a room, you instantly reminded me of her too.'

'That must have been very annoying. No wonder you took instant umbrage with me too. But as we seem now to share so many unexpected similarities, I fear we are now unbelievably doomed to be friends.'

'I fear we are.' And more unbelievably that felt wonderful.

The carriage slowed as they turned back towards Covent Garden and the driver knocked on the roof. 'Another lap, sir?'

Piers looked to Faith who reluctantly shook her head. 'As tempting as it is to ride up and down the Strand with you for ever, I only went to fetch some water, so my sister has likely already sent out a search party.' Her hands went to her riotous hair. 'Do I look a complete fright?'

He couldn't resist adjusting the flower she had haphazardly pinned in it as the hackney came to a halt at the same place it had collected them, simply for the excuse to touch her again before he had to let her go. 'You look beautiful, Faith.' Only now, he realised that beauty wasn't merely skin-deep. 'As you always do.'

'The consummate diplomat to the bitter end, for that was exactly the right thing to say.' She beamed at him, looking a little vulnerable still but no longer broken, and something odd happened to his heart. 'Thank you for saving me tonight. And for...well...everything else.'

'It was no bother. After all, that is what friends do.'

He held out his hand to help her alight from the carriage, with every intention of doing only that. But something strange came over him as she stepped towards him, staring deeply into his eyes and without thinking he dipped his head, and instead gave in to the overwhelming, uncharacteristically reckless and foolish impulse to taste her lips.

Chapter Fifteen

Mrs Roberta Brookes made a triumphant return to Covent Garden last night, leaving several theatregoers clinking champagne glasses in celebration at the beauty of her performance. However, clearly Lord R. imbibed a little too much, because a little bird told me he tripped on the stairs and fell, with such force, he managed to break his nose...

Whispers from Behind the Fan
March 1814

They had both hastily agreed to blame the heat of the moment.

A perfectly reasonable explanation after their short but emotionally charged carriage ride, when they had both been a little too honest with one another and were likely both still staggered that they had been so.

After Piers had apologised profusely for over-stepping the mark, which he really hadn't done at all as far as she recalled, they had both also reasoned it was also more a friendly kiss than a meaningful one. More platonic than passionate, more relief at unburdening themselves than a declaration of anything more, even though they both knew that was stretching the convenient lie they were desperately telling themselves a bit too far. It might well have been the heat of the moment, even though Faith had grave and lingering doubts believing that unsatisfactory explanation, and it might well have been brief and relatively chaste all things considered, but there had been absolutely nothing platonic about that kiss.

That short but profoundly intimate moment between them had altered things and burned like a furnace.

So intensely Faith was reeling from it still. Close to two whole days since she had willingly stepped into his arms, pressed her mouth against his and lost herself in it, her body still hummed with awareness and scandalously tingled with need. And as much as she might want to deny it, that kiss had also meant something. Although she wasn't anywhere brave enough to admit exactly what it had meant even now, it had felt both profound and somehow inevitable—right even—though that had to be inconceivable.

Surely?

She sighed and smothered her brush in some French green then dipped the tip in some burnt umber to mix on the canvas rather than on her palette, to add some texture and shadow to the ground on this first layer before she added the finer details of the grass and wildflowers on top. It was a technique which wasn't the least bit traditional, but it worked for her. Landscapes were never made of one solid colour in real life, even the smallest lawn contained a wide spectrum of varying shades, so she found this method was the best way to achieve similar results in her paintings.

She used the fat brush to blend the colour in to what was already there, thankful that this first stage of the picture did not require much concentration because she wasn't capable of that this afternoon. Her mind was too cluttered with her changing feelings towards Piers and that kiss.

The truth was, she still didn't know quite what to make of it or how she felt about it beyond curious, flustered and off-kilter, and until she could neatly package it in her mind as something entirely transient and not the least bit momentous, a slip that meant nothing beyond the fact she hadn't been herself, she was supremely grateful that she hadn't had to face him yet.

Her father insisted they never worked Sundays to please her mother, so she had been spared the awkwardness yesterday, and Isobel had lamented he had left for Whitehall so early she hadn't seen him at all so far today either. Now that the last vestiges of the daylight were rapidly disappearing, Faith was hopeful she would have at least another full day's reprieve before they collided, because she still had no earthly idea what to say or how to behave around him.

Hopefully longer.

Because, heaven help her, she had sighed contentedly against his mouth. Pressed her body wantonly against his. Greedily run her fingers through his hair, anchoring him in place so their tongues could better tangle and been left thoroughly and obviously breathless once the kiss was done.

All nowhere near friendly gestures no matter how one dressed them up, and he would know that too.

'Faith—I've been thinking about the light.' Her father's sudden appearance in the ballroom made her jump. 'I still want it coming from the left of the picture to illuminate the family on the path, but I don't want it to be too bright. More a three o'clock in the afternoon sort of sunlight than the midday sort. A tad dappled rather than blazing. I want shadows.'

They had been over this repeatedly and it irritated her that he still did not trust her to carry out his wishes, even though she disagreed with them. He had overruled her idea of capturing the family in the middle of one of their summer picnics oblivious of being painted. He did not like the idea of the children laughing and flying kites, of the ladies lounging on the ground soaking up the sun. That, he had decreed, was too informal for an important family like the Writtles. Instead, he envisioned them posed among nature in their finery, sat facing the viewer on artful tree stumps or fanciful ruins which they could lean against. The nine figures dominating the foreground of the huge canvas with the scenery reduced to a pretty backdrop.

'I do understand, Papa.' Even though she had no excitement for the composition he was meticulously planning. It was too contrived for Faith, who always preferred the real and the candid. She gestured to the sea of green she had already begun layering. 'As you can see, I've purposely kept the left side of the landscape lighter, the base tones brighter where the sun's rays hit it.

We can obviously add more highlights once you paint in the figures.' If he ever decided on the final positions he wanted the family to be so formally and traditionally arranged in, which did not promise to be any time soon. He had made the poor things sit through four variations so far and still wasn't happy.

'I know you understand the ground level composition well enough, Faith, but it's the clouds I need to discuss with you.'

'I thought we had agreed on the clouds.' Faith's talent might not surpass her father's in much, but her clouds were infinitely better and he had frequently said so. 'You agreed to trust my judgement.' Because clouds were fluid and ethereal wisps which formed on the breeze, not rigidly planned structures.

'And I do.' He grabbed one of the big folding ladders they used to support the scaffold and dragged it noisily towards her. 'I shan't interfere with the shape or the position or even the structure of the clouds, but you are going to need to know exactly where I envisage the sunlight to fall to get the shadows in them exactly right.'

'I understand completely where you want it.' He was already killing all her joy for the foreground, if he murdered the background this was going to be the dullest picture she had ever worked on. 'There really is no need for you to labour the point.' But he had that stubborn glint in his eyes as he unfolded the ladder while staring up at the delicate blue hue she had spent most of last week meticulously applying to resemble a perfect summer sky.

'It wouldn't hurt to mark it on the canvas.' He grabbed some charcoal from her box and began to climb the ladder. 'If I don't, I shan't rest tonight. I shall toss and turn...' The ladder shook.

'Papa! At least put the ladders up properly. Let me get the other so we can lay a board between them for stability.' She dropped her palette and brush on her work table and went to fetch the other but he didn't stop climbing.

'This will take but a moment, Faith, so do stop faffing.' Because he hadn't placed the ladder quite close enough, he began to lean precariously towards the canvas. 'Now I see it just here...'

'Oh, for goodness sake!' She abandoned the second ladder to hurry towards him. 'Let me at least steady the bottom or you are going to fall...' Before she could grab it, it wobbled again, then folded in on itself, sending her father, her worktable and the entire contents of her paint box flying.

He hit the floor with an ominous thud and immediately screamed in pain as jars of pigment and bottles of thinners and oil shattered around him.

'Oh, Papa!' She crouched among the carnage as he writhed in agony, the ladder now on top of him and his leg still caught between two rungs. 'Are you all right?' He groaned, in obvious pain. 'Where does it hurt?'

'Everywhere!' He angrily swatted away her hands as she tried to keep him still. 'It hurts blasted everywhere. My leg...my back...' He tried to sit and instantly winced.

Behind her, the ballroom doors suddenly crashed open revealing a startled Isobel and an even more startled Piers. He took one look at the scene and ran towards them, so fast his boots skidded on the polished wooden floor as he came to a halt beside her.

'What the hell happened?'

'He fell from the very top of the ladder before I could get there to steady it.'

Piers nodded, quickly taking control of the situation in a calm, measured way she envied. 'Please try to stay still, Mr Brookes...let me take the weight of the ladder while we figure out how best to proceed.' He turned to her, his eyes flicking tellingly towards her father's leg before silently conveying to her he was concerned about it. 'It might be badly sprained.' Although his pointed stare suggested he feared worse. Now that she looked at it, he was probably right. It was twisted at an odd angle. 'I do not want to risk moving it until we can do so without jarring anything.'

'Faith—can you clear away the worst of this glass?' Several shards of which were dangerously close to her father's head. 'Isobel—fetch my parents. Tell my mother *exactly* what has happened and tell her to round up some hefty footmen. Ask my father to send for Dr Freiberg from Harley Street with all haste. *Not* our usual physician—we need someone who specialises in bones.'

Faith cleaned up as much of the glass as she could until the Countess of Writtle rushed in with a battalion of capable staff who she commanded like Nelson at Trafalgar, and the next frenzied few minutes seemed to happen in a blur around her. She sat cradling her father's head, doing her best to keep him calm and still while Piers organised the footmen to carefully remove the ladder. Then, as they anxiously awaited the doctor, he asked him question after question.

Did you bang your head? Are you dizzy? Is your vision blurred? Can you feel your toes?

* * *

A physician rushed in.

He had a kind face, slate-grey hair and a neat, pointy beard. When he spoke, his reassuring voice was heavily accented. German perhaps? Or Russian? Faith had no clue but whatever it was, bizarrely Piers seemed to know the language because he spoke to the man in a rapid tumble of foreign words as he pointed to her father's leg gravely and explained the entire situation.

By this point her Papa was past caring about anything beyond coping with his pain. His face was ashen, his skin clammy and his eyes closed. He could talk through gritted teeth if he had to, but it seemed like too much effort.

Impotently, she watched the doctor cut away his trouser leg and remove his shoe and stocking, then covered her mouth with her hand so as not to alarm her poor Papa with a gasp when she saw the angry bruising and swelling on his shin. The limb was misshapen, confirming all her worst fears. She did her best to soothe him as he was thoroughly examined, and the doctor's nimble fingers carefully checked him from head to toe. He asked the exact same questions Piers had, except he made her father prove he could move his fingers and toes. Finally, he dripped a few drops of laudanum in his mouth, enough that she could feel the exact moment when the tenseness left her dear Papa's shoulders and his body relaxed.

As his breathing became heavy, the doctor finally addressed her.

'His leg is broken. It feels like a clean break.' The physician smiled at her. 'This is good, *liebling*. I will reset it here while he sleeps. I suspect he has fractured his right wrist too as it took the brunt of his weight when he landed. This is also good because it saved his head. I see no signs of concussion—yet. I will have a better idea once he comes around after I have set his leg. I have given him enough laudanum to keep him comfortable while I do that as it will not be pleasant, but I would rather do it correctly now than give the bones any time to set badly. The rest, I think, is just bruising. Perhaps some strained muscles too. And, no doubt, some severely damaged pride. All will heal, I promise, although the pride is always the trickiest, especially if the patient is as stubborn as I fear your father is.'

'He had a bee in his bonnet and wouldn't wait for me to hold the ladder.' If her father hadn't been unconscious on the floor, she would have given him a piece of her mind. 'I could see it looked precarious but…' She huffed out a frustrated sigh. 'Typically, he wouldn't listen.'

'He is a man, *liebling*, and all men think they are invincible and think they know best. It is our curse and you ladies should pity us for it.'

'Mama is going to have his guts for garters for his stupidity.' Faith looked to Piers, suddenly very conscious that in all the uproar, she had completely forgotten her mother would want to be here. 'Has anyone sent for her?'

'She is on her way.'

As if that was all it took to conjure her, her mother's panicked voice came from the hallway. 'Oh, Augustus! Oh, my dear! Oh, my poor darling! What have you done to yourself?'

Faith brought her frantic mother up to speed, and when she insisted on taking her place cradling his head, she stood close by while the doctor reset his leg, then strapped it between sturdy splints. Once that onerous task was done, and with her now lucid father shouting his disgust, Piers, the Earl and the footmen gently slid him on to the hastily removed linen cupboard door which they used as a makeshift stretcher to carry him upstairs.

Chapter Sixteen

After a full-blown and noisy tantrum just before ten, Dr Freiberg reluctantly agreed a very belligerent but not concussed Augustus Brookes could be transferred to his own bed in Bloomsbury that night.

While Piers thought it too soon and a good deal too late at night for such shenanigans, he also sympathised with the man. Mr Brookes had at least three weeks of bed rest ahead of him, followed by several more weeks and possibly months of convalescence and that would be less tedious in his own surroundings. There was nothing worse than being ill in someone else's home. He had once endured a week in a baking inn in Lisbon after being struck down by a horrendous vomiting illness. In the gaps between being bent doubled in agony he whiled away the time pining for his own sheets and ceiling. While this house wasn't infested with cockroaches and hotter than hell itself, Augustus Brookes would feel less self-conscious and beholden in his own place.

His leaving was likely also a blessing for their entire household, not that he would say that out loud while Faith and her family were sat in his drawing room, because the tempestuous artist had already proved himself to be a very trouble-some and demanding patient and the soprano wasn't much better. Flustered, her theatrical tone was so high-pitched it could shatter glass and she did seem to be one for being flustered as a matter of course, even though everyone else, bar her husband, had calmed down hours ago. Even Faith and both her sisters had apparently had enough of her parents and had taken refuge with his family in the drawing room while their biggest and most well-sprung carriage was read-ied to transport an invalid.

The physician was adamant the only way his patient could be safely moved so soon after he had strapped him up was lying flat on his back. Which meant that much to their precise and per-nickety housekeeper's disgust, the door which had only just been reattached to her precious downstairs linen closet was being pressed back into service and was in the midst of being un-screwed as they spoke.

'I am so sorry about the delay to your tableau, my lady. We were so looking forward to working on it.'

For the second time, Faith was apologising for something which wasn't her fault because his mother had been obviously and visibly disappointed by the delay. She had wanted to show off, and doubtless brag about, her coveted Brookes masterpiece at the ball she always held on the first of May, but with the great artist out of action for heaven knew how long, that wasn't going to happen. The wrist he had fractured was the one attached to his painting hand and the damage to that bothered him more than his broken shin bone.

'It cannot be helped, Faith dear. I shall just have to have another ball in the new year so I can show it off then. I am sure your father will be as right as ninepence long before then. Dr Freiberg was confident his injuries will only set him back a few months.

A few months.

Which of course also meant Piers was unlikely to see Faith again this side of the summer. He hadn't considered that consequence until now and it depressed him immensely. While common sense told him this was likely for the best, because he frankly needed some serious distance to get over his current foolhardy obsession with her since their kiss, another part of him, the masochistic, optimistic, thoroughly besotted, idiotic part of him was devastated by the blow.

He realised, with a start, that he already missed her and she was currently sat opposite him. Still in her shapeless painting smock, her hair curling all over the place where most of it had long escaped its pins, he was fairly certain he had never seen anything quite as lovely in his life. And now that he knew how her mouth tasted, he already recognised she was going to be difficult to forget in the interim. Nigh on impossible probably, because it had been one hell of kiss. A perfect, passionate, earth-shattering, foolhardy kiss which never should have happened.

One he wanted to regret, but couldn't, even though he bitterly regretted the circumstances. After pouring her heart out and confiding her darkest secret to him, when she had tentatively offered the hand of friendship, he'd responded by hauling her into his arms and kissing her like a starving man at a banquet. Making absolutely no secret of his desire to be more than her friend. Although, as much as he had flagellated himself for his mindless, crass stupidity in the hours since, reminding himself that no matter what he desired, vibrant women like her weren't suited to mundane men like him, she had kissed him back. And it had been so splendid, he couldn't think of another kiss he had indulged in which topped it.

Which of course made it all the more awkward. Because despite their mutual polite protestations afterwards that it had been a silly heat-of-the-moment slip which meant nothing, born out of their mutually fragile emotional states at opening up to one another so honestly, the insistent and blatant bulge in his breeches hadn't been nothing and it hadn't been friendly.

Instead, it had loudly proclaimed his ferocious, decidedly unfriend-like lust for her and there was not a cat's chance in hell she hadn't felt it. Especially as Piers had hardly been subtle about it. He had even groaned his appreciation as he had tugged her lush body tight against his needy one. A guttural, carnal moan before he had greedily plundered her mouth some more.

No wonder she was having trouble meeting his eyes tonight. Not that that seemed to make his seek hers less.

'I shall arrange for my father's men to remove the redundant canvas and restore the wall this week so that your lovely ballroom still looks its best. Fortunately, I had only just finished the base layers, so we shan't be throwing away anything important.'

His mother brushed this away. 'There is no need to throw it away, we can store it somewhere until you return.'

'Alas, it is so large, even if stored with the utmost care, my lady, it would probably warp. We shall doubtless have to start it afresh when my father is recovered anyway—but fear not, I have saved the dimensions, and that will certainly help speed things up once he is ready.' Her gaze flicked to Piers briefly, the swirling emotion in them unfathomable. 'Hopefully towards the end of summer.' Was she relieved to be shot of him? Disappointed? Still mortified by their too short but too enlightening foray into passion?

Milton, their unflappable butler, coughed politely at the door. 'The carriages are ready, my lord.'

'Splendid.' Piers stood, grateful for something else to do rather than mull over his own awkward situation, then went to war with his wayward eyeballs, forcing them to face anyone who was not the woman they fervently longed to gaze at. The one he doubtless owed another grovelling apology to if he ever managed to get her alone. 'Then we should get going.'

They had already planned everything meticulously. Once the footmen had carefully loaded the prostrate artist into the biggest carriage with his wife, the ladies would leave in the Brookeses' own conveyance and Dr Freiberg in his. Between them, they would carry the bushel of footmen needed to transport Augustus Brookes at the other end. Piers was going to follow on his horse to oversee things. Not that he really needed to oversee things, but it did not feel right to abandon the family to the aftermath of the accident when it had occurred at his home. Besides, if he hadn't insisted on accompanying them, his father would have, and he wanted a chance to talk to Faith even though he had no earthly clue of what to say, any more than he had any clue of what he really wanted when his head, his heart and his body all now apparently craved entirely different things.

Manoeuvring the patient down a long flight of stairs and into the carriage took significantly longer than any of them could have imagined, and the usually short ride to Bloomsbury took much longer because Dr Freiberg insisted on taking the lead and kept the motley convoy sedate on purpose in case any jarring undid his good work. That meant it was close to midnight when they finally arrived at the Brookeses' town house on Bedford Place, a stone's throw from the British Museum.

Like pall-bearers, Piers and the three footmen carried Augustus Brookes to his bedchamber, then left the ladies to get him comfortably settled. But while the footmen and the press-ganged linen closet door immediately left in the carriage, he lingered downstairs, trying to fool himself he was dawdling in case he was needed.

Feeling like a spare wheel, he accepted their housekeeper's offer of tea and took it all alone in the strange drawing room. A room which resembled nothing like his parents' drawing room at home. Even if he hadn't known anything about the family, he would have guessed they were all artistic simply by the decor. It was an eclectic mix of bright colours and patterns, unusual objects and a plethora of art. The bold choice of the busily patterned fabric used to upholster the enormous but comfortable sofa should have clashed with the plain but equally boldly coloured turquoise chairs—but didn't. Unusually, a very ornate and gilded pianoforte dominated one corner, the curled pages of well-loved sheet music stood on the stand and were piled haphazardly on the stool. One wall was positively smothered in paintings, portraits mostly and obviously from Augustus's talented hand.

While a striking, almost angry seascape hung in pride of place above the mantel, depicting one fragile-looking and solitary frigate being tossed about on foaming black waves while a tempest raged in the vivid orange sky.

He was there, twiddling his thumbs for a good half an hour before he heard Dr Freiberg on the stairs. 'The sleeping draught should keep him peaceful till the morning, then he can have two drops of the laudanum for the pain but no more. I want him lucid when I return in the morning and I examine him again.'

'Thank you, Doctor.' The sound of Faith's voice made his foolish heart sing. 'For everything.'

'It is no trouble, *liebling.*'

Instead of making his presence known, Piers remained out of sight while he listened to them walk towards the front door. Only when he heard it quietly close did he poke his head into the hallway. As if she sensed him, she turned and smiled as she came towards him.

'How is your father?' He whispered this, hoping he would have a few moments with her without an audience before he bade her farewell for lord only knew how long.

She made sure the drawing room door was

shut before she answered, her own voice hushed. 'Comfortable at last, thank goodness, but in the highest of dudgeons. He has my mother running around up there catering to his every whim.'

'And your sisters?'

'Very sensibly escaped the hideous ordeal to go to bed a good ten minutes ago. My father is always unbearable at the best of times when he is unwell, but seeing as this is all his own fault, he is keen to milk my mother's sympathy to distract her from tearing him off a strip for his stubborn stupidity and he has decided the best way to do that is to be a martyr. But as she chose him as her husband and took an oath to love him in sickness as well as in health, I am happy to take the coward's way out and leave them both to it. Does that make me a bad daughter?'

'It sounds eminently sensible to me.' And he couldn't think of another thing to say. Apparently, neither could she because the sudden silence was deafening. 'I feel I should apologise again, Faith, for the other night. I am not sure what came over me...' Lord, this was mortifying. 'But I certainly shouldn't have...'

'I thought we had agreed to blame the heat of the moment and forget about it?'

'Only because you were being too kind to tear me off a strip when I undoubtedly deserved it.

You were in a bit of a state and I...well, I suppose I took advantage.'

'Oh, dear...are you going to be a martyr like my father? Taking advantage would have been offering to rent me a little house here in Bloomsbury, or taking shocking liberties with my person, or dragging me back into the hackney to have your wicked way with me.' Her expression was amused as she folded her arms. 'It was just a kiss, Piers. One that I recall we both played an active part in and certainly nothing to feel guilty about or to lose any sleep over.'

If only she knew how much sleep he'd lost because of her already, and precious little of it due to guilt. 'I just wanted to check you weren't angry with me.'

'Your annoying habit of always leaping to the rescue makes it impossible for me to be angry with you. You have been a brick today. A very tolerant and calm one, all things considered, when both my father and my mother would try the patience of a saint.'

'I am not burdened with an artistic spirit like they are.' It was the most diplomatic answer he could think of which did not inadvertently insult either of her parents. 'This room appears to be a testament to that talent.'

She chuckled, pretending to be offended. 'Is

that your polite way of saying they use sheet music and portraits instead of wallpaper?'

'Perhaps—but oddly it works. I like all the family portraits especially.' He gestured to the cluster of three identically shaped baby pictures. 'They seem to chart every stage in you and your sisters' lives.'

'Hardly a surprise when our father is England's premier portrait painter.'

'He paints premier landscapes too.' Piers pointed to the seascape over the mantel. 'That is perhaps my favourite painting in the room.'

She regarded him oddly, as if questioning his sincerity, then her lovely mouth slowly curved in a smile. 'That's not my father's work, Piers—it's mine. And clearly you know very little about art as it only has pride of place over the fireplace because it was my crude first attempt at oils and my parents have always been encouraging and knew my poor fourteen-year-old's confidence would be devastated if they hadn't hung it somewhere. My compositions are much better now. I promise.'

He scraped his jaw from the floor. 'If you painted that well at fourteen, I can only imagine how brilliantly you must paint now. Because this is wonderful, Faith. Truly wonderful.'

He could see she wanted to believe him but

doubted herself. Her teeth were suddenly worrying her plump bottom lip as if she were nervous, then she took a deep breath. 'Would you like to see some? Only I cannot decide which picture to submit to the Academy for judging and I'd value your opinion.'

She grabbed a lamp and led him down the hallway, then down a short flight of steps to a tiny room next to the deserted kitchen which smelled of paint. 'This is my studio. Papa's is upstairs.' A scruffy, empty easel stood in the centre, splattered in every conceivable colour of the rainbow. He could make out the shadowy forms of various canvases leaning against the walls beneath cluttered shelves filled with jars of pigment powders and bottles of oils. As she lit some more lamps, she smiled shyly. 'I've never shown my paintings to anyone outside the family before—apart from the judges at the Royal Academy that is. But as the judging for their exhibition is a highly secretive affair, conducted behind closed doors and done by faceless men I've likely never met, they don't really count. Please be gentle…but not dishonest. I'd hate for you to humour me as this competition is important. Careers are made on the back of it.'

She went to the stack of canvases and retrieved two, keeping them close to her body so he couldn't get a glimpse. 'Don't look. Better still turn around. I need to display them side by side so you can judge them together.'

Piers did as he was told, and faced the door instead, until his eyes were drawn to a large canvas propped in the corner. Even lying on its side, the vibrant painting drew him in, the colours of the huge expanse of sky so striking he tilted his head at a right angle to study it.

It was obviously London. He could see the shadowy outline of St Paul's towering over the plethora of church spires and rooftops of the city, the first rays of sunrise shooting fragmented highlights on the cathedral's dome and picking out traces of London Bridge stretched over the inky River Thames. But this wasn't a picture celebrating London, it glorified the sunrise. Basked in it. Understood every nuance of the way it crept over the horizon, changing the sky he had taken for granted all his life into a spectrum of colours his mundane eyes could never fully contemplate unless guided by another's brilliance. Red and orange were reflected in the river while green and brown tones were picked out in the water and bounced up on the heavy grey clouds above. Purples and lilacs blanketed the horizon and blended with the greys and midnight blues as they battled to banish the night and herald in the new morning. So beautiful he felt his heart quicken—a staggering reaction to mere paint he would not have thought possible.

'All right…you can turn around now.'

He did, expecting to be similarly dazzled, and wasn't. Both pastoral scenes were lovely, stunning even if one hadn't just witnessed complete perfection, but they paled against the magnificent sunrise. He smiled because she was anxiously awaiting his judgement and he could tell by the fear in her troubled eyes as he stared at them stood on the seat of a battered chesterfield she had placed them on, that entrusting him with this was a momentous thing for her. 'They are both wonderful.'

'But which do you prefer?'

'That is an impossible decision to make—especially when one knows nothing about art and is clueless about what those judges want.' The diplomatic answer annoyed him because he understood his opinion meant a lot. She had never entrusted anyone outside her close family circle with her work, but he did not have the heart to tell her neither picture stood out.

'My father always says that if he were a judge, he would choose only the submissions which spoke to his heart. He believes good art should be a visceral experience. Something about it should conjure emotion and call to your soul...'

'Then that makes this a very simple decision to make.' Because this meant the world to her, he had to be sincere, even if that sincerity hurt her. 'Neither do.' Her shoulders slumped and he felt wretched. 'But this does.' He turned her by the shoulders and pointed to the sunrise. 'That painting is breathtaking, Faith.'

'Oh, I couldn't submit that.' She was too quick to dismiss it. 'It's too...'

'Bold? Unique? Hypnotic? Seductive?' All adjectives which also perfectly summed up her too.

She offered him a half-smile at that assessment, obviously flattered at the compliments despite all her self-doubt. 'I was going to say it was too radical for the Royal Academy.'

'I am sure that the same charge was also levelled at Michelangelo and Raphael, and likely your own father when he started out and dared to paint faces that actually smiled.'

'Perhaps but...'

He touched his finger to her lips, a huge mistake because it made his blood heat and his body want, and then it made him mourn the imminent loss of her more.

'I suspect your indecision is born out of the fact you have no visceral or emotion reaction to those two other paintings either. But you care about this one, Faith. This picture matters to you and that is why you are scared. I can see it in your eyes.' Eyes he was currently drowning in. Eyes he wanted to drown in. Eyes his suddenly wanted to stare at for ever. A new and troubling realisation which rocked him to his core. 'What does your heart say?'

Chapter Seventeen

Faith felt decidedly strange.

Not quite dizzy or anxious, though she was undoubtedly both of those things now that she stood alone on the Strand and was seriously considering marching back inside Somerset House and withdrawing the submission she had bravely handed over mere moments ago. Understandably, there was also a large dollop of fear tossed into the mix combined with some undeniable excitement that she was finally trusting her gut and listening to her heart. Because Piers had been right, the sunrise over London was the most honest representation of her work.

She had poured her whole self into that picture, and assuming she would never dare show it, had been bold and reckless and gloriously untraditional in its execution. It was more of her than either of the two others she had been struggling to choose between. Both those landscapes were, she realised now with perfect clarity, unsatisfactory and insipid compromises as they had both been created specifically to appeal to what she thought the judges wanted to see and not what she loved to paint. Whereas the sunrise was all her, laid bare on the canvas, intensely personal and easily bruised by criticism, so it wasn't really a huge surprise that she was a little overwhelmed.

But beneath all those turbulent, wholly understandable emotions, there was a deep seam of sadness. A despondency which had nothing whatsoever to do with the painting because it had begun long before she had waved Piers away last night. Even as she watched his horse turn out of Bedford Place, she found herself wishing she was brave enough to throw caution and common sense to the wind, call him back and act on the overwhelming impulse to kiss him goodbye as she had wanted. But as the strange intimacy in her studio had lingered, some inexplicable force daring them to acknowledge there was more between them than friendship as they drew out those final moments for longer than any friends ever would, she had sensed they had both shied away from that truth.

Just as they had also quickly shied away from the poignant and loaded moment which had occurred out of the blue, when she had first asked his opinion and he had pressed his finger to her lips, asked her what her heart said and the entire world seemed to shift and tilt on its axis. Because in that moment, her bruised and wary heart answered. It was barely a whisper—a ghost in the distance or a subtle change in the breeze—but she heard what it said loud and clear.

It wanted him.

Instinctively, Faith had panicked at the revelation and stepped away, reminding herself of all the reasons why her stupid heart was wrong. Or perhaps he had been the one to step back first as he too had looked suddenly troubled and all at sea? She couldn't clearly remember, but the mutual hesitation and withdrawal changed the atmosphere around them even though they nonchalantly pretended nothing was amiss as she walked him to the front door, when everything was. Fate had thrown them together, made them question everything they thought they understood, then separated them cruelly with one freak and unnecessary accident much too soon.

In the end, neither of them had really acknowledged that the goodbye was a decisive ending to something intangible which had barely started—if it had started at all. They had hidden their regrets beneath a thin veneer of detached politeness. She had thanked him for all his assistance with her father, he had said that he looked forward to them colliding again some day in Grosvenor Square once her father was healed, and then he left. Leaving Faith alone on her front steps with her thoughts and her regrets and the achingly empty void of things unsaid and desires unfulfilled.

It had all felt wrong.

Unsatisfactory.

Unfinished.

Deflated, she stared aimlessly at the river, then took her time walking the short distance to where the family carriage waited on the corner of Surrey Street.

'Are we headed straight home, miss?' Their driver helped her in.

'Yes.' Then she wavered as a new idea formed. 'Actually, I need to make a brief stop at Grosvenor Square first.' She had intended to send a message detailing when her father's workmen would come and remove the canvas, but if she delivered it herself, then perhaps she could steal a moment with Piers to tell him she had been brave and taken his advice, and then perhaps...

Perhaps...

The carriage lurched forward, and she huffed out a sigh. At least to herself she should admit the truth. There was no perhaps—she simply needed to see him. She would work out exactly why another time and then lecture herself about the need for caution, prudence and patience over the overwhelming desire to dive in head first with all haste.

Milton, the Writtles' butler, was obviously surprised to see her but he smiled in welcome and didn't bother checking to see if the family wanted to receive her. As he took her coat, he reached for a letter on the side table. 'You have actually saved me a job. Her Ladyship asked me to have this sent to you not more than half an hour ago.' Before she opened it, he grinned. 'It's an invitation to tea...*tomorrow*.'

'Oh...would it be better if I come back then?'

'To be frank, Miss Brookes, I think she will enjoy the distraction. It's been one of *those* days and she is in dire need of cheering up.'

Before Faith could ask why, Isobel suddenly flew down the hallway. 'I knew you wouldn't forget our lesson!' Which of course, with everything else going on, Faith had entirely.

'Grandmama said she would remind you about it tomorrow at tea, but as tomorrow is Wednesday and we always have our lessons on Tuesdays and Thursdays, I told her there would be no need and set up my easel in readiness regardless. You are teaching me clouds today, aren't you?'

'Of course! Big, white, fluffy ones.' She allowed the little girl to drag her down the hallway towards the drawing room, grateful that she now had a more believable excuse to be here than the flimsy one she'd arrived with.

'I told you she would come!' As they burst through the door, the Countess smiled and stood, but there was something about her cheerful expression of welcome which did not quite ring true.

'How lovely to see you, dear! And what perfect timing. I only just this minute scratched out an invitation as I have something important to talk to you about.'

Faith waved the unopened missive. 'Then I am all ears.'

'I shall get to that in a minute. First, I wish to enquire about your poor father. How is he today?'

'Considerably more belligerent than he was yesterday, which none of us thought was possible after all the fuss he made here last night, but comfortable now, thankfully. Dr Freiberg is confident he will make a complete recovery.'

'Oh, I am glad! The poor thing took quite a tumble and I have been worried sick about him.'

The Countess gestured for her to sit, and when the impatient Isobel pouted from her chosen spot beside her waiting easel, rolled her eyes. 'Miss Brookes and I are going to have a civilised cup of tea together first, young lady, as we have much to discuss.'

'But we are supposed to be learning clouds today!'

'Which you can still do *after* we have had tea and conducted our discussion.'

'It is me she has come to see after all and I have been waiting all morning for Miss Brookes to arrive.'

'Then another half an hour won't hurt will it, Isobel? In the meantime, practise what she taught you last week quietly or I shall send you back next door to your mother.' Admonishment issued, the Countess turned back to Faith. 'And speaking of mothers, how is yours today?'

It was Faith's turn to roll her eyes, because they both knew her mother had been a nightmare too yesterday alongside her father. 'My mother veers between making a huge fuss of him while he tragically plays the martyr and laps it all up or lamenting his stupidity for climbing an unsecured ladder in the first place while he sulks. It is all very tiresome, but I suspect they both enjoy the drama of it all. But Mama has asked me to pass on her heartfelt thanks for all the trouble you and your family went to yesterday on Papa's behalf.' Which was true in a roundabout sort of way because her mother would have had she known Faith was coming here. 'Dr Freiberg has been a complete godsend. It has been most reassuring for all of us knowing dear Papa is getting the very best care, so we especially thank you for fetching him.'

'I can take no credit for that, my dear, as I had never met the man before yesterday myself. It was Piers's quick thinking to send for a bone specialist and thank goodness he knew one.' The Countess paused while the tea tray was brought in accompanied by a tall Sèvres cake stand piled high with delicious-smelling warm scones. 'Although, to be fair to my son, he does seem to know a lot of *very* useful people. He met the good doctor at a dull dinner hosted by the new Bavarian Ambassador to London a few months ago. Dr Freiberg hails from Munich apparently, or so Piers said, and is much revered in medical circles. He teaches at the London Hospital as well as running a successful practice in Harley Street. Apparently, doctors travel from all over the country to hear his lectures on all bone-related things.' She smiled as she poured the tea.

'He and Dr Freiberg had quite a long, dull chat at that very dull dinner, by all accounts.'

'In German, I presume.' Faith took the proffered cup and saucer and balanced them on her knee. 'I wasn't expecting to hear that yesterday. It was very impressive. I am no judge, but to my untutored ears, Lord Eastwood sounded fluent.'

'Oh, he is, dear.' The Countess smiled, obviously proud. 'To be frank, that always surprises me too whenever I hear it, but Piers has always had an ear for languages and excelled at them at Cambridge. Heaven only knows who he inherited that talent from because it certainly wasn't me or his father. But, as it did yesterday, it sometimes comes in handy. Dr Freiberg's English is reasonable, but Piers's German is better so I think it helped expedite matters.'

'It did.' Undoubtedly. 'I shall be sure to thank your son for all his help before I leave.' And now she had a genuine excuse to interrupt Piers. 'He went above and beyond yesterday, and we all owe him a huge debt of gratitude.'

The older woman's face clouded. 'I am afraid you shall have to save your thanks for another time, Faith, as he is not here. He left for the Continent first thing this morning, on urgent government business, for heaven only knows how long.' She inhaled deeply, then forced a smile as she blinked away the hint of tears which still glistened in her eyes. 'He's probably bobbing across the Channel in a packet as we speak.'

'But there is a war raging on the Continent.' A terrible thought which made Faith feel suddenly sick. 'Please tell me he isn't going anywhere dangerous!' She was struggling to sleep enough thanks to Piers and the complicated and warring emotions he created, she did not need to add constant worry and fear into the churning mix now too.

'France.' The Countess's pained expression made the nausea worse. 'Paris, I think, or at least that is what I believe I overheard the messenger say.'

'Isn't Paris Napoleon's main stronghold?' Filled with enemy soldiers and guns and flying bullets. Which really didn't bear thinking about.

'It is.' The Countess made no attempt to hide her own concerns this time. 'Right in the terrifying thick of things. Though as usual, Piers refused to admit that before he left, even when I asked him outright if he was headed towards a battle! But the wretch plays his cards very close to his chest, as you know, especially when it comes to his government work. Which, of course, does not help me one jot from worrying myself sick every single time he goes away.' She poured her own tea badly, sloshing half into the saucer, before she put the pot down and used the task of vigorously stirring in the sugar to compose herself.

'The only thing I console myself with this time is that he is accompanying the Foreign Secretary, so it cannot be *that* dangerous. The war must be close to an end as Castlereagh wouldn't be headed towards the front otherwise, and he certainly wouldn't be dragging my son again so soon unless the end of the war is finally in sight and there was a treaty with the French in the offing.' A task which sounded dangerous. 'Piers is his right arm in all treaty negotiations and has been since Reichenbach when he convinced the Prussians and the Austrians to change sides.'

This was all staggering news to Faith. If he was negotiating treaties for the government, his work really was of significant importance. Significant *national* importance. 'But I thought he was involved in just getting supplies to our troops?' A nice, safe occupation he could do in an armchair. One she had been so dismissive about when they had first met.

'Is that what he told you?'

'He also mentioned, in passing, he was arranging a state banquet at the palace next month and wasn't particularly happy to be doing it.'

'All true, dear, as he does spread himself too thin and work too hard but...' The Countess rolled her eyes. 'How typical of Piers to gloss over the fact he is also currently the *only* man in the government who speaks *all* of the languages of every nation around the dratted negotiating table.'

'All the languages? You mean he speaks more than just German fluently?' Although that was impressive enough.

Isobel poked her head from behind her easel. 'Uncle Piers also speaks French, as well as Portuguese, Russian and Italian. And he speaks Arabic too, but he doesn't get to use that very much nowadays because he has to spend so much time translating the intercepted enemy documents.'

'I didn't know he translated intercepted documents too!' Even the Countess was surprised by that nugget of information. 'Did he tell you that?'

'Of course not. It's a big government secret.' Isobel rubbed her brush over the cake of ultramarine Faith had taught her to use sparingly when painting a sky. 'But when he is busy, he forgets I am under the desk and he does tend to mutter when he's irritated about something, and the Russians, especially, have been very taxing of late.'

'It is rude to eavesdrop, Isobel! You know that.'

The Countess wagged an admonishing finger while Faith stared at her tea stunned as she tried to digest it all.

'I had absolutely no idea he was involved in such things.'

'Nobody does, dear. Because he never confides a single thing in anyone.' Not strictly true, when he had confided a great deal of intensely personal information to Faith on the night that he saved her and then kissed her breathless. 'Getting anything out of Piers is like drawing blood from a stone and in his case that stone is granite! I only know all that I do because I have become very adept at listening through keyholes.'

'But you just said it was rude to eavesdrop!' Isobel was incensed by this double standard. 'Why are you allowed to do it and I am not?'

'Because I am his mother, dear, and that affords me certain rights which mere nieces do not have.'

'Sometimes I think adults make up the rules as they go along.'

'And when you are an adult, Isobel, you will be afforded the luxury of doing the same but not before.' She turned back to Faith. 'When you have children, dear, never teach them to speak.' Then she smiled. 'But enough of all my woes, Faith. I didn't invite you to take tea with me so I could bemoan my vexing son's frustrating choice of career or make you listen to my arguments with my precocious granddaughter. I invited you here because I really wanted to discuss that huge canvas still hanging in my ballroom.'

The abrupt change of topic momentarily threw her. 'I have already arranged for some men to remove it tomorrow, my lady.' Not that she wanted to think of something so trivial when she had just been bombarded with a staggering amount of new, and potentially devastating information about a man who was already so much more than a friend. A conundrum of a man who was currently bobbing across the Channel in a packet, towards goodness knew what danger and how many stray bullets. 'It was too short notice to have them come and remove it today. But if it is bothering you then, I could dismantle it this afternoon so we can clear the room and get it out of your way.' It would at least give her something practical to do while she worried about Piers, which had now banished all trace of her earlier anxieties about her Royal Academy submission.

'Oh, I don't want it removed, dear!' The Countess seemed amused by the suggestion. 'I want it finished. Preferably before my May ball as was originally agreed.'

'That is impossible, I am afraid.' And slightly

ridiculous that it even needed explaining again, but as the Countess was worried about her son, she smiled kindly as she did. 'Not only is my father completely immobile and likely to be so for the foreseeable future, but Dr Freiberg examined my father's wrist again this morning and in the cold light of day has confirmed that not only is it fractured as he suspected, but he has broken some fingers too. He will not be able to hold a brush properly for at least two months.'

'But you can.'

'Of course *I can*. And while I would be more than happy to continue painting the background if that is what you would like me to do, it is only fair for me to state that it could be months before my father is well enough to attempt to add the figures to the composition, especially if his leg takes longer to heal as Dr Freiberg warned broken legs inevitably always do...'

'I know all that.' A tea plate, now loaded with a fat scone bursting with jam and cream, was thrust unceremoniously into her hands as the Countess grinned. 'But Piers told me you draw a damn good portrait yourself, Faith. He was positively gushing about your painting prowess when he arrived home last night, so much so he brought it up again this morning before he left. In fact, he said he had a *visceral* reaction to your work, which is astounding when one considers he isn't normally prone to such effusive praise and rarely has any obvious reaction to anything—let alone a *visceral* one.'

'He said that?' Another battlement in her defences against him crumbled. 'That was kind of him.'

'And if he says you are as good if not a better artist than your father, then I am inclined to believe it as he is not one for faint praise either. He also said I'd be a fool not to take advantage of it.'

'I am not really sure that I follow...'

'Then I shall come straight to the point and say it plain.' The Countess smiled, slathering another scone with enough cream to fill six. 'It would be such a shame not to have it finished now that it has been started, wouldn't it? I have already waited a year and am far too impatient to wait another six months on top, so I was wondering if you would take on the commission instead, Faith?'

All the air left her lungs in a whoosh. 'Me?'

'I am sure your father will not mind, and if he does then I will happily commission another family portrait for the drawing room once he is better.' The older woman suddenly noticed the state of her scone and frowned as she discarded it. 'Or perhaps, on second thoughts, he should paint just me and my husband to avoid any duplication? Even in a house as big as this.' She flicked her wrist towards the wall as she leaned forward to pick up her cup instead. 'Two enormous family tableaus are probably a tad too much, even for me, and I sincerely doubt I will be able to pin Piers down for two sets of sittings when getting him to sit for this one has been nigh on impossible.' She took a sip of her tea and scrutinised Faith for several moments over the rim of the cup. 'Although something tells me he'll be considerably more agreeable to them now...'

Faith's head was spinning as she tried to take it all in. Excitement at the challenge warred with outrage at the implications. It did not take long for outrage to win.

'While I can mimic my father's style very well as far as the scenery is concerned, I cannot mimic his portraits and, all that aside, you should know I am not the slightest bit comfortable about painting a picture and then passing it off as his.' That was fundamentally wrong and dishonest no matter how she looked at it. 'Nor will I ask my father to condone it or sign it.'

'Good gracious!' The Countess threw her head back and laughed. 'I am not asking you to commit a fraud, Faith, nor am I suggesting *you* paint a forged Augustus Brookes tableau for my ball-room.'

'Then what are you asking me to do?' Because Faith was staggered if she knew.

'I am commissioning *you*, Faith—to paint a uniquely *Faith Brookes* tableau for my ballroom.'

'Me?'

'Yes, dear. You.' The Countess calmly sipped her tea again with amusement as she watched her absorb it all.

'Why would you do that?'

'It was my son's idea, so you have him to thank. Or perhaps murder. As there is no denying I would not blame any reasonable person for doing the latter. He is beyond exasperating.'

'I don't know what to say, my lady.' Or what to think.

About Piers, or Paris or the Writtle family portrait. It was all so surreal and unexpected. All so overwhelming and terrifying.

'Well, I for one hope you say yes.'

'So do I,' said Isobel with an angelic smile. 'Then you can finally teach me how to paint clouds today like you promised.'

Chapter Eighteen

Lady Bulphan has assured us that all fevered speculation concerning the youngest Miss B. from Bloomsbury, and a handsome cavalry officer in her orangery last night, is completely unfounded...

Whispers from Behind the Fan
April 1814

When his carriage finally turned into Grosvenor Square at a little after nine at night, Piers purposely made it stop well shy of the house and entered via the servants' door at the back instead. He needed a few minutes of blissful quiet staring at the familiar walls of his study before he faced the inevitable inquisition from his family. After what felt like months of incessant negotiation and arduous travel instead of the three and a half weeks he had actually been away, he was exhausted, demoralised and utterly done. Even dragging his dilapidated carcase up one flight of stairs and falling face down on his mattress currently felt like too much work.

Milton spotted him, so he asked him not to say anything to his mother for ten minutes while he unloaded the unwieldy documents in his bag into his desk for safekeeping, and quietly trudged down the dim hallway alone intending to do just that after refusing the offer of a brandy. Because the lamps were burning low, he noticed the bright slice of light streaming beneath the ballroom's double doors and slowed, his heart quickening at the mere thought of Faith.

Had she accepted his mother's offer? Had his mother even made it? He had no idea. Just because he had made sure to sing her praises before he left, did not mean his mother had taken heed. Her heart was set on an Augustus Brookes masterpiece and his…well, after three and a half weeks of constant pondering, yearning and arguing with himself about the perils of rushing headlong into things when he knew better, he was prepared to concede that while he did believe Faith was a better artist than her talented father, his recommendation that she replace him on the commission had been entirely selfish.

He had no earthly clue what exactly it was he wanted, he was too jaded to hope, too wary to rush into anything after so short an amount of time and too damaged to listen to just his heart without the rational counsel of his head, but he knew with every fibre of his being that he wasn't ready to say goodbye—even for a few months. He had lost count of how many times since he left for France that he had prayed that they hadn't. He needed her here. Her comforting presence. Needed to be able to talk to her whenever the urge took him, or to look at her, or even just to know she was across the hall rather than across town and completely out of his life.

He paused at the doors and dropped his satchel. The only way he would know for sure if his mother had listened and commissioned Faith was to check. If the canvas was still in place, then perhaps he would see her tomorrow, and if it was gone, he would not and their lacklustre goodbye all those weeks ago on her doorstep in Bloomsbury had been it and their unexpected but lovely interlude was over. It was really that simple, or at least it would be if his head did not caution one thing while his foolish heart cried for another.

The butler reappeared with a balloon of cognac on a small silver tray. 'I figured I'd bring you the drink anyway, my lord. You look as though you need it.' As he came level he bent and picked up Piers's discarded satchel. 'I shall put everything in your study and leave you in peace to gather your thoughts. You will be pleased to know that your mother is in the middle of a spirited game of whist, so I shan't disturb her till she's done. I estimate that gives you at least twenty minutes.'

'Thank you, Milton.'

'And then I shall arrange for a hot bath to be drawn so that you can escape in a timely manner.'

'I see your skills at mind reading are still sharp.'

'Indeed they are, my lord. As sharp as ever.' The wily retainer smiled. 'And because I have a feeling it might interest you, Miss Brookes is also still here tonight, my lord.'

Milton's unexpected words were like a balm to his soul. 'With my mother?' Because all at once he needed to see her, even if that meant forgoing the necessary bit of quiet he needed to centre himself after forty interminable hours of constant travel.

'No, my lord. She's in there.' He gestured to the ballroom with an incline of his head. 'She seems to always be in there nowadays, but tonight apparently, she is working particularly late because she wanted to finish the tree she has been painting. I was about to tell her that her carriage has arrived to take her home—unless you'd care to tell her?' He did not wait for an answer, instead, with a knowing grin he sailed past.

Alone again, his mouth suddenly dry and his breathing already erratic, Piers cracked one of the doors open and felt all the remaining residual tension seep from his body in a relieved rush. Faith was stood on a low scaffold clutching a huge palette in one hand and wielding a brush with brisk precision in the other. Swathed in a shapeless smock beneath which the typically bold hem of a turquoise dress poked out of the bottom, complete with brightly patterned slippers which shouldn't match but did, she was humming softly, her body swaying in time to the unrecognisable tune. Her hairstyle had long collapsed, and strained heavy against the pins which clearly struggled to hold it after so many hours of diligent service, while one endearing stray curl bounced next to her ear. The most beautiful sight for sore eyes and his drank her in.

He could have watched her for ever, but she must have sensed someone was there and turned around, and her lovely face broke into a spontaneous and dazzling grin.

'You're back!'

'I am.' And he probably looked a complete mess. He hadn't shaved in days. Hadn't bathed in more. The dusty coat and crumpled shirt he wore

were the same ones he had donned yesterday before he had stepped on the Royal navy ship in
Calais. As a gentleman, good manners dictated
he probably should have rectified all that before
he saw her, but he did not have the strength. 'I
wasn't expecting to see you here.'

'Why not? It was you who convinced your
mother to give me the commission, wasn't it?'

'I did but...' God, he'd missed her. 'I assumed
you'd have gone home hours ago like any sensible person would.'

'Your mother wants it finished by the May ball
and this is my first commission.' She shrugged,
her violet eyes shimmering with something
which he wanted to believe was more than her
being pleasantly surprised to see him. 'I am a
little obsessed with it, as you can see.'

He forced his gaze to flick to the canvas and
take in the colours and the shapes she had created. 'That is a damn good sky.' Probably not the
correct words to use in front of a lady, but the
best he currently had. And it was a damn good
sky. Faith's unique talent drenched every realistic
and gossamer cloud. 'The tree is splendid too.'

'But not splendid enough, hence it is the vexing source of my current obsession.' The smile
suddenly faltered and another intense emotion
whirled in her eyes. 'I have also been completely

obsessed with the news from the front...you've been busy too apparently. Was Paris as dreadful as it sounded?'

'I don't think I saw the city at its best.'

'But Napoleon has gone... The war is really over?'

'For now.' Piers wanted to believe it would last for ever, but he was a realist. 'Paris and his own government turned on him. He's been deposed as Emperor of France and been exiled to Elba.'

'You don't seem happy by that.'

'He still retains the title of Emperor, has complete sovereignty over that island, an army of four hundred loyalists and an annual income of two million francs. Hardly a punishment for all the havoc he has caused, nor much of an incentive for him to behave. They afforded him too much power so I fear it is only a matter of time before he breaks the latest peace treaty and goes on the rampage again exactly as he has done before. We tried to argue that, but everyone is so battle weary they refused to listen.'

She put down the palette and the brush and nimbly jumped down from the scaffold. 'And *they* are?' She didn't walk towards him, preferring to stand awkwardly several feet away and twiddle with her hands.

'The rest of our motley group of make-do

allies—Austria, Prussia, Bavaria. But Russia mostly. The Tsar wanted it done and dusted as fast as possible, and wanted all the credit, so the treaty was too rushed.' And too damn flimsy whichever way you looked at it. 'In the end, after much to-ing and fro-ing, and a great deal of table bashing and sabre rattling, Castlereagh refused to sign it. So I suppose technically, even though we are no longer at war with France, Britain is still at war with Napoleon even though all the hostilities have ceased.'

'I didn't know that.'

'It will be in tomorrow's papers because I was the lucky messenger who got to bring back the mediocre tidings. But at least that meant I got to come home.'

'And are you and your armchair in one piece?'

'Just about.'

'Were you shot at?'

'Only a couple of times. Thankfully, they all missed.' He tried to sound flippant. Trying to play the ordeal down rather than admit that there had been moments in the midst of that battle, albeit as an observer on the periphery, where he had genuinely been fearful for his life, but she saw right through the bravado and her lovely eyes filled with tears.

'Oh, Piers... I've been so worried about you.'

Then with no warning whatsoever, she launched herself at him, looping her arms tightly around his neck as she cuddled him close. 'I feared you might never come home.'

'You didn't need to worry.' Although Piers was ridiculously delighted that she had cared enough to. He hugged her tightly back, needing the contact, feeling choked at her concern but trying not to allow his silly heart to read more into it than that.

'I've been a complete nervous wreck. That's why I've been painting every hour that God sends. Every time I allowed myself to think, I kept conjuring images of you lying dead somewhere.' She stepped back just enough to run her hands over his face and shoulders as if she needed categoric physical proof he was unharmed. 'You look thinner. And so very tired.'

'Nothing a good meal and a good night's sleep won't sort.' Although he already felt a million times better just because she was here. 'I missed you, Faith.' He didn't mean to say it, but the words tumbled out before he could stop them. 'Probably a great deal more than I should have.' More truth, and perhaps closer to home than he was comfortable admitting, but he felt he had to admit it. Or he was too tired and overwhelmed to hide it.

'I missed you too.' A single tear trickled down her cheek as she lovingly cupped his face. 'So very much.' Her palms smoothed over his shoulders again and down to his chest. 'And I'll kill you if you ever make me worry like that again!' She shook him by the lapels, her body trembling. 'If you as much as think about ever heading towards a battle again, I shall tie you to your bloody armchair and nail it to the floor! Do you hear me?' Then she grabbed those same lapels and pulled him to her mouth.

It was an angry kiss. A relieved and heartfelt kiss, filled with so much emotion it actually hurt, yet it was precisely everything Piers needed in that moment. He just hadn't realised it until his lips found hers. More than sleep, more than sustenance, more than even air, he needed Faith and nothing more. A realisation which would have been terrifying if he hadn't already become so lost in her nothing else mattered.

Vaguely, as his body and heart rejoiced, he was aware of them stumbling back towards the wall which held the canvas. His palms hungrily traced her curves then he filled his greedy hands with her bottom as his tongue tangled with hers, his desire flush against her hips, obvious and gloriously rampant. She moaned into his mouth, her own hands exploring—his back, his chest, his behind—and he lost all sense of time and reason in the carnal fog which engulfed them.

He must have hoisted up the smock at some point, and loosened the laces on her dress, because suddenly her breasts sprang free of the tight bodice which held them. He reverently caressed them, teasing her pebbled nipples with his thumbs as she thrust them into his hands, basking in the way she writhed and mumbled her pleasure at his touch. One of her legs hooked around his and he ran his hands over her thigh, enjoying the silken texture of her skin above the silk top of her stocking. She wriggled her hand between them to boldly stroke the length of him through the straining fabric of his breeches and somehow, his fingers lazily found her core through the damp curls which hid her sex and her eyelids fluttered closed as she opened for him and he stroked her.

So soft.

So wet.

So wanton.

So utterly perfect.

She smiled against his mouth. Whispered his name. Kissed him deeply as her nimble fingers went to the buttons on his falls. Then instantly stiffened at a sound in the hallway.

The unmistakable sound of several pairs of rushing feet.

'Piers! My darling!' They had barely managed to jump apart when the double doors crashed open and his entire family spilled in like lava. Thankfully, the capacious painting smock concealed all evidence of Faith's gloriously sensitive bare breasts and his dusty greatcoat hid his rampant ardour enough, that if his mother noticed anything was amiss, she did not show it as she grabbed him and instantly began to fuss. 'Thank God you are home!'

Chapter Nineteen

'Why are you using a knife and not a brush?' Isobel watched Faith pick up a tiny sliver of the paint she had just mixed on the palette on the tip of the blunt-topped blade.

'Because I am putting the final details on this bark and I want texture. I want the viewer to see a real tree and if they run their fingertips over it, I want them to feel it too.' It was the last bit of detail she wanted to put into the scenery before she started on the figures which were currently only faint outlines on the huge canvas. She knew she was procrastinating as adding texture was something she usually did as a final flourish, but painting faces still felt like the exclusive domain of her father and she was terrified hers wouldn't measure up. It wasn't the only thing frightening her.

Her intense and uncontrollable reaction to Piers last night was really playing on her mind, to such an extent she had been on tenterhooks all day wondering what she might say to him, or him her, when they finally collided. It was already past three and he still wasn't up. According to Isobel, he had apparently slept right through both breakfast and luncheon. Not that that was a surprise when he had clearly been exhausted. Beneath the rough but very attractive beard he had grown, his skin had been pale and there had been deep shadows etched beneath his compelling green eyes.

Yet as appealing as he had been all dusty, windswept and dishevelled, that had not been the reason why she had fallen on him so ravenously and kissed him until she was breathless. She also hadn't done that because of the heat of the moment or from relief that he was home in one piece—although both those factors had undoubtedly played their part, as had pure unadulterated lust. She had wanted his hands on her body and still wanted his hands on her body. She supposed she should be ashamed of that but wasn't because it felt right.

It was none of those things which had stopped her sleeping. It was something more terrifying than that. It was because her reckless, headstrong and often misguided heart was convinced that it had fallen in love with him. Just as it had, with equally petrifying speed, fallen for Rayne. And no matter how many times she told herself Piers was different—that this was different—the unwelcome revelation had sent her wary, jaded head into a blind panic.

Because it was too soon.

Even if she counted the long weeks he had been away, she had known him for a grand total of six and a half weeks, and they had spent less than two hours in all that time alone.

Which meant she couldn't possibly know him, even though her heart screamed that she did, and certainly not enough to throw caution to the wind once more when everything about her blossoming relationship with Piers seemed to echo the devastating one from her past. She couldn't do that again!

Wouldn't do that again.

At least not until she was truly sure she wasn't making another hideous mistake.

She sensed him before Isobel squealed her delight and rushed towards him and turned around in time to see her launch herself at him and watch Piers spin the delighted child around by her arms. Until his eyes lifted to Faith's and he lowered the girl gently to the ground.

'Run along, brat. I need to talk to Miss Brookes.'

'Why can't you talk to her while I'm here?'

'Because it's none of your business. But if you scurry away and wait for me in the drawing room without letting slip to my interfering mother or my dreadful sisters that I am up, then I shall take you and Elspeth to Gunter's as soon as I return.'

'Can I have a violet *and* a rose ice?'

'I will even throw in a chocolate if you leave right this second.'

His besotted niece beamed at him. 'Consider me already gone, Uncle Piers.'

'And close the door on your way out.'

Faith waited until they were alone before she spoke. 'This all feels very serious.' As well as worrying. But there was no point in skirting around the issue. 'I assume you want to talk about last night. Shall we blame the heat of the moment again?'

'Well, there was certainly a lot of heat.' His smile did not quite reach his eyes. 'If we hadn't been interrupted, I'd have had you up against the wall and we would have probably been caught.'

'One of us would have come to our senses long before then.' Although she did not fool herself it would have been her. Not when her body still ached to feel him buried deep inside her.

'No we wouldn't have. I wanted you so badly I had lost all reason and you...' He sighed as he ran an agitated hand through his dark hair. 'I am pretty certain you wouldn't have stopped me either, Faith.'

She felt her cheeks heat at that truth and looked away, using the excuse of dispensing with her palette and knife to cover her embarrassment at her blatant wantonness. 'You are suddenly very cocksure in your abilities at seduction.'

'Am I wrong?' His fingers sought hers and he tugged her to face him, and she saw the same need and turmoil mirrored in his eyes.

'No. I can be stupidly reckless sometimes and forget all inhibitions.'

'And I love that about you.' His gaze was intense, as heated suddenly as it was wary. 'I'd like to think things would always be like that between us…if there was an us.'

Instantly, her foolish heart quickened. 'What are you saying?'

'That I find there is rather a lot I love about you. So much that calls to me and makes me question everything that I thought was chiselled in stone for ever.' He stared down at their intertwined fingers and then gently pulled his away. 'So if you are amenable to it, I have a proposition for you.'

Foolish hope turned to fear and bitter disappointment. 'If it is to rent me a little house in

Bloomsbury, then frankly, you can go to hell, Piers.'

He seemed stunned at the suggestion. 'It isn't. I am not the mistress type. I've never had one and am fairly certain I never will. Besides, I have too much respect and affection for you to insult you that way.'

'You have affection for me?'

'A little.' All the colour seemed to bleach from his face at the admission. 'Am I daring to hope too much that it might be reciprocated?' His Adam's apple bobbed as he swallowed, suggesting he was nervous about her answer. That charming uncertainty proved her undoing and she smiled to put him out of his misery.

'I have some affection for you too.' She held her thumb and index finger an inch apart. 'Just a tiny bit.'

His relief was palpable. 'That's what I thought… I mean hoped. I mean, I'm hardly the most scintillating and exciting prospect and you are…' He waved his hand in her general vicinity. 'Well, you're rather…um…wonderful actually.' He scrunched up his face as if mortified at his own words. 'Can we sit, Faith? Please?' He gestured to the plank she had stretched between two ladders. 'Only I'm having the devil of the job not hauling you into my arms and I'd really rather talk to you reasonably, if undoubtedly very in-articulately, before I risk losing all sense of reason again.'

She sat at one end, and tellingly, he then sat right at the other. 'What is your proposition?'

'These have been an odd few weeks...unexpected and...um...quite eventful. What with your father's accident, and Napoleon and everything.' The stuttering, awkward Piers had returned with a vengeance and she adored it. 'And I think it is fairly safe to say, these feelings have crept up on us both unawares. Well, at least mine have. I am probably assuming quite a lot to expect you to be feeling it with quite the same intensity.'

He stared at her then, so longingly, she could feel the intensity of those feelings all the way down to her bones. 'And if you do miraculously share that, then I also suspect you are as confused and apprehensive of it all as I am. We've both been down this rutted road before and we've both fallen in massive potholes and neither of us ever want to fall in one again. This has all come on so fast. I think perhaps too fast...'

In his own endearing and inarticulate way, he managed to say exactly what she was feeling. 'It has. So fast my head is spinning and that all feels too uncomfortably familiar. I don't want to feel blinded by lust to the detriment of common sense, Piers.'

'Me either. When in truth we hardly know one another, and I cannot afford to make another mistake. Not after the sheer magnitude of the last one. The scars are just too deep to blithely run ahead.'

Faith nodded. Strangely relieved and disappointed by his pragmatic and cautious response to their passion of only hours before.

'But it also feels different from before…to me anyway. Like it could be love…if we give it a chance to be. Or is that just me?'

Her own heart seemed to melt at his words. 'I feel it too.'

'It's petrifying isn't it? I can't quite believe I actually want to try to entrust another with my poor, battered heart again…but I would like to try. Even though trying scares the hell out of me because I am not even sure I am capable of trusting again. But I want to and I hope you do too.'

She nodded again, smiling soppily this time because he was smiling soppily too.

'Therefore, I came here to propose we give it a fighting chance.'

'And how do we do that?'

'The old-fashioned way…with a proper courtship once this painting is finished and our everyday lives return to normal. All this enforced proximity muddies the water too much to trust anything. The lust is all well and good, but we have never even been out for a walk, Faith, let alone discovered if we can tolerate one another's company for longer than a few stolen moments.'

'This painting is going to take me another month before its finished. What do you propose we do in the interim? Ignore one another?' Because that was inconceivable after the last three weeks when she had missed his company so very much.

'We could always work on that friendship we started on a few weeks ago? We could chat, gradually get to know each other properly, perhaps even go for the odd walk during daylight hours in densely populated public places which ensure we have to adhere to the strict rules of propriety.'

'And if the lust rears its ugly head again and we find ourselves plastered against each other in another passionate embrace?'

He answered with a heated stare which was so molten, Faith's mouth dried and her body yearned at the sight. Then he huffed out a frustrated cross between a sigh and a groan and stared at the heavens as if praying for strength. 'Then we struggle through piously as best we can, with gritted teeth until the time is right and we are certain that this thing between us is not just lust—but trust and love too. And then I'll happily take you up against any wall you fancy at the merest click of your seductive fingers, you minx.' Then he stood, looking every inch like a man who was struggling not to carry out that delicious threat right at that precise moment, and stuck out his hand instead for her to shake. 'Do we have an accord?'

She took it and shook it, marvelling at the way such an innocent, platonic gesture from him still had the power to make her suddenly weak-willed body want his so very much. 'We do.'

'Good. Then grab your coat and whichever ridiculous bonnet you've paired with that canary-yellow dress today, and come and take a friendly walk with me to Gunter's. I've already arranged two eagle-eyed chaperons to protect your virtue for the duration—and I'm starving.'

'Can I have a violet *and* a rose ice too?'

He hoisted her up, his eyes dipping hungrily to her lips, before he scowled and tore them away. 'If you step lively, and stop looking so damn tempting, woman, I'll even throw in a chocolate.'

Chapter Twenty

Piers stared at the letter again disbelieving.

There was nothing like the mention of Constança to royally spoil his mood, and things had been going so well of late. Already he could taste the bitter bile in his mouth which he hadn't missed at all. The unique taste of anger laced with shame and still oddly tinged with unfathomable jealousy, that only his former wife could muster. Odd because he wasn't the least bit jealous of the Duke. That pompous fool was welcome to her. It was more a jealousy which he rationally understood stemmed from never feeling quite good enough—another thing which he linked directly to her. He had certainly never felt that way before he met her and, thanks to Faith, hadn't been feeling much either lately. Things had been going too well really, so he might have guessed Constança would do something entirely spiteful simply to ruin it.

Not that she knew about Faith, of course. While they navigated the unfamiliar and unexpected waters of their fledgling relationship, tested the boundaries of their mutual fears and preconceptions, and figured out how to inform both sets of their parents of the increasing possibility of their impending courtship, no one did. They needed neither his mother's meddling and her mother's outright hostility, nor the inevitable scandal they were bound to create, to put more pressure on what was already a huge and momentous step for both of them.

In the wee small hours of the morning his demons still reared their heads to remind him that he and Faith were chalk and cheese in many respects. She was bold, spontaneous and outgoing and he was sensible, cautious and introverted. But during daylight hours when it was just them, she made him feel interesting and attractive and almost confident about himself again—which was staggering really, after he was convinced his marriage had knocked all that out of him.

The letter still clutched in his fingers pulled him reluctantly back to Constança. His tentative week-old blossoming romance aside, he wasn't in any way fooled that his former wife's decision to accompany the Portuguese delegation to London, for the banquet he happened to be organising, was any sort of coincidence. Any more than her new husband's place in the same delegation was a coincidence. She was headed here on purpose, freshly married to her Duke, and doubtless dragging along their infant son too, simply to rub his nose in it.

And the worst part was, if one ignored the uncomfortable fact that there wasn't a damn thing he could do about it, he only had himself to blame. If he hadn't taken her with him when he had been posted to the Royal Court of Dom João, then she never would have met the Duque do Covilhã and she wouldn't be able to still haunt him now.

But then again, he wouldn't be divorced either and free to pursue Faith. And as terrifying as that unforeseen and unfathomable state of affairs still was, it was eminently more pleasurable than being shackled to Constança for all eternity.

'Every cloud...' Especially as he was beginning to think the damage to his bludgeoned heart wasn't as permanent as he had originally feared. As each day passed, it seemed to heal a little bit more and would stubbornly continue to do that despite Constança.

Blasted Constança.

The fresh acid in his stomach churned some

more. 'God help me.' No matter which way he looked at it, her imminent arrival was beyond depressing. His former wife caused upheaval and upset like most people breathed. Mostly to him.

'Is everything all right, Uncle Piers? Only you've been muttering to yourself for at least twenty minutes.' In his misery, he had completely forgotten Isobel was under his desk.

'Just more banquet nonsense.' That blasted dinner was the bane of his life. The irony wasn't lost on him that if he hadn't suggested that in the first place, then this miserable letter wouldn't exist. Yet another regret to go with the other five hundred he already had under his belt which also actively involved her. 'But at least, now that I finally have a complete list of the Portuguese delegation, I can finish the stupid seating plan.'

Or completely rewrite it more like. Piers had originally allocated the twenty guests of Dom João to seats nearest to him purely so he could act as a translator if any of them needed one. Now that he knew one of those seats would hold the bottom which he would have been delighted never to have to see again, it put a decidedly different slant on things.

'Well, that's a good thing isn't it? It will all be done and dusted.'

'As usual, there is now another fly in the ointment.' One that was giving him some serious indigestion. As there was no point hiding from any member of his family, even from one of the youngest, that the woman they loathed above all others was coming to town, he passed the letter to his precocious niece so that she could read it for herself. He waited several moments for her to scan the list of names and heard her sharp intake of breath when she reached it.

'The witch is coming!' She scrabbled out from her camp, her immature face furious on his behalf. 'The evil witch is coming here? How dare she?'

'Well, apparently, she dares.' Of course she dared. It was such a typically Constança thing to do. Even without the need to gloat at him, which probably would have been incentive enough, the chance of attending a state banquet was too good an opportunity for such a determined and shameless social climber to miss.

'Grandmama is going to be furious!' She stamped her foot. 'I am furious!'

And with that, she took off with the damning missive to hunt his mother down.

Wearily, Piers trailed behind her to the drawing room, arriving just in time to hear his mother's bark of outrage as she leapt to her feet. Opposite her was Faith, sat awkwardly behind her easel, the charcoal in her fingers still poised over her sketch and her lovely eyes filled with sympathy.

'This is absolutely outrageous! After everything she has done!' His mother scrunched the letter in her hand as if she were already strangling his former wife and enjoying doing it. 'You must put a stop to it, Piers! Inform the witch that she cannot come. Better still, inform her that if she ever sets one foot on English soil, I shall not be responsible for my actions and a piece of my mind won't be the only thing she will be receiving!'

'Sadly, I cannot stop her from coming because she is part of Dom João's delegation.' And if his calculations were correct, she was also already ensconced on the royal ship sailing somewhere in the vicinity of the Bay of Biscay. His guts griped again and he resisted the urge to rub them. 'His ship is expected to dock at Portsmouth by Saturday and we expect them in London by Monday.' Which gave him seven interminable days to dread it. 'If not sooner.' Perhaps it might be prudent to get the kitchen to boil up some of the foul tea the physician in Porto used to give him to calm his roiling stomach? He hadn't needed the putrid concoction of basil, mint and fennel in two years, but it was better to be safe than sorry.

'But you are in charge of the banquet!'

'Which is in *his* honour, Mother. Dom João invited Constança and so she must have a seat at the table. I genuinely have no say in the matter.'

'But you will also be sat at that table, my darling.' Concern was written all over his mother's face. 'All on your own. I cannot bear the thought!'

He shrugged, resigned but not quite as furious as he had thought he would be by this inconvenient turn of events. 'I was dreading the damn dinner anyway, so I dare say a bit more hideousness hardly matters in the grand scheme of things, and it's just one meal and one miserable evening.' One utterly torturous evening— if he discounted all the preliminary talks which he would doubtless be expected to sit through where he would be constantly facing his illustrious replacement, and the welcoming and leaving receptions. 'I am sure I can deftly avoid her for the rest of their visit.' He would certainly give it a damn good try. Piers now realised his life was much happier when an entire continent sat between them.

'Then I shall accompany you to the banquet! And your father will too! We won't leave you to march into the lion's den alone.'

'That is very thoughtful of you...' Piers emphatically shook his head. 'But I am going to have to say no, Mother. While I appreciate the gesture, and lord only knows I could do with the moral support, I dare not allow you and Constança in the same room. Especially when the purpose of the banquet is to honour our Portuguese allies, not to insult the delegation because you want to give one of their number a piece of your mind.'

'Oh, it's not just one of them I'd give a piece of my mind to! That scoundrel who married her deserves a punch on the nose and the Prince Regent, Dom João, would also receive a few choice words. It's outrageous that he brought her after the huge favour you did him!'

'And you have just proved my point entirely, Mother. We've only just ended one war in Europe—let's not start another one.'

'Then at least take one of your sisters, Piers! You'll need a friendly face in that nest of vipers, as well as someone to protect you from that harpy as I wouldn't put it past her to say or do something spiteful.'

'Take me.' Isobel held up her hand. 'I would make an excellent escort, Uncle Piers, and I'd stick up for you if the horrid witch dared try anything.'

He smiled and stroked her hair. 'I'm sure that

you would too, brat—but sadly, state banquets are adult-only affairs.'

'What about me?' Faith grinned, her lovely eyes alight with the fire of battle on his behalf. 'You've been my knight in shining armour, so I would be delighted to return the favour with some friendly moral support. As you know, I am entirely capable of being both pithy and disdainful if the situation warrants it, so I am more than a match for any harpy and a nest of vipers. I am also famously charming—or so it says in the gossip columns—so I might well be an asset on the night too.'

She would undoubtedly be an asset and a friendly and dear face. The acid in his gut calmed as she smiled. 'It will be a very long and very dull diplomatic dinner...' And Piers wanted to hug her for her offer. There was no way the damn banquet could be completely hideous if he had Faith by his side.

'Are you suggesting I am incapable of diplomacy, Piers, or is this your subtly diplomatic way of saying I am too scandalous a prospect for a state banquet?'

Was that a test? Probably, but she didn't need to worry on that score. Who wouldn't be proud to have her on their arm? He was counting the blasted days until the damn family portrait was done so he could strut around with her by his side. And then, hopefully... He did not want to run before he could walk. And as frustrating as it was taking their relationship one day at a time, every day so far had been utterly perfect.

'I am not suggesting either. I am merely pointing out that your noble act of altruism will come at a cost and you will probably live to regret it. The speeches alone are enough to send anyone into a stupor and I can pretty much guarantee you will have to sit next to someone either very pompous or very boring. Likely both. And then, of course, my escorting you to something so important is bound to make the newspapers after all the furore we caused with that waltz.'

Was she ready to dip a toe in that murky water? Was he? With their individual insecurities still not completely gone, and his former wife currently bobbing on the ocean towards them, did they need to put that added pressure on their relationship so soon?

'Society will put two and two together, Faith, and make four.' Instead of one hundred and sixty-three. Which was another momentous step because this time there would be some truth to the inevitable gossip. Hopefully, a great deal of truth in it. Such a public declaration would mean they would go from almost courting to officially courting. There would be no denying their intentions then.

He could see she understood the stakes perfectly, but being Faith she brushed it off with a saucy shrug. 'I am game if you are.' But her eyes said she wanted to be there for him when he faced Constança and that alone meant the world. 'Especially if it saves your mother from creating a diplomatic disaster. Nobody wants another war—not when you've only just stopped the last one.'

'Then it's settled!' Never one to miss an opportunity to matchmake, and already doing her utmost to thrust them together at the minutest pretence, his mother treated the solution as a fait accompli. 'Faith shall be my emissary and will protect you from Medusa.' She beamed at her for good measure, making no secret of the fact that she saw this as a sign that there was something between them as she suspected. 'And I cannot help but be delighted that the sight of you on Piers's arm will severely put the shameless hussy's nose out of joint. She always was so hideously vain and full of herself; it will do her the power of good not to be the most beautiful woman in the room.'

* * *

'He is escorting me to a state banquet, Mama, not Sodom and Gomorrah!'

Faith couldn't understand her mother's objections, especially since her attitude towards Piers had softened considerably since he had stepped into the breach after her father's accident. Only two days ago, she had conversed amiably with him over tea after he had called upon them to check on her father. At least that had been his believable excuse then. He had admitted the next day, when he had dropped into the ballroom for one of their many daily chats, that he had simply wanted to see her and had to use his initiative because it was a Sunday. Thoroughly charmed, after he had left, her mother had even remarked upon what a lovely and thoughtful gentleman he was and that she was prepared to concede, now that she knew him better, that she had been quite wrong to call him a beast.

'Which is precisely why I take issue with it! At any sort of normal society function, I would happily give him the benefit of the doubt, but this is a *state* banquet, at *St James's Palace* no less. And in the presence of *royalty*. It is bound to be overwhelming!'

'And?'

'And while you are in the grip of awe at being

so close to the monarchy and are dazzled by all the grandeur of the palace, a girl of your humble background might be more susceptible to a seduction in such an unfamiliar environment.'

'Oh, for goodness sake!' She was sorely tempted to tell her overprotective mother that all Piers had to do was not shave or look a bit windswept, and she was already thoroughly seduced. Instead, she lifted her mother's expensive Sèvres teapot from the breakfast table and pointed to it. 'I am not sure my background is that humble, Mama!' Because they all knew the Sèvres was her second-best pot and that she only ever deigned to use her beloved Wedgwood Queen's Ware if they had company she wanted to impress. The Wedgwood had certainly been wheeled out for Piers last Sunday. 'And if Lord Eastwood had seduction on his mind, then he certainly wouldn't have insisted I bring one of my sisters as a chaperon!'

A thoughtful caveat he had insisted upon when he had taken up her offer, and one she was both touched by and furious at in equal measure. It was beyond frustrating that he was determined to be a gentleman when every day she was becoming increasingly more tempted to embrace the wanton side of her. Until the doubts crept in of course and she remembered he wasn't from her world.

'Don't look at me.' Hope did not bother lifting her eyes from her breakfast. 'I have already made plans to visit Grandfather in Whitstable next week. I need some quiet writing time if I am ever to get my book finished. This house has become Piccadilly Circus since Papa's fall.'

'That's just selfish, Hope!' Their mother instantly turned on her. 'How could you do that when your dear Papa is still practically immobile and it is all hands on deck here at the moment?'

'Ooh...let me think?' Hope tapped her chin sarcastically. 'You and Charity are out every evening at the theatre, plus the two afternoons when you also have matinee performances every Tuesday and Saturday, not to mention all the rehearsals you seem to need. While Faith is out from dawn to dusk working on her illustrious commission...which really means it's mostly only my hands on deck—but apparently I am the selfish one because I am daring to still pursue my dreams too? Who knew stealing a few peaceful days in Whitstable was a capital offence!'

Her mother had no answer to that perfectly reasonable summary of their current family situation, so went back to lambasting Faith. 'And doubtless there is going to be more gossip and speculation if you are seen out in public with Lord Eastwood again! Especially after your fool-hardy waltz—gossip which has only just died down.'

Gossip which would flare back up again soon enough regardless of the banquet, if things be-tween her and Piers proceeded in the wholly pleasant manner that they had so far. Because alongside the persistent and heady lust, and their growing friendship, was something which was dangerously bordering on something more than a little affection. It was so all-encompassing, she was eager to start their official courtship, which was a miracle in itself because she had closed off her heart so thoroughly after her devastating experience with the snake.

'If they are not gossiping about that, they will resort to gossiping about someone else around this table like they always do. So what if it's me next week? It was Charity's turn last week.' Although Faith wasn't entirely convinced her youngest sister was as innocent in that persistent rumour concerning her and a dashing cavalry of-ficer at the Bulphan soirée as she had fervently proclaimed. She had definitely witnessed Char-ity sneaking out of the orangery instead of the retiring room where she had claimed to be head-ing a half an hour before, and she had certainly looked very pleased with herself about something.

'Thank you for dragging *that* up again!' Charity glared as she folded her arms. 'And there I was about to offer my services as your chaperon seeing as Hope is off to Whitstable and abandoning us all.' A comment which earned her a scowl from their mother.

'*You* apparently need a constant chaperon, young lady! So it will be a cold day in hell before I allow you to be one! Out of all my daughters, you are the one I wouldn't trust to behave herself as far as I could throw her!'

'Well, that is hardly fair when I have at least offered to step into the breach! Hope is only headed to Whitstable in the first place because she said she'd rather gargle broken glass than sit through a dreary state banquet! Had you heard of her plans prior to five minutes ago?' This earned her a narrowed glance from their middle sister which Charity met with an unrepentant shrug.

'Then *I* shall have to be her chaperon!' Her mother slapped the table, her expression as pious as a nun's. 'I shall cancel both of next Tuesday's sell-out performances, or worse, send out my useless understudy, and disappoint all those loyal and devoted opera fans who have spent their hard-earned money on those tickets and I shall be forced to abandon your poor *broken* father to an entire night all by himself seeing as the rest of the family do not care about his welfare. Because somebody sensible needs to go and protect Faith from ruin!'

At this impassioned comment, from his new wheeled chair at the head of the table, her father finally dropped the morning newspaper he had been hiding behind and reluctantly came to everyone's rescue.

'There is no need for all that, Roberta. You are worrying unnecessarily again and imagining a crisis where there isn't one.' He patted his wife's hand. 'We are now all agreed Lord Eastwood is a decent sort despite his unfortunate scandal, and you forget he does Faith a great honour in inviting her to the banquet. How many years have you despaired of our dear daughters being excluded from Almack's? Of being looked down upon by certain sectors of society who always think they are better than them? Than us?'

He chuckled as if he found it all wonderfully amusing. 'And yet here she is, trumping that fusty prejudice with a trip to the palace! What a splendid coup for this family! I, for one, am thoroughly looking forward to the stories in the newspapers the day after—because for the first time the name Brookes shall appear in the Court

Circular instead of the gossip columns. Won't that be a turn up for the books? And if Faith is mentioned in the gossip columns as well, I sincerely doubt they will be able to make too much mischief when she will have been in the presence of the highest echelons of the government and the Portuguese Royal Court—not to mention Prinny himself—all evening.'

'But what if they make insinuations about her and Lord Eastwood?'

'Would it be so terrible if they did?' The words slipped out before she thought better of them, earning her a strange look from both Hope and Charity. 'I can think of less agreeable gentlemen to be linked with.'

'He might well be more agreeable than I gave him credit for, but he is still a D-I-V-O-R-C-E-E, Faith! That is never going to change.'

'Who foolishly married the wrong woman, Mother, when he was young and impetuous—but then nobly set her free. To the detriment of his good reputation and standing in society and despite all the unfair censure and scandal, so that she could marry her aristocratic Portuguese lover and give birth to *his* heir in wedlock!' Technically, it wasn't her secret to tell, but she couldn't bear the thought of her own family judging him unfairly for something which wasn't his fault. 'Piers is...'

'Oh, for goodness sake! I'll go!' Hope surged to her feet with such force, the china rattled. 'I'll forgo my well-earned peace in Whitstable to be Faith's chaperon next week! I'll protect her precious virtue even though I *would* rather gargle glass than waste an entire evening sat at a dreary banquet! Then the thronging masses who have spent all their hard-earned money to fill every seat in the Covent Garden theatre can still enjoy the *magnificent* Roberta Brookes in *Così fan Tutte*, and seeing as Charity is apparently able to forgo her *important* role in that splendiferous production for the banquet, she can stay at home next Tuesday evening, and we'll all breathe a huge sigh of relief knowing that for at least one night she can't be distracted by any more cavalry officers and our poor *broken* Papa won't be abandoned all alone!' Then she glared at their mother. 'Now will you all please shut up about it?'

'How dare you take that tone with me, young lady!' And all at once, her mother's face was purple again.

Chapter Twenty-One

If my calculations are correct, dear reader, then the Duke of Aveley's Ball is destined to be the first crush of the Season! As his mother has apparently sent out no less than three hundred gilt-edged invitations...
Whispers from Behind the Fan
April 1814

'I believe I owe you a huge and grovelling apology.' Edward Tate's handsome face was contrite as he kissed her gloved hand. It was the first time she had seen him since the Renshaw Ball and her subsequent enlightening first waltz with Piers. 'I caused a horrendous scene, I was unspeakably rude and I behaved like a child. I am heartily ashamed of myself, if that helps grease the wheels of your forgiveness.

'Obviously, if that is not enough, and lord only knows it shouldn't be after I acted so abominably, then I am prepared to do whatever penance you think fit. I shall wear a hair shirt, flail my bare skin with birch twigs, I shall even pen a long and tragic poem about all my failings and my utter remorse for my actions and send it to *The Times* to publish with impunity if that is what it takes.' Then he got down on both knees and stared up at her piteously, not caring that they were in a packed alcove behind the refreshment table and at least thirty people were openly watching.

'I am sorry, Faith. Please be my friend again.' His face was so mischievously pitiful, she couldn't help but laugh.

'Get up, you idiot.'

'Only if you forgive me.'

'I forgive you! Now get up.'

He stood and smiled. 'I hear huge congratulations are also in order. The Writtle commission...that is quite a coup.'

'Thank you. Although it came at the cost of poor Papa's broken leg, so I do not feel that lucky. But it is a wonderful opportunity.' Which all came thanks to Piers. 'And Papa gave his blessing that I took it over, so that eases my guilt a little that my good fortune came at his expense.'

'I visited him earlier, did he tell you?'

She nodded. 'That was very thoughtful of you.'

'He seemed in good spirits.'

'He is happier now that his fingers have healed enough that he can sketch again, and his leg is also mending well, so we are hopeful he will be back on his feet in a month—albeit still with crutches.' She smiled and dropped her voice. 'I hear congratulations are in order to you too.'

He barely nodded back. 'They are—though it's not public knowledge yet and likely won't be until we can work out a way to tell Catherine's father about our engagement. A task I am dreading, as I am sure you can imagine. He's not the most approachable sort.'

'I've always found the Earl of Burstead terrifying.'

'We all do. It well might be Gretna Green at this rate as he had her earmarked for a marquis at the very least, so the prospect of his only daughter settling for a lowly, ever so slightly scandalous jobbing poet isn't likely to go down well. Especially after he banned her from seeing me when he thought we were getting a little too *friendly*.'

'Let me guess…you saw her anyway?'

'I tried to abide by his wishes…we both did for two long years and tried to move on to more acceptable pastures new…' He winced a little, clearly apologising that his pursuit of Faith hadn't been entirely heartfelt. 'Because he threatened to disown her and banish her from the family completely. He is that callous we are in no doubt he will still carry out that threat once the truth is out. But we have both come to the conclusion we would much rather be scandalous, shunned and impoverished but blissfully together than hideously miserable and apart because...' He huffed out a sigh, his handsome face filled with such sadness for a moment until his eyes drifted across the room to Lady Catherine and the sadness was instantly replaced with love. 'When your heart has picked its soulmate, there is absolutely nothing that can be done about it.'

Instinctively, her gaze flicked to Piers, who was typically stood alone in the opposite alcove watching the dancers, doing his very best impression of a man determined to blend into the wallpaper and doubtless counting the minutes until he could escape. She already knew him that well. He wasn't one for crowds, and likely never would be. But when you got him alone...

She found herself smiling. As much as Faith enjoyed parties and balls and crowds and noise, she always had the best time alone with him. There was no point trying to deny any longer that she was in love with him. As each day passed, and they spent more time together, another of her reservations melted away. Not that they had spent much time together this week. Poor Piers had been swamped with banquet preparations, so busy he'd only been able to snatch a few minutes here and there. The fact that he was here only because she was, was lovely, especially when he hated social functions so much.

As if he sensed her watching, he turned and their eyes met across the crowded room, and her heart seemed to skip a beat. Good heavens, he was handsome! But it wasn't just his broad shoulders and smouldering, compelling eyes which warmed her. It was simply him. Inside and out.

It was funny, she had always feared her judgement in men was skewed, but she now knew in her heart that Piers was different. It too had met its soulmate. A momentous revelation she was still trying to pluck up the courage to tell him, and likely would have too if he wasn't still so determined to stick to the strict parameters of their unsatisfyingly platonic friendship for the duration, rather than succumb to the simmering lust which still bubbled no matter how much they tried to ignore it. Not that Faith could ever really ignore it. She had never felt so ripe and wanton and ready to sin in her life.

'How go things with your Viscount?' Edward was grinning and had clearly seen the yearning written all over her face, so there was no point in denying it.

'It is going well...we are going to attempt a proper courtship once the painting is finished. Piers wants to do things traditionally and completely above board.' Although she had pretty much decided that once the courtship commenced, she was going to actively encourage they indulge the lust too. 'Neither of us want to rush into anything.'

'Do his family know?'

'They have their suspicions.'

'And are they disappointed by his choice?'

From anyone else, she would have taken great offence at the question, but Edward came from her world and understood better than most the stark difference between being tolerated by the aristocracy and welcomed into it.

'So far, they are doing everything in their power to actively encourage it.'

Margaret had even tried to force Piers to pencil his name into her dance card this evening for both waltzes and he flatly refused to even agree to an impersonal cotillion. She understood and appreciated why. He wanted to spare her the speculation while they tentatively found their feet. For him, their relationship was intensely personal and private—not in the clandestine way that Rayne had insisted upon—he merely wanted them both to be sure before they made things public. And they both knew that their waltzing together could be dangerous.

Still…dangerous or not, she would have loved to waltz with him again tonight.

And maybe she still would? If she brazenly took his hand and tugged him to the floor, he wouldn't be able to refuse her. Then, if they twirled breathless enough, perhaps she might even convince him to forget his iron reserve long enough for her to tempt him out on to the Aveleys' secluded terrace and throw caution to the wind.

Her pulse quickened at the thought.

'I am happy for you both and delighted that his family approve of you—because I always have. I hope we are allowed to remain friends when I am a social outcast and you are a countess.'

'Of course we will.' The speed of her answer shattered another one of her doubts. 'Piers cares little for rank and I will always be a Brookes at heart and we Brookeses have never been strangers to scandal.'

'I hope you are right. But just in case I am not, how about one last dance for old time's sake? From one scandal to another? While I tell you the entire turbulent and tumultuous tale of my illicit romance with the woman of my dreams.'

Piers had watched them talk, reassuring himself that Faith had absolutely no interest in the frilly Adonis at all, but then the poet led her out on to the dance floor, and something snapped. It was primal, wholly irrational, and no matter how much he tried to tell himself it was just a dance, the sight of her waltzing in another man's arms sent him into a jealous rage. Because the Adonis wasn't just any other man—he was a man who had never made any secret of the fact he wanted her.

And the waltz wasn't just any old dance. It was exclusively their dance.

Or so he had foolishly thought.

But watching them now, his hand around her waist, hers on his shoulder, all much too close for comfort, there was something about the way the pair of them were looking at one another which made the acid in his gut, which he had battled for a week, churn with a vengeance.

Their eyes locked while deep in conversation, which then set the familiar alarm bells ringing. Only this time, instead of just listening to them and accepting them and pragmatically preparing for the aftermath, they clanged like a battle call, invading his brain until the irrational voices at the back of his mind controlled it.

It was then Piers kicked himself for not writing his name next to the first waltz on her dance card as he had desperately wanted to, and to hell with all the gossip and speculation such a possessive move would have caused. In fact, those previously ignored voices made sense. He should have written his name next to both waltzes! All the dances! Carved his name in huge letters across her dance card and guarded her like a sentry to prevent any other man from daring to come near. Then perhaps…

What the blazes was the matter with him?

This violent reaction was neither sensible nor rational. The toxic new voices dangerous and nonsensical. Thanks to the blasted banquet on the morrow, he'd been working too hard again, and that, and the looming prospect of seeing his former wife again had obviously set his nerves on edge. He wasn't normally a jealous person. Jealousy was a futile and base emotion which only ever caused grief! It wasn't logical or pragmatic. It wasn't measured or sensible. When he knew in his heart it wasn't fair to transfer all the negative feelings Constança churned within him on to Faith.

This was just one dance. And if she had been

dancing with any other gentleman than the ridiculously handsome Edward Tate, he would have reacted in a much more pragmatic and sensible way. He'd have watched the dance simply to enjoy watching her, then counted the minutes until he could have her all to himself again. Well away from the crowds which always made him self-conscious.

Feeling better, he glanced at them again and in horror glared as the poet said something to her which touched her heart. Piers recognised it by the way her head tilted and even from his spot in the alcove, yards away from the dance floor, he saw that her lovely violet eyes were filled with something which looked dangerously like regret, before she tenderly cupped his rival's cheek and he realised he was done for.

A wave of acid burned his throat as the poison permeated his brain. *What a blasted fool he was!*

Of course she would ultimately choose her handsome poet over him! Some things were as inevitable as night following day. Even in his rage that made perfect sense. Edward Tate was charming and erudite, interesting, fascinating, talented. A man who stood out from the crowd and revelled in it. Like Faith, he was nauseatingly unique. Flamboyantly so. Whereas Piers was merely Piers.

Predictable. Mundane, staid and unexciting.

The poet kissed her hand and they parted, and his poor heart wept when he watched her watch him leave with a winsome smile. And like the colourful social butterfly she was, she was soon engulfed by the crowd, laughing and chatting and blithely unaware she had just destroyed him.

He considered leaving then, before he punched a wall in his anger, or better still a poet, but the now distant voice of reason screamed over the noise of the blood rushing in his head, urging him to stay and to give her the chance to explain. In despair, he listened. Took himself out on to the terrace to get some air while he tried to get his emotions in check, reminding himself that Faith wasn't Constança.

Oh, God, how he hoped Faith wasn't like Constança! He couldn't go through all that again.

'I knew I would find you hiding somewhere.'

The sound of her voice had him spinning around. She was smiling. Not one of her usual smiles. It was the sultry one. The one he had first seen when he kissed her in the carriage, and when he had filled his greedy hands with her sensitive naked breasts, the one she gifted him whenever the lust between them reared its head…

Only this time it wasn't him that had caused it.

How could it be when he had purposely avoided her all night? Because he hadn't trusted himself not to look at her like a man hopelessly in love looks at his woman, and inadvertently alert the whole damn ballroom to that undeniable fact.

Hopelessly in love?

Good grief!

The terrace spun around him as he absorbed the truth. All too fast. All too terrifying. He felt his lips curl as the rushing blood in his head drowned out all else, hating himself for feeling so out of control. 'How could you?'

He was being pathetic! Of course he was... He was tired. Overworked. Off-kilter. Up in the air. Organising a damn banquet when he couldn't even bear to dance one dance at a ball... Hopelessly in love.

She had the gall to appear confused instead of contrite.

More damn alarm bells!

'How could I do what, Piers?' It was a convincing performance, he had to give her that, much better than any his former wife could have managed. But then the theatre was in her blood. And he was an idiot. An irrational, overwrought and oversensitive idiot. 'What's wrong?'

She touched his arm and he tugged it away. It wasn't logical. It wasn't fair. But it was visceral.

'I saw you! Dancing with Edward Blasted Tate! Flirting with Edward *Blasted* Tate!' Something vile and spiteful had taken over his tongue, making him lash out instead of listen. He barely recognised himself. Loathed himself. But vented the poison anyway.

'Was it the pretty apology?' The sarcastic tone he was using disgusted him but he couldn't seem to stop it. 'I saw him on his knees. Did he write you a poem? Did he confess his undying love? Did he tell you he couldn't live without you?'

'It was a dance, Piers.' She reached for him again and he stared at her hand as if it were a cobra before she let it fall away. 'Just a dance.'

'It wasn't just a dance, Faith. It was a premonition. History repeating itself.' The distant voice of reason begged him to shut up but he couldn't listen. Wouldn't listen because the madness had completely possessed him. 'Thank God it came before I did something stupid!'

He slapped his forehead with his palm, pacing now because he worried that if he didn't move then the surge of raw emotions might explode out of him. It forced the cogs of his mind to restart and the strategist within him emerged, scrabbling, trying to fathom a way to save things. A way to stop himself from destroying everything with his own long-buried insecurities while preventing all the hurt from happening again. He was so tired of hating himself. 'Maybe we can fix this?'

'Are you comparing me to your *wife*?'

'Never dance with anyone again! Not ever, do you hear me?' Even to his own ears it sounded like an unreasonable request.

'I am *not* Constança, Piers!' There were tears in her eyes now. Tears he had put there. Tears which broke his heart. 'How dare you compare me to her!'

'How can I not?' There were probably tears in his eyes too. Because something was clouding his vision and stopping him from finding himself in the smog. 'She was like you. Beautiful. Talented. Ambitious. A siren who blinds hapless men with lust and then discards them when they fail to measure up.'

'Listen to yourself!' She shook him by the lapels. 'You are not being rational.'

He knew that. Felt it. Hated it.

Yet it apparently made no difference.

'I cannot compete with him, Faith. He dazzles while I sit behind a desk in an armchair—just as you say. He's brilliant and talented and exceptional and I...'

'Speak seven languages fluently, Piers. That is no ordinary feat.' She shook him some more.

'You convince countries to sit around tables and talk. End wars. Negotiate treaties. Organise banquets and keep state secrets. Rescue damsels in distress and step up in every crisis. You are a rock and the calm in the chaos. You make little girls adore you and you are so exceptional, so very special that you make jaded, wary, cynical women love you even though falling in love terrifies them...'

'I forbid you to ever see him again.'

A test.

One he prayed with all his heart she would pass.

A single demand she would readily agree to if she did not still harbour feelings for Edward Blasted Tate.

She blinked. Her body as still as a statue and he held his breath.

'You...forbid me?'

The pause felt more significant than any pause ever had before. As if his feet were on a cliff edge and his very survival depended entirely upon her answer. The tight knot of nerves now swollen so large and so painful, it was closing his throat.

'Go to hell, Piers!'

And then, in an outraged rustle of brightly coloured petticoats, she was gone, leaving Piers to tumble into the terrifying abyss alone, suffo-cating on his own irrational stupidity and hating himself more than he ever had before.

Chapter Twenty-Two

It appears that the romance between Miss B. from Bloomsbury and her handsome poet is most definitely back on. If their passionate waltz at the Aveley ball wasn't delicious proof enough, dear reader, I have it on good authority that the besotted gentleman has already visited her father, and we all know what that means...

Whispers from Behind the Fan
April 1814

Faith stared at the magnificent silk gown laid out on her bed and wondered what on earth to do.

Technically, she still had an invitation to St James's Palace, and while she was unfamiliar with royal etiquette, she was fairly certain it wasn't done to fail to turn up to a state banquet. On the other hand, because Piers had left Grosvenor Square long before she had arrived there this morning, the horrible argument between them was unresolved and after the irrational and explosive way he had behaved last night, she was no longer certain he would want her at the banquet. Would the Brookes carriage be turned away at the gate? Would he really have rescinded her invitation? Because he had been that angry, she really didn't know.

Yet as furious with him as she still was, she couldn't leave him to face the banquet or his former wife all alone. Not when he had rescued her from Rayne and not when his mother was relying on her to protect him from the witch.

Unaware of the rift between them, Margaret had insisted on taking tea with her this afternoon and had spent the entire hour telling Faith horror stories about Constança. Painting a picture of Piers as a man who returned from Portugal a shadow of his former self. Withdrawn, wary, all the stuffing knocked out of him, lost and convinced it was all somehow his fault because he wasn't quite enough. And then she had taken Faith's hand, her eyes filled with gratitude, said she couldn't be more delighted that they had fallen in love even if they weren't yet ready to admit it to the world and thanked her for bringing her son back.

Bringing him back.

Three words which felt very significant, and which made her wonder if his uncharacteristic outburst last night had more to do with his past with Constança than his present with Faith.

'Aren't you dressed yet?' Hope wandered in looking beautiful, in an impressive emerald silk concoction which the theatre had rapidly made for the occasion, exactly as they had Faith's, as a favour to their mother. While both gowns were stunning, Hope typically filled hers out better and her sister's enviable curves would doubtless draw every male eye tonight exactly as she always did—much to her own disgust. Hope loathed being appreciated for anything except her clever mind. 'The carriage is waiting outside.'

'I am thinking about it.'

Her sister rested her shapely bottom on the corner of the dressing table and frowned. 'Is this about your tiff with Lord Eastwood last night?'

'How do you know we had a tiff?' Because Faith certainly hadn't mentioned it to a soul. Mentioning it meant confessing there was more going on between her and Piers than the easy friendship which she had claimed.

Her sister grinned. 'We writers are very adept

at surreptitiously watching people. When you reappeared from your tryst on the terrace, you were sporting that brittle, tight smile you always wear when you are angry but determined not to make a scene and when poor Lord Eastwood finally emerged, he looked positively ashen.'

Her heart clenched at the thought. 'Ashen?'

'You had obviously torn him off a strip over something. And if my observational skills are as good as I think they are, I also suspect it had something to do with your waltz with Edward.'

'He was jealous.' Ridiculously so. Worryingly so. 'Heaven only knows why.'

'The poor thing adores you. He thinks the sun rises and sets with you... And I think you return the sentiment.'

Faith aimed for nonchalant back, not in any fit state to have this conversation when her mind was still reeling, the clock ticking and she still had no earthly idea what to do. 'He's rather likeable once you get to know him.'

'I think you are currently suffering from more than a mild dose of *like*.' At Faith's instant defensive expression, she smiled kindly. 'You forget that I know you, sister. And I have eyes. I have seen the way you look whenever you mention him, and I hear the admiration in your voice each time too. Not to mention the mooning you do in the evenings sometimes on the odd occasion you grace our drawing room with your presence nowadays. And, of course, you accidentally called him Piers instead of Lord Eastwood when you leapt to his defence last week...' The smile turned into a knowing grin. 'Or the fact that I saw you kiss him on the steps of the theatre on Mother's opening night when you said you felt unwell...'

'You did?'

'You had been gone for ages and I was worried about you.' The smile melted into concern. 'Especially after I saw that lying scoundrel Rayne leer at you across the theatre. I loathe that libertine.'

In that moment, Faith realised her dirty secret perhaps wasn't quite as secret as she had presumed. 'I suppose you know about him too.'

'Of course I do. So does Charity by the way. And she also knows about Piers.' At Faith's shocked expression she sighed. 'We're sisters— and sisters can always be relied upon to go out of their way to thoroughly know each other's business. Just as we both know that Charity *did* have a tryst in the Bulphans' orangery with that cavalry officer last week, we both knew the pair of you had a little romance when he was Papa's pupil. It did not take a genius to work out it had ended badly. His marriage was a fairly decisive end and neither of us will ever forgive the leech for breaking your heart.'

Stunned, Faith slumped on her stool. 'Do Mama and Papa know too?'

'Do you think Lord Rayne would still be alive if they did?' Her sister shook her vivid copper head. 'Our parents would have had him hanged, drawn and quartered. We both covered for you before they got suspicious—because that is also what sisters do. And we both agonised over consoling you after it ended. The only reason we didn't was because you seemed so determined to pretend nothing had happened, we didn't want to ruin that brave façade.'

Then she reached out and squeezed her hand. 'I am so sorry about that now because I did not realise until a couple of years later that your little romance involved considerably more than a few stolen kisses. Had I known the full extent of his treachery, I would have hanged, drawn and quartered him myself, and I would have enjoyed it.'

'How did you discover we were lovers?'

'The leech himself told me when I spurned his advances two summers ago.' Her sister's face hardened as Faith blinked in shock. 'He responded with his trademark callousness, and said my refusal hardly mattered in the grand scheme of things, as he supposed that seeing he had already sampled all the delights of one Brookes daughter, the other two would be much the same... I never shared *that* part of the tale with Charity. Some things are too private—even for sisters.'

'Thank you.' Although she felt queasy knowing just one knew. 'I was a fool.'

'You were nineteen and he took advantage of you.' Exactly what Piers had said, and thanks to that, only recently had Faith begun to forgive herself for that foolishness. 'And you will be pleased to know that I was so furious at him, and so disgusted by his vileness that I told him so. Then I hit him so hard with my fan that I blackened his eye... Although I wish I had broken his nose like Lord Eastwood did. That would have felt marvellous.'

'Did you witness that too?' Faith obviously had no secrets left at all.

'Not first-hand—but it didn't take much to piece it all together because he staggered into the foyer with his nose dripping blood everywhere at the same moment as I did when I came to check on you. Moments later, I watched you disappear into that hackney, so obviously being a good, diligent sister, I waited until it returned...'

'Oh...' Her sister knew about Rayne and Piers and had kept it all to herself. 'But why are you telling me all this now?' She sat heavily on the mattress. 'You might have picked a better moment. Or is this a timely reminder of what an idiot I have been in case I am stupid enough to fall for a man like that again.'

Hope sighed. 'I am telling you now because I wanted you to know that I fully intend to be a very neglectful chaperon tonight if that is what you would like me to be. Because I've never seen you look at a gentleman like you do Lord Eastwood and because he obviously makes you happy. Even Charity has noticed that, and she's so wrapped up in herself at the moment she barely notices anything.' She leaned forward and took both her hands. 'And because I would hate for you to use one unfortunate mistake in the past as a barrier if you have found a worthy man who will treat you with all the love and respect you deserve to be treated with. If Piers is the one, then take the chance.'

Suddenly, Faith needed her sensible sister's opinion more than anything. 'After our argument last night, I am not sure he is the one. I think...' Her voice trembled. 'I think it might all be over between us?'

'Because of one argument?'

'It was a very bad argument.'

'Mama and Papa have had some stinkers over the years, and they have always made up and emerged stronger from them.'

'He compared me to his wife... Not directly but by implication. He suggested, that because I danced with Edward, then I would inevitably have affairs exactly like she did. It was horrible. He was horrible.'

'As horrible as Rayne?'

'Of course not! Piers is nothing like Rayne.'

Hope smiled. 'And how long did it take you to work that out?'

'A little while...'

'But you initially suspected he was exactly like him, didn't you?'

Faith threw up her hands. 'What difference does that make?'

'That if you still carry all that doubt after five years, then it isn't inconceivable that it might take Piers a while to be able to let go of his.'

'That is what worries me. He was so angry, but so passionate about it, it has made me wonder if he isn't over her at all. He loved her once... maybe a part of him still does?'

'Do you still have affection for Rayne?' A ridiculous question and she let her face show it.

'How could I after what he did, Hope? I hate him.'

'Yet he still held the power to upset you at the theatre.'

'And your point is?'

'That those old wounds linger long after the love has died. From what you've told me, that woman put Piers through hell. Arguments, dalliances…she made him a cuckold, then publicly discarded him in favour of another man. His scandalous divorce was less than a year ago— it's still raw and he suffered tremendously as a result. He was unfairly maligned and is still ostracised for it—and now the woman is here, and he has to face her again…' Hope shrugged, palms spread.

'Are you saying I should forgive him for being so beastly to me simply because she was beastly to him?'

Her insightful sister shook her head slowly. 'No, Faith—I am asking if you think Lord Beastly is worth the effort of forgiving? Because surely that is the crux of all this.'

Piers stood in the receiving line, listening to the names being called, feeling utterly wretched.

All the familiar emotions of self-loathing which only Constança elicited paled into insignificance against the sheer grief of losing Faith. Worst of all, it was all his fault. She had simply danced with a man and he had reacted like a lunatic from Bedlam, making outrageous accusations and unreasonable demands, so terrible he had no clue how to apologise for them. Or even if she would allow him the chance to apologise.

'His Excellency Herr Christoph von Lieven, the Russian Ambassador...'

He had wanted to last night, but by the time he was rational enough, the ball was long over and he had taken himself too many miles away. Then he had intended to head to Bloomsbury the moment the sun came up and beg for her forgiveness, but was called to Whitehall almost as soon as he got home to translate an urgent communiqué and then he was called here, to St James's Palace, to deal with last-minute arrangements and the day had run away with him as everyone stole his time.

If his valet hadn't had the wherewithal to send his dress clothes for this evening to his temporary office here several days ago, he would be stood here now in the same crumpled suit he had worn last night, still on tenterhooks wondering if she would come so he could fall on his sword and beg for her mercy and know that he still had a chance, but was wholly prepared that she wouldn't. Even though he now realised she had told him that she loved him, but at the time he had been too overwrought and overwhelmed and controlled by the poison to hear.

Why would she when he had basically accused her of being as loose with her sexual favours as Constança?

'His Excellency Louis, Duc de la Châtre, Ambassador of France…'

And all because of one dance, and not the first one he had happily watched her dance at that damn ball from afar. Neither the cotillion nor any of the country dances had turned him into an incensed and irrational idiot. In fact, he had enjoyed watching them all. The way she moved, the animated way she spoke, her smile…

Just the waltz.

With the handsomest man in the damn ballroom, one Piers already knew she had no romantic feelings for, but threat enough that he had lost all reason. The most frustrating thing was that he knew if he hadn't been so unsettled by the return of blasted Constança, he never would have reacted so badly. Why the blazes did he keep allowing that blasted woman to get to him? It had been two years! A lot had happened in those two years. The change to his life just in the last six months alone had been exponential.

He wasn't the same man who had returned to England humiliated, angry, broken and embittered. In the two months since Faith had come into his life, a great deal of that bitterness seemed to have gone and the anger appeared to have subsided and he did not feel anywhere near as broken any more. Cautious, yes—but even that was fading beneath the rosy glow of optimism that had suddenly appeared out of nowhere. Like grief, the raw pain which had been his marriage was now more a dull ache, so his reaction last night was ridiculous. He was long over Constança. Or at least he hoped he was. And he loved Faith.

'His Excellency Dom Domingos António de Sousa Coutinho, Conde do Funchal, the Portuguese Ambassador...'

He stiffened at the announcement of the Portuguese delegation, his stomach instantly churning as he braced himself for the reunion he was dreading. Then felt a hand slip through his elbow.

'Relax your shoulders and smile, Piers.' Faith's fingers stroked his rigid bicep which instantly deflated at her command. 'Do not give her the satisfaction of seeing you rattled.'

'You came!' Emotion choked him. Relief

mixed with hope all wrapped in love. 'I didn't think you would after the awful way I behaved last night.'

'Oh, I am still fuming about last night, be in no doubt about that, and we will be having words about it later, Piers, and you *will* explain yourself for behaving so out of character.' She slanted him an irritated glance then softened it with a half-smile. 'But I couldn't leave you to face the witch all alone and I made a promise to your mother and to Isobel to protect you, and we Brookeses always keep our promises—even when fuming.'

'Thank you.' He was so relieved to see her, he could barely speak. 'You look beautiful.'

An understatement.

He had never seen anything so breathtaking in his entire life. The plain but bold coral bodice caressed her curves like a second skin, the demure scooped neckline showing only enough cleavage to make his collar feel tight, while the skirt skimmed her hips in a waterfall of liquid silk overlaid with an ethereal, gossamer fabric threaded with filigree strands of gold. A simple, single collar of identical diamonds drew attention to her graceful neck, the matching droplet earrings sparkling in the pale moonlight. But as always, it was her hair which drew his eyes. The wayward copper-gold curls were pinned loosely to her head, the only adornment a single hot-house rose the exact same vibrant shade as her gown. All so typically Faith. However, it was her sheer beauty on the inside which left him entirely undone. It was that which he couldn't bear to ever lose. And he wouldn't. Whatever it took, he had to make it right.

She beamed at his compliment, and that gave him more hope. 'Well... I didn't want to show you up on your big night. Especially as my presence here is bound to cause a veritable frenzy of gossip for us tomorrow. If one is destined to be a spectacle anyway, one should always stand out, don't you think? Hope and I both came fully prepared to dazzle.' She gestured behind with a tilt of her head and he saw her sister. But while the redhead did indeed look lovely, and seemed to draw every male eye in the room, to his she was no match for the woman on his arm. 'It was her who convinced me to come, in case you were wondering. She seems to think you deserve a second chance.'

'Do you?'

She poked her lovely nose in the air. 'I suppose that depends on how pretty your apology is later.' She had already forgiven him. He could see it in her eyes. Feel it in her touch. Loved her all the more for her benevolence. She didn't play games and never would.

'It'll be prettier than your poet's was, I promise.'

'It had better be.' But she cuddled closer against his elbow, a wall of strength and comfort in his hour of need.

'Their Graces Dom Alfonso Perreira do Sousa, the Duque do Covilhã of Portugal, and his wife Dona Constança Perreira do Sousa, the Duquesa do Covilhã of Portugal...'

'And Piers, even though I am still rightly furious at you...' Faith's whispered tone so deliciously close to his ear was teasing, pulling him away from the line-up. 'Do feel free to look longingly at me as soon as the witch enters, so that I can stare longingly back and let her know in no uncertain terms that I consider her loss, my gain. Not that that will be much of a problem because you look exceptionally handsome tonight. A little too handsome, truth be told as it's giving me some decidedly scandalous ideas...' Those reassuring, saucy, gloriously flippant words from the woman of his dreams couldn't have come at a better time.

Because the woman of his nightmares was headed straight for them, positively dripping in jewels and dragging her Duke—and to Piers's and his stomach's utter delight, he didn't feel a damn thing.

Not for Constança at least.

His feelings for the clever, kind, loyal and thoroughly wonderful seductress on his arm was a different matter entirely.

Chapter Twenty-Three

They say there is no smoke without fire, gentle reader, which obviously begs the question... Why did the infamous Lord E. have the newly betrothed Miss B. from Bloomsbury on his arm at the palace last night? And what happened to her poet? After two breathless waltzes in recent weeks, with two entirely different gentlemen, we await further clarification of this intriguing conundrum with bated breath...

Whispers from Behind the Fan
April 1814

'*Olá, Piers...querida...já faz muito tempo.*'

For Faith's benefit, Piers made a point of answering in English. 'Yes, Constança, it has been a long time. You look well.'

As much as it galled her to think it, his former wife did look well. In fact, to her complete disgust, she was a staggeringly beautiful woman. She was petite, almost a full foot shorter than Faith, with big dark eyes, jet-black hair and overt womanly curves which, frankly, put hers to shame. And she had the sort of effortlessly breathy voice and undulating way of moving which turned every male head in the room.

Her husband was every inch a duke in his bearing, glancing around the room as if every aspect of it and the people within it displeased him. His appearance did not quite measure up to his superior manner though. He was short and poorly proportioned. A pair of skinny legs in shiny satin breeches held up a significant paunch while the padding in his ostentatious peacock coat did little to conceal his stooping shoulders, any more than the fussy lace spilling from his sleeves disguised his dainty, effeminate hands. He was such an underwhelming specimen, it left her wondering what hot-blooded woman in their right mind would ever consider swapping Piers for this?

'Marriage and motherhood suits me.' As she purred, she hung on her haughty husband's arm and openly looked Faith up and down, and despite the vast difference in their heights, still managed to do that while looking down her nose. 'Is this your wife?'

'Not yet...' She had no idea what made her say

it, other than she wanted to put her stubby, smug rival firmly in her place. 'But I will be.' Beneath her palms she felt Piers's muscles twitch at her lie, but to his credit, his face did not give his shock at her unexpected outburst away.

'Your...' The Duquesa clicked her fingers and turned to Piers. 'How do you English say *noiva*, Piers?'

'Fiancée.' Piers turned to her and simply quirked one dark eyebrow, his mossy eyes amused, clearly waiting for her answer.

'I am his *particular* friend.'

'Yes...' Now he looked as if he wanted to laugh. 'Indeed she is. But where are my manners. You must allow me to introduce you. Constança, this is Miss Faith Brookes. Faith, this is Dom Alfonso, the Duque do Covilhã and his wife, Dona Constança, the Duquesa.'

'It is a pleasure to meet you both, your Graces.' Faith slowly dipped into a polite, if begrudging, curtsy while the other two barely inclined their heads in acknowledgement. Clearly already bored, the Duke immediately wandered off to greet the rest of the line, leaving the three of them alone.

'That is a pretty *flower* you have in your hair, Miss Brookes.' The witch flapped her hand towards it smiling as if butter wouldn't melt in her mouth, then made a show of patting her own artful coiffure, in case Faith hadn't noticed the enormous tiara dripping with rubies balanced upon it. More rubies shimmered in the chandeliers stretching her ear lobes and a big fat one nestled between the plump, generous breasts straining against the neckline of her heavy crimson beaded gown.

'Thank you, your Grace.' She smiled innocently, reminding herself this was a diplomatic dinner before the wasp inside her ran free. 'As Piers will tell you, I have always loved roses. They are the most beautiful flower, don't you think? I've always much preferred their natural simplicity over fussy, artificial embellishments.'

The other woman blinked rapidly, clearly unsure whether it had been simply a bland comment about a flower or an outright insult over all the flamboyance weighing down her neck, and while she was perfectly content to let her flounder, Piers diplomatically changed the subject.

'How long are you staying in London?'

'A week. We sail next Monday. It is nice to be back. It reminds me of *our* honeymoon.' Then she reached over to brush his arm, a little too proprietorially for Faith's liking. 'It would be good to catch up before I go.' Then she proffered the same hand like a gift, obviously waiting for it to be kissed. As Piers bent to do so, she flicked Faith a dismissive glance, letting her know in no uncertain terms that she considered her no rival. 'I shall have the arrangements made tomorrow for a private meeting. It has been too long since we have spent any time alone...*querida*.' She allowed her eyes to linger on his for several moments before they turned to her and instantly hardened like jet. 'It was nice to meet you Miss... er...' Then the witch clicked her fingers again, pretending she had clean forgotten. 'Brookes.'

Then she undulated away like a queen.

'She hasn't changed a bit.' Piers smiled, looking a bit bemused by the odd exchange. 'That's exactly the Constança I know and loathe.'

'What does *querida* mean?'

'Darling.'

'Ahh...interesting.' And completely galling. 'I assumed it would be something like that by the way she batted her lashes at you.'

'You aren't...jealous, are you? Because Constança bats her lashes at every man and tosses around such endearments like confetti...'

'Of course not.' Even though it corded around her throat and turned her vocal cords waspish.

'Are you sure?' His eyes were dancing with

amusement. 'Only you sound a little peeved.' And he looked ridiculously pleased that was the case.

'Of course I sound peeved, Piers. I am still furious with you for yesterday!' Thankfully, before he called her out on the lie, the trumpets blazed.

'His Royal Highness Dom João, Prince Regent of Portugal...'

As Piers had warned, the banquet was a painfully long affair. At least it felt that way to her as she was still too preoccupied with all thoughts of Piers, the events of last night and her feelings towards him to properly enjoy all the pomp, luxury and spectacle. Hope was right, before she bared her heart and confessed her love she needed to know for sure he was over Constança and his outburst yesterday had been triggered by his own insecurities. And if that were indeed the case, which she hoped it was even though the sight of his beautiful former wife had challenged Faith's own insecurities, she needed to hear that Piers recognised it. As much as she loved him, she wasn't prepared to enter into a marriage with a man who could never trust her. If he forbade her from dancing with a man, then what would be next? Would he stop her talking to them? Painting them? She had always enjoyed her independence, and had no intention of giving up her artistic ambitions—even for marriage.

After the meal, the tedious speeches seemed to go on for hours, not helped by the fact that many were effectively repeated twice. Once in the native language of the speaker, and then again translated into English, or Portuguese or German or Russian or French. Piers seemed to be called upon to do most of that, and did so with such confident and commanding dignity that she felt immensely proud of him. After an eternity, the guests were left to mingle, and while she and Hope met some very interesting and some very illustrious people, including the Regent himself, she only managed to collide with Piers briefly because his superiors kept him busy. Each time he tried to talk to her, someone stole him away.

Eventually, somewhere around two in the morning, the crowd began to thin. Certainly enough that she could see him across the room. As their gazes locked and he once again started towards her, Hope yawned.

'I'm going home.' Before Faith could argue that she hadn't yet had the chance to clear the air with Piers, her sister surprised her. 'Here's the key to the back door.' She rummaged in her tiny silk evening bag and slipped it into her hand.

'Make sure you are back by six at the latest or you know there will be hell to pay.'

'You cannot go home without me! Mama is bound to be waiting up and she'll have a fit if she realises I am unchaperoned.'

'Mama has two performances on a Tuesday and that always makes her tired, and in case she wasn't, Charity has strict instructions to make sure her traditional night-time toddy is a stiff one. On the off-chance that failed, she was going to send an urgent message here.' She smiled. 'Instead, she sent me this an hour ago.' She retrieved a small folded note from the reticule and waited while Faith read it.

Our mother is snoring next to our father and I should like it noted that you both now owe me.

'Will you send the carriage back for me?'

'I figured Lord Beastly would see you home. Once you've sorted everything out, of course.' Hope grinned. 'He hasn't taken his eyes off you all night by the way.' Then she kissed her cheek. 'Nor has he once glanced at his hideous former wife. I've been surreptitiously watching him like a hawk…just in case we were both wrong and he isn't worthy. Goodnight, Faith. And be in no doubt, you owe me too.'

He reached her as Hope disappeared out of the door. 'Where is your sister going?'

'Home. Without me. She wanted us to be able to talk.'

'That was decent of her.' He looked nervous. Awkward. 'We do need to talk. I was an idiot and I am so sorry about...'

'Lord Eastwood...' The Master of the Household scurried towards him. 'Might I have a word...'

Piers shook his head and grabbed her hand. 'Not yet, Sir Hulse... I am a bit busy. I'll come and find you in a minute.' Then he tugged her to follow him. 'I swear I haven't had one single moment's peace all day!'

They were headed towards the courtyard, when someone else spotted him and gestured that they also needed a word, and he groaned and changed direction, taking her towards a large winding staircase which they practically sprinted up, and then down a long hallway to a big white door. Impatiently, he unlocked it, then once they were inside, put the key back in the lock and clicked it shut.

The dimly lit room was dominated by a long, narrow dark oak table which filled its centre, strewn with papers and flanked with ten very sturdy chairs. The only other furniture were two huge wingback armchairs and a small occasional table sat in front of an ornate fireplace, above

364 The Viscount's Unconventional Lady

which was an old oil painting of somebody regal looking in the sort of long, curly wig favoured by King Charles II.

'At least while the door is locked, I can pretend I am not here. Unless you shout too loud of course. I dare say I deserve it.' He rocked on his heels, looking thoroughly wretched, apparently suddenly having no clue what to do with his hands. 'The way I treated you was indefensible. I have no idea what came over me.'

'Yes you do.' She sat in one of the wingbacks and sighed. 'And if I am going to forgive you properly, I should like to understand it. Even if I might not like what you have to say.'

Chapter Twenty-Four

The plot thickens...as I have it on the highest possible authority that the Duquesa do Covilhã was once none other than the Viscountess Eastwood too! And with the sour looks being exchanged between her and a certain Miss B. from Bloomsbury, who is likely, I am told, the next to hold that tarnished title, this reporter eagerly anticipates the exciting prospect of reticules at dawn...

Whispers from Behind the Fan
April 1814

Where to start? How to explain his irrational behaviour? Baffled, Piers sat in the chair opposite and tried to make some sense of it all. Without thinking, his hand went instinctively to his stomach, waiting for the inevitable biliousness and bile, and when that didn't come, he sighed.

'Would you believe me if I said that it was down partly to indigestion?'

She snorted her disbelief. 'I certainly wasn't expecting that...but I am intrigued to hear how?'

'I panicked, Faith—though you have to know not intentionally.'

'I don't think anyone ever panics intentionally, Piers.'

'True, but...' He huffed his frustration and reached for her hand. 'But I am a born diplomat. I use reason and logic. You said it yourself last night, I am instinctively the calm in the chaos. I've always been reserved. I don't like scenes or arguments or enjoy any of the negative emotions which go along with them...so I suppose the most natural way for me to deal with the glut of all that within my marriage was to suppress it all.'

'And that gave you indigestion?'

He laughed at the stupidity of it all. 'It was anger. Self-loathing. I felt trapped and foolish and ashamed by it all. I suppose it is also in my nature to endure, because that is what we do here isn't it? We strap on our stiff upper lips, paste on a brave face and stoically soldier on. The whole of England is stuffed with couples making the best of a bad lot simply because they know they are stuck with one another. But Constança wasn't from my world, so my reaction to the death of our relationship was anathema to her and because I wasn't from hers, I couldn't bear all the histrionics and the fury. Ignoring it all seemed a more palatable option, at least at first.'

'You hoped it would go away or did you hope it would get better?'

He pondered it for a moment, then shook his head. 'That's the thing—I knew then it wouldn't go away or get better, it was already too far gone for that. But I convinced myself I could carry on and not care.'

'You still loved her?'

'Good grief no! I despised her. I couldn't bear to be in the same room as her nor she me. But I also couldn't leave her... I had made my bed.'

'So you soldiered on.'

'Rightly or wrongly, yes I did. I didn't believe I had any other option. But as time moved on, I grew to hate the person I became with Constança more than I despised her. Does that make sense?'

'Love and hate are inextricably intertwined.' She sighed. 'Just look at me and Rayne.' Somehow, he had known she would understand. 'I loathed myself too after that.'

'I was so damn disgusted and furious at myself it was making me ill. Bile in my mouth, this awful, painful knot here.' Piers pointed to his throat which was now blissfully knot-free. 'Then Lisbon happened and I was posted back to London, and without Constança in my life all those pains went away. Or they mostly did. Every single time someone mentioned her, or I had to think about her as I did during the divorce trial, they returned. So I dealt with them by *not* thinking about her and never talking about her and I now realise that gave her power over me. The moment I knew she was headed here it resurfaced again and typically I tried to ignore it. I rationalised, quite logically, that those buried insecurities had absolutely nothing to do with us and would go away as quickly as she did.'

'That plan went well.' Faith did sarcasm so well. 'If all it took was one silly dance to make your thick head explode.'

'Something snapped when I saw you dancing with Edward Tate and sent all the suppressed emotion shooting to the surface like steam in a kettle. Because I realised something earth-shattering, Faith... I realised that I wasn't just falling in love with you—which already seemed daunting enough as you know—but that I was already *in* love with you. Hopelessly in love, in fact.' Her spontaneous and delighted smile at this revelation warmed his heart. 'And in my panic, all those buried nagging doubts became entangled with how I felt about you. I suppose, deep down, among all that destructive and obstructive self-loathing, I still feared history might repeat itself.'

Her lovely face was full of sympathy. 'Do you still?'

'That's the damnedest thing of all. Even as I said those awful things to you, I didn't truly believe them. Not here.' He touched his heart. 'Where it matters.'

'Good, because Edward...' Piers placed his finger on her lips.

'You don't need to explain, Faith. You never need to explain. A relationship without foundations built in trust is doomed to collapse and only a complete idiot believes he can prevent that from happening by forbidding inconsequential nonsense like dances. Or stupidly trying to dictate who you can see or not see. I am not an idiot...not usually at least...and that is not the sort of relationship I want for us.

'I also realised that the fact I was panicking was also significant. It meant that despite my reserved, staid and pragmatic character, even I cannot suppress my emotions when the stakes are high enough. And while my idiotic jealousy was completely misplaced and wholly unwarranted, it made me realise I would do anything to fight for us.'

She smiled as her thumb stroked his palm. 'That was quite a pretty apology, but how do I know it won't all flare up again if somebody mentions Constança or something I do reminds you of her?'

'Because it only took one look at Constança to confirm without a shadow of a doubt that it could never possibly be that way with you. I was really dreading seeing her again. All week, the mere thought of it unsettled me—another reason for my panic—but instead it turned out to be the best thing that could have happened. Because I saw her and felt *nothing*.' It was like the entire weight of the world being lifted from his shoulders.

'No hate. No anger. No stomach pains. No bile. No anything except indifference and the overwhelming relief that she wasn't a part of my life any more. In a strange sort of way, it released me from the prison I've been locked in, one entirely of my own making, and proved it was long past time I moved on.' He took her hand, marvelling in his good fortune that fate had sent him her when he had least expected it. 'I know this is fast. I know this is reckless. But you would make me the happiest man in the world if that could be with you.'

She stared down at her fingers and then deep

into his eyes. 'Then what are you waiting for? Just kiss me, idiot.'

He did not need her to ask twice, and scooped Faith off her chair and into his lap with such speed she giggled as she clung to him. But then her laughter turned to a contented sigh as he brushed his lips over hers. 'I'm going to do more than kiss you, woman!'

Like all their kisses, this one heated quickly and she welcomed that, wrapping her arms tightly around his neck so he could properly plunder her mouth. But unlike those others, and despite the palpable lust hanging heavy in the air, neither of them were in a rush. They both understood that this time things were different. They no longer needed to be wary, didn't need to shy away from it, didn't need to apologise for the sheer intensity of their desire. They kissed instead like two people who knew exactly where it was heading, and revelled in it all the more as a result.

'What time do I need to get you home?' His mouth barely lifted from hers.

'Before the house wakes at six.'

He reached beneath her and pulled out his pocket watch and then smiled wolfishly as he glanced at the dial. 'That gives us three whole hours.' His talented lips found her ear. 'And I don't intend to waste a second.'

As he kissed her, his hands roamed lazily over her body until they found the hem of her gown, then they wandered beneath it, smoothing up her leg with aching slowness, then back down again taking her stocking with it. Then he did the same with her other leg. When both were completely bare, his finger went to the pins in her hair, removing them leisurely one by one, twirling his fingers in the curls as his tongue tangled with hers.

Faith unknotted his cravat and unwound it, then nuzzled his neck with her teeth while she pushed his jacket from his shoulders, enjoying the feel of the corded muscles beneath his shirt and the way they bunched at her touch. His waistcoat went next, and because she was impatient, so did his shirt and she felt his rapid heartbeat beneath her palms as she explored his bare chest, then tasted it with her lips. 'It has just occurred to me that you have deftly avoided sitting for me and I still need to sketch you.'

'You have sketched me.'

'For my father's tableau—not for mine. I want to draw you differently.' She tugged him to stand, her fingers reaching the buttons of his falls. 'I want to draw you naked...'

His mouth paused on her shoulder. 'You cannot put me naked in my mother's portrait.'

She pushed the waistband from his hips, then boldly traced the shape of him. 'It's not for your mother's portrait. It's a picture just for me.'

His compelling eyes darkened, and his breathing became erratic. 'You can draw me naked any time you want as long as you are naked too.'

'Oh, I think I can guarantee that.' Wantonly, she turned her back to him and lifted her hair in invitation, enjoying the way his fingers became clumsy in his haste to unlace her dress. She let the garment slither to the floor in a puddle of silk at her feet, gasping as his fingers brushed her bare skin as the final set of laces of her corset were undone. Then turned and watched his eyes rake her body encased in only her thin chemise.

Still, he refused to hurry, preferring to tease them both by exploring her curves thoroughly again over the flimsy barrier of her chemise. Smiling as she shuddered when his thumbs finally found her pebbled nipples and she thrust her breasts towards his hands. He trailed soft kisses down her neck and across her collarbone, pushing the chemise away only as far as he needed to expose her shoulders to his lips.

Again, it was Faith who hastened things, wriggling out of the garment and then feeling beautiful and powerful as he devoured her with his eyes until he simply had to touch her.

Trailing just the pad of one finger, he traced the shape of one bare breast. 'That is a pretty flower you have in your hair, Miss Brookes.' Then he smiled wickedly as he retrieved it and used that to slowly trace her body instead, until she growled her impatience and he tugged her to his chest. The feel of his skin on hers was divine, his mouth on hers sublime. She pressed her hips against his hardness and felt him tremble.

That was when the lust consumed them and they let it have free rein, clinging to each other breathless—mindless—shameless until even that wasn't enough. She tried to drag him to the floor and he shook his head. 'Not there…not yet.'

'The table?'

Then she smiled and hauled her body upwards so that her legs were hooked around his waist. 'The armchair first…obviously.' And as they laughed at the irony, he carried her to it, fell back on to it while she straddled him and then kissed her some more.

Hot, fevered, desperate kisses turned poignant and tender, then stopped completely as they sensed the significance of the moment. His eyes locked with hers as she shifted her hips to take him and remained locked as her body encased him to the hilt. Then lost themselves to passion. The world blurred, tilted and disappeared altogether, taking all the past and all the pain and all the doubt with it and leaving only the breathless promise of tomorrow in its place.

Chapter Twenty-Five

Two hours later, Faith sighed contentedly against his chest, wondering how they came to be under the table. 'I feel cheated.'

Half-asleep, he kissed the top of her head. 'How so?'

'I was promised staid, dull, reserved and unexciting, and that was anything but.'

She could hear his smug smile in the tone of his voice. 'Clearly you bring out the worst in me.'

'Or the best. You are particularly wonderful in an armchair.'

'It's where I am at my best.'

She propped herself on her elbow to stare down at him, and his fingers idly toyed with the curtain of her hair. 'The one in here is particularly comfortable. Do you think the palace would sell it to us?'

'I'll have a special one made to its exact specifications and it will have pride of place in our house.'

'Are we going to have a house?'

He chuckled. The delicious rumble vibrating through her skin. 'I was going to rent you a little one in Bloomsbury...'

'That'll be nice. We can share it until I leave you for a duke.'

'I absolutely forbid you from ever leaving me or my trusty armchair.'

She trailed her finger down the intriguing arrow of dark hair on his abdomen. 'You... forbid me?' She smiled at his sharp intake of breath as her fingers drifted lower. 'You can go to hell, sir. Unless we are now officially courting, Piers, in which case I might make just one exception...'

He turned her to lie beneath him so swiftly, she gasped. 'What say you we bypass the courting and dash recklessly, rashly, lustfully and scandalously headlong into for ever instead?'

Faith smiled contentedly against his lips.

'I'd have to finish your mother's picture first, of course—but then I'm game if you are.'

In a shocking but not unforeseen revelation, the long-suffering Lady R. is petition-

ing Parliament to divorce her husband on the grounds of his cruelty, adultery and rife drunkenness! This comes hot on the heels of Lord R.'s hasty resignation from his government position in Whitehall, after rumours of his alleged affair with the French spy Madame d'Pellitier surfaced.

A source close to the government refused to speculate on whether or not Lord R. was under suspicion of passing state secrets to Madame d'Pellitier across the pillow before she fled back to France, but did confirm that he believed the philandering Lord had indeed returned to his estate in early April, after complications arising from the broken nose he sustained while inebriated at the Covent Garden theatre made it impossible for him to carry out his duties.

In more pleasant news, alongside the much-anticipated unveiling of their spectacular new masterpiece at their Annual May Ball which received much critical acclaim, the Earl and Countess of Writtle also confirmed society's worst-kept secret last night by announcing the engagement of their son.

Lord Eastwood and the artist of the aforementioned lauded masterpiece, Miss Faith

Brookes, will tie the knot this very week-end! She is to be walked down the aisle by her father, the famous portraitist Mr Augustus Brookes, to an aria from Così fan Tutte *sung by her mother, Mrs Roberta Brookes, the famous soprano. Her two sisters will be bridesmaids and the groom's niece, Miss Isobel Filbert will be her chief bridesmaid.*

Another work of the soon-to-be Viscountess Eastwood, entitled Sunrise over London, *will also be exhibited at the Royal Academy this summer to much fanfare after it left the judges overawed by its magnificence. However, do not wait until then to commission her for your own masterpiece, as I am reliably informed there is already a huge waiting list for the unconventional Miss Brookes's exquisite paintings.*

And while I am on the subject of the unconventional Brookes family of Bloomsbury, dear reader, another delicious rumour also found its way to my ears this morning. Only this one involves the middle daughter, Miss H., who was apparently involved in an altercation in the Writtles' garden during the exact same ball!

Although what the fiery redhead was doing

alone, in the dark, in the small hours of her sister's engagement ball, with the dissolute new Marquess of Thundersley is anyone's guess...

Whispers from Behind the Fan
May 1814

* * * * *

LET'S TALK
Romance

For exclusive extracts, competitions
and special offers, find us online:

f facebook.com/millsandboon

⊙ @millsandboonuk

🐦 @millsandboon

Or get in touch on 0844 844 1351*

For all the latest titles coming soon,
visit millsandboon.co.uk/nextmonth